LIKE WE CARE

A NOVEL BY
TOM MATTHEWS

bancroft
press

Baltimore, MD

Published by Bancroft Press ("Books that enlighten")
P.O. Box 65360, Baltimore, MD 21209
800-637-7377
410-764-1967 (fax)
bruceb@bancroftpress.com
www.bancroftpress.com

Cover and interior design by Jim Versace
jversace@jimmyversace.com
www.jimmyversace.com
Author photo by Gilpin Matthews
ISBN 1-890862-36-3
Library of Congress Control Number: 2004100701
Printed in the United States of America
First Edition

1 3 5 7 9 10 8 6 4 2

For Chip,
Who did not make it out

Today's teenager is tomorrow's potential regular customer, and the overwhelming majority of smokers first begin to smoke while still in their teens… The smoking patterns of teenagers are particularly important to Philip Morris.

—Philip Morris
internal document

I'm not supposed to be like this.

—"The Wrong Child," R.E.M.

Pop

He felt something give. He remembered that.

Also the white hot sting of bone breaking, and the explosion of metal-flake stars that filled his head for that moment or two before he lost consciousness.

And then he remembered Todd Noland standing over him, desperately, eagerly wanting to know if he was all right. Todd Noland, who had always just been there, had always just wanted to know that things were going okay for him. Kind of like his mom or something.

He had hurt Todd Noland in the past, hurt him bitterly. Todd had naïvely attempted to bridge the chasm that precluded them from being friends, and stirred up the usual hateful sense of fun in his gang. The razor wire that separated high school cliques had been strung for a reason, and anyone who thought he could just stroll across the divide was begging to get his ass kicked.

Todd didn't fit, and there was just no way—with so much at stake, with so much going right—he could allow Todd's gangly attempts at friendship to rattle things up. Todd had to be sent back to where he belonged, as harshly as possible.

He owed the guys that much.

Still, he remembered Todd standing over him, relieved to see him hovering there with the towel and the ice and the oddly mature look of comfort that calmed him down when he was really, really scared.

He noted that. And then he passed out again.

He was Joel Kasten, lying there on the ground.

He was a high school junior.

He was seventeen years old.

The break was in his lower left jaw, the high fastball hurled by Hawthorne East's pitcher having smashed the side of his face with the force of a bat being swung for the fences.

Opposing pitchers had been coming in tight on Joel throughout the season, instructed by their coaches to crowd Dickinson's star batter by any means possible to keep him from making contact with the ball. Any team that hoped to have a chance in the post-season had to find a way to shut Joel Kasten down.

Joel was a pure power hitter, the sweetest swinging batsman any of the locals would ever see outside a Major League ballpark. Locking onto the ball with the unerring efficiency of the military's most advanced radar tracking system, Joel could—within the 46 feet between mound and plate, within the blink of an eye it took for the ball to find safe passage through the strike zone—make all calculations necessary to determine whether to swing or lay off.

And if the instinct said go, the boy swung. In ten years of playing ball, going all the way back to rookie league, Joel Kasten had almost never gone down looking. Better to commit and swing, take the third strike and cede this encounter to the pitcher, than to just stand there and do nothing. Like a *dick*.

As the season wore on, there looked to be no stopping Dickinson. That year's team was blessed with great pitching and better than adequate fielding, but more than anything it had Joel. Even beyond his bat and his effortless prowess at third, Joel brought to the team and its fans a genuine star-like quality, that intangible aura of a winner, whose raw, gangly handsomeness and scruffy humility came to personify the team itself.

The team fed off Joel, the fans fed off the team, and as the Dickinson Eagles took the field against the East Hawthorne Vikings for the final, tie-breaking game of the Illinois state finals, there appeared little doubt that Monday morning would find the state trophy displayed proudly in Dickinson's well-stocked trophy case. Joel's hometown of Berline, a Chicago suburb with about 45,000 residents, expected no less.

So what else to do but take Joel Kasten's head off? Or at least that was the rumor, from the instant that Joel's jaw exploded and his skull snapped back and his body hit the ground in a cloud of dirt and chalk.

Many wondered why Kyle Hoffstetler was brought in in the eighth inning when starting pitcher Bobby Lerner had a one-hitter going, his only slip-up a Joel Kasten homer in the third, which accounted for all the scoring on either side. Many wondered, for that matter, why Hoffstetler was still on the team at all, having been arrested the weekend before for what his lawyer was calling a consensual sex act and the girl was calling gang rape.

Whatever: it worked. With Joel out of the game, the Vikings were able to mount a limp ninth inning rally against a deflated and troubled Eagles squad. As the victors leapt upon Kyle Hoffstetler in a great homoerotic pile on the pitcher's mound, his parents and his lawyer pushing in to offer their admiration and affection, Joel was being admitted to the emergency room at St. Hobart's. He wouldn't regain consciousness until just before noon the next day.

Too Many Veronicas

Frank Kolak's fist hovered over the stapler, the fleshy part of his other hand having assumed the position. He shouldn't have to do this. He had strong suspicions there was something seriously wrong with this behavior.

And yet that start, that sting…

He hammered his fist home, driving the needle-like tooth through his flesh. Just as Veronica Jefferson walked into his classroom.

"Damn!" he shouted, not at being hurt but at being caught. Conveniently, it looked like it was because he was hurt.

"Veronica. I'm sorry." He brought the wound to his mouth, easing the pain with the balm of his spit.

"Damn, Mr. Kolak. That looked like it hurt."

"Yes," he replied. As near as he could recall, this was the first evidence that 17-year-old Veronica had any cognitive skills whatsoever. Had party hats been available, a celebration might have been in order.

"Where's your mother?"

"My mother said to tell you she wanted to be here to discuss my grades, but her boss wasn't going to spring her ass every time one of her kids was in trouble," she said listlessly, noting her teacher's disapproval. "That's what she *said.*"

Mr. Kolak sank into his seat with a defeated sigh. "Good lord, girl," he thought to himself. "Here we are, two black Americans, together on this journey, trying to elevate ourselves to a better place. A place we deserve.

"And while I don't have all the answers, I know more than *you.* So since I'm here every day anyway, blowing words into the air to the benefit of seemingly no one, could we not make a pact—just you and I—that if you will drop this anger and this feigned laziness and understand that I simply want, with all my soul, to see you excel, I will teach you?"

But instead he simply said: "You are failing Social Studies."

She set her jaw bitterly. "Mr. Kolak, I can't learn this stuff. I don't need this stuff. I'm fixing to be a hairdresser. What do I need to be knowing about all these dead men you keep throwing at us?"

"'These dead men' made the world you live in, and the future you're stuck with," he pleaded. "Don't you have any interest in how you got here?"

"*I* take the bus."

It was like another staple, this time through the heart.

"You want to drive a car? You want to *own* a car? You want to drive your car into a white man's gas station, hit the full service line 'cause you can afford it, have him run out and say, 'Yes, ma'am, how can I help you?' and then speed off, saying, 'Sorry, old man, I'm taking my business to the black brother up the street 'cause we finally got it all figured out and we're taking care of our own. Later for you, suckah!'"

She stared at him dimly. Can anything be so wasted as a metaphor cast upon a teenager?

She blinked, so he knew she hadn't fallen asleep.

He gave up. "When's the baby due?"

"February!" Finally, a light. This sullen, disconnected child all of a sudden was radiating good cheer and purpose. The baby would be her happiness.

He stared at her. "As you sit here this very moment, rejecting what I am trying to give you, you are sentencing that child to a life even more ignorant and doomed than your own."

He caught himself and winced. What a horrible, hateful thing for a teacher to think.

He lowered his eyes and discovered that he was bleeding all over various piles of homework. How was he going to explain *that*?

Props to the KKK

Hutch Posner had it going on because he had pulled off that most rare and spectacular early 21st century art form: the successful ante-upping concept rip-off. He had spotted a trend that was paying off handsomely for someone who had done the actualst hard work of breaking new ground. He had stolen it with such bloodless, chromium-sleek panache that even his competitors were awed—routinely offering him millions to come over to their side to work his magic on the network that he had learned and looted from in the first place.

Because Hutch Posner understood. Which is to say, he didn't. Couldn't have. Had no more foresight or boldness of vision than the guy who came up with the guy who came after Vanilla Ice. He had been just one more creativity-free heat-seeking scorpion who had idly suggested just one more crass exploitation to throw into the unquenchable maw that is public demand.

Just a jot on a notepad, thought #17 of 37 that he had brought with him during that first creative meeting following the acquisition of Decade Zero by MediaTrust, the cable colossus:

"Teens hate."

Didn't they? From the benign (I hate my parents, I hate my looks, I hate my brother, I hate my sister, I hate my school, I hate my town, I hate my life, I hate myself) to the lethal (pick the schoolyard slaying of your choice), wasn't the average teen feeding off hate like oxygen, devoting nearly every conscious moment trying to turn idle, listless contempt into a lifestyle choice? Wasn't this just the angriest, most pissed-off collection of brats ever to stroll this earth, happy only when consuming (whatever: drugs, mall effluent, those weaker than themselves), but otherwise dissatisfied, let down, denied?

Like there wasn't a buck to be made *there*.

What Hutch had proposed—and, again, he was just spewing out this crap—was the next generation in music television, free of the divas and the boy bands and anything that struck the eye or ear as soft. Melodic. Kind.

Spike the vein of cruelty and naked aggression that informed most of what was passing for popular entertainment, and mainline it to American youth. Maximum hardcore. Balls out extreme. All savagery, all the time.

Take the sugar out of their older sibling's MTV, which long ago had become a bloated and slick revenue-generator, eager to pimp to American youth whatever their jaded little souls desired, and just give with the nasty:

Nothing but seething skate punk thrash—the nü metal—with its breathtaking crunch-laden *Achtung!*, doing no less than transposing the goose-step into a pulsating, head-thrashing, fist-pumping white boy hootenanny.

And, of course, rap—the more gangsta the better. Take a white racist's worst possible caricature of a dope-selling, gun-slinging, cracker-hating, poon-snatching pimp, throw him in the studio with some samples, a drum loop, and a rhyming dictionary, and watch the money fall from the sky. Let the brothers take the first taste off the top—they're the ones, after all, selling out their culture with Stepin Fetchits for the new millennium. There's plenty left over for The Man.

The beauty part was that despite the seeming chasm separating the two—the white metallers and the black gangstas—it was the hateful, simple-minded hooliganism of both which bound them together. That, and the fact that it was all being sold primarily to white, cash-flush teenagers in the suburbs.

That was the thing about hip-hop: for all the grammar-deficient speechifying about keeping the music real for the homies on the block, their act was largely subsidized by white teen poseurs who couldn't have cared less about the hard street truths spun by these sons of Tupac, and who damned sure wouldn't be living anywhere near or offering employment to any one of their black brothers when they inherited the world in a few years.

It was this dynamic, this market paradox, which got Hutch the second meeting. The next meeting up. The meeting at which a half-assed whim might actually solidify into a MediaTrust-funded development deal.

— —

To make this happen, Hutch knew what was required—more than an embellishment of his initial concept, more than a demonstration of why he was the man to launch an entire new network in the venerated MediaTrust constellation.

What he needed was an icon. A graphic image. A brand-setting piece of eye candy that would crystallize his vision into a single, trend-defining logo with just as much credibility on a $45 T-shirt as when displayed proudly in a shareholder's report.

In the world in which he traveled, you needed to sell neither the steak nor the sizzle. Make the *concept* shine and the public, in its endearing eagerness to constantly be boned up the ass by corporate hucksters, could usually be counted on to bend over.

At that second meeting, now nearly four years ago, the state-of-the-art projection computer whirred silently as he began his sell.

"I want to plant a flag in the youth market, a flag that will fly proudly and defiantly, bearing two things: a name and a logo. A logo and a name. A network identity rendered in a single graphic image that will be just as evocative as the name Tupac, as raw and indelible as the tattoos on Fred Durst's arms. (Note: Fred Durst and his band Limp Bizkit mattered when Hutch sold the network; they do not anymore. They get to keep the tattoos.)

"Limited as we are by the three- and four-letter acronyms or quasi-acronyms that define the cable universe—CNN, ESPN, VH1, MTV—I want to break the form as much as possible and push the envelope like a motherfucker."

(Hutch had been practicing this last bit for the past week while driving in the Beemer, knowing full that as a white man out of the Ivy Leagues, this patois had no business coming out of his mouth. But if he was going to sell himself as the godhead of this vulgar, inappropriate network, he was going to have to pull it off. Up until the words actually left his lips, he was prepared to employ the fallback "Push the envelope like a certified bad-ass," but he sized up the tenor of the room and went for it. Judging from the wizened nods he received in return, he figured he had made the right call. Fact was, everyone gathered there fancied themselves ready to push the envelope like a motherfucker. What higher calling was there?)

"And to define this branding statement, to forge this network identity around which we intend to rally our desired demographic, I looked to an inspiration just a little outside the box.

(Hold for the dramatic pause.)

"I looked to the KKK."

Uh-oh. Envelope pushed too far. Hutch felt the air sucked from the room as those around him instinctively readied to fire back with rote, politically-correct platitudes.

Which was the intent.

"Now, hold on," Hutch urged with a sly grin. "I'm not talking about the KKK itself, which I'll be the first to say is off the hook. *Totally.*"

Jeff Bradley, the only black man having reached this power tier, squirmed uncomfortably. Hutch had given Jeff a lot of thought, wondering how his spiel would play with this member of the team. But the fact was that if anyone present had much concern for the side effects of crass, improper behavior, they were in the wrong business. Hutch knew that Jeff would know that if his idea were to take wing, Jeff would be positioned to take a lead role in the hip-hop half of Hutch's universe.

You make your compromises. You scoop up the gravy.

"No, I am talking about the KKK as a branding device," he said, nodding to Brad Stein, who was entrusted with running the computer. Three stark Ks now filled the screen. Those who had been willing to hear Hutch out began fidgeting all over again.

"Think about it," he soldiered on. "The Ku Klux Klan barely even exists anymore, just a handful of hate-filled crackers getting together in a mobile home down South a couple times a year to suck up the moonshine and bitch about the big, bad black man."

Jeff Bradley stared a hole in his notepad.

"But the *power* of their name hasn't diminished one bit. It still works. It's those three hard consonants—*KKK*—that drive it all home. Right?"

Nobody knew quite how to respond. Jeff Bradley worried that this momentary pause in Hutch's presentation was inviting everyone to recite the letters in unison, proving they had lost none of their luster.

John Viceroy, the MediaTrust liaison who would be crucial to Hutch's success, cleared his throat. "We cannot call a network KKK."

"That's got to be trademarked," added Jill Ebert, his beautiful, toadying Number Two. "Right?"

Hutch laughed, everything playing out as he had scripted it. "I don't want to call my network KKK."

"Good. Then I guess you can put me down for a box of T-shirts." It was Jeff Bradley, chiming in with just the right mood-lightener at just the right spot. Hutch could've kissed him.

"I'm just talking about the importance of the right selection of letters. It got me to thinking of the dynamic power of those three hard consonants—KKK—but, frankly, nothing else has the same impact. BBB? TTT? DDD? I mean, forget it, right?"

The room stirred, getting caught up in the exercise.

"How about XXX?" This was Roger Viner, always the one to go for the most obvious, insipid joke. The year before, he had cleared 500K as one of MediaTrust's most promising bright young thinkers. He was 22 at the time.

"You know what?" Hutch shot back. "Come back in eighteen months, and basic cable will be ripe for something that in-your-face down and dirty. The first network that can appropriate the illicit edge of hardcore pornography without the negatives is going to capture the entire market.

"We're just not there yet. *Not yet.*"

Jill Ebert scrawled a note to *her* Number Two: "Poll and focus group 'XXX' as possible net and/or product name component."

John Viceroy, spying her note, scrawled his own note: "Great note!"

"So I bagged the hard consonant construct," Hutch continued, "but I wanted to maintain the triplicate, just for the cleanliness of the image.

"I started thinking about what this network would be about, what its focus and its mandate would be, and it wasn't hard at all to distill it down to three words. (He met the eyes of everyone at the table, ending with Viceroy.)

"Rap.

"Rock.

"Revolution."

As scripted, Brad Stein pulled the trigger and the screen blossomed with the genius payoff of Hutch's presentation, a stark, undeniably riveting graphic of three R's, rendered in a distressed, raw-edged font.

The first R was backwards, an inadvertent salute to the illiteracy of much of Hutch's target audience. The third stood correctly, a jagged scar (Hutch originally wanted a bullet hole) portraying the hiply hardscrabble lives suburban teenagers fancied themselves living. The R in the middle jutted forward in an amazing 3-D rendering. The money Hutch had paid that uptown graphic artist had been well spent.

It was a masterful icon. You could instantly envision it on the backwards hat of a skate punk, brazenly proclaiming his individuality by sporting the same mass-produced corporate wear that all the other skate punks were wearing.

Hutch could feel the adoration in the room. He set for the kill.

"Meet the—"

"It sounds like a pirate." It was Roger Viner, chuckling.

Hutch kept his cool. "What?"

"Ar-ar-*arrrrrr*. It sounds like Long John Silver."

The room began to titter. Hutch felt a needle prick between his third and fourth vertebrae.

"No, I don't think—"

"Yeah, it kinda does," concurred John Viceroy.

"Arrrrrrrrr! Avast ye scurvy dogs!" Mitch DeLong, Vice President of Why The Fuck Does He Have To Be In This Meeting?, picked up the merriment, squinting his left eye and growling like a grizzled sea captain.

The room dissolved into "Arrrrrrrrrrs!" These richly paid, cutting-edge seers of cable's future were cutting up like a bunch of second graders.

All except Annie McCullough, Hutch's assistant, who watched as her boss deflated, and with him her own chances for promotion.

She grabbed an art pad and started scribbling. She was ready for this.

"Okay, so the icon needs some retooling," Hutch said through a forced smile, trying to be a good sport. "But let's agree that my concept—"

"It's strong, Hutch. It's very promising," John Viceroy said, the enthusiasm already leaking out of him like slime from a rotting tomato. The fact was that Viceroy, like most of those present, didn't like Hutch all that much. And in the pack dog climate that defines men at this level of power, better to belittle and diminish than concede that a competing alpha male may actually be onto something.

Let it lie for a few weeks, Viceroy knew. Then he could revive it and grab some glory by plucking it from the discard heap.

"Let's take it up next time."

"No!"

Hutch knew that he couldn't leave this room without a guarantee of the next meeting up, the face-to-face with the programming powers who could put his idea into active development. To "take it up next time," to essentially have this same meeting twice, would spell the end of his dream. Momentum was everything when you flew at these heights.

"Let me just—"

There was a tug at his sleeve. Annie, more determined than he had ever seen her, needed a moment.

"Not now!" Hutch hissed.

She was not going to be denied; he was bright enough to see that. He put up a finger, requesting a brief time-out. The rest of the room, having already been subjected to Hutch's pitch for going on half an hour, welcomed the chance to stretch their legs, grab another bottle of water from the communal fridge, and make more pirate noises.

"This is your icon," she said with a sexy forcefulness that he would've admired if it had come from him. As it was, he was deeply annoyed.

"Annie…"

"You are losing them. If they leave the room on this note, you're dead anyway."

Dammit. She was right. He took the sketch pad from her.

Like all brilliant logos, it attacked with a narcotic efficacy. No matter how great the resistance—and Hutch's couldn't have been greater—it instantly fused itself to that pleasure receptor that made the beholder believe he was in the presence of corporate benevolence and only the most well-intentioned strain of mass consumerism.

It was that good.

He tried to fight it: "It's not three letters!"

"Hutch. It works."

Yes it did.

In that instant, he ran all the angles: The network was still *his* idea. Annie had merely come up with a label to stick on it. She would make her contribution known, and probably become a more legitimate part of the team than he would've envisioned, but everyone would still know he was in the lead chair on this one.

And besides, if she were promoted in rank, it would look more appropriate if he wanted to hook up with her, which is something he wanted to do more and more lately. If this thing flew, she'd be working around the clock, way too busy to devote any time to that rock star wannabe she'd been sleeping with.

The long, crushing hours, the aphrodisiac that comes from fighting the same battles side-by-side, the occasional words of insincere praise when she really needed a boost, her grateful smile in return. This could all break nicely, nookie-wise.

In, like, four seconds, he worked all this out.

And above all else: He could not let Viceroy out of this room.

The rest of the team was resettling in their seats. When the final ass was planted, new business would commence. Hutch strapped himself in mentally for the play of his life—unless this idea flopped, and he'd have to come up with more of this bullshit for next week's meeting.

Instinctively knowing that some theatrics were in order to reenergize his pitch, he took the art pad and slowly stood on his chair. He was recalling that movie *Norma Rae*, the scene that made Hutch and his Poli-Sci classmates giggle because they were sure they could see Sally Field's nipples under her sweaty T-shirt.

As his colleagues and superiors looked at him curiously, Hutch looked down upon them like Moses cradling the commandments.

"Gentlemen, I give you the next generation in music television."

He displayed Annie's work, her heart about to burst from her chest.

Those gathered there beheld what she had brought forth, what she would not be credited with for nearly six months.

There was a respectful silence, maybe an impressed gasp or two. It worked. It simply worked.

$R^2Rev.$

Rap. Rock. Revolution. Perfectly good words bastardized and rendered totally unintelligible, anchored by what would soon be commonly referred to by the creative team as "that little floaty two thing." *Adweek* would eventually proclaim it the new Nike swoosh.

The precise font would be subjected to months of focus testing. The debate over whether it should be "*Rap, Rock,* Revolution" or "*Rock, Rap,* Revolution" would trigger ferocious battles, which would ultimately be resolved when black staffers—led by that bastard Jeff Bradley—threatened to call in the NAACP and Al Sharpton unless "Rap" got top billing.

But still...

It looked cool. It sounded cool. Like a hot new drug.

$R^2Rev.$

Hutch Posner climbed down from his chair into a whole new world.

He avoided Annie McCullough's eyes.

Closed

They kept Joel in the hospital for three days, because the bash to the skull had doctors concerned about the severity of the concussion. Every physician Joel saw seemed to delight in telling him that had he crouched three inches lower, the ball would've caught him right in the temple and, well, he could be dead.

Joel, who got hip to irony in ninth grade English, saw the irony here: if he had lowered his stance, done what every coach since age seven had tried to get him to do, despite the fact that the way he stood in the box—rod straight, coiled for action—worked just fine, thank you very much, he'd be just another dead teen. He'd be consigned to the "Lest We Forget" page of the yearbook, like poor old Dennis Stark, who accidentally sliced open his wrist with a box-cutter and bled to death in a dumpster behind Target, trying to save up for a used Toyota.

There in the hospital bed, Joel snuggled up with his irony, pleased with himself for having ferreted it out on his own, proud—as he was more and more these days—that despite his jock swagger and his hard-partying rep, he was actually getting smarter.

He wished there was someone in his vast clique with whom to share this wry observation on the capriciousness of life, but the fact was that his entire gang had to rally merely to be defined as something other than retarded. Any mention of the word "irony" to the likes of Wad Wendell would no doubt lead straight into a discussion of Wheaties, as in "I don't need no iron-y foods like Wheaties since I started bootin' the andro, dude!"

But the fact was he wasn't going to be sharing much with anyone for a long time, anyway. Maybe three months.

His jaw had been wired shut.

In addition to losing two permanent lower teeth, the bone and hinge that drove his mouth had been shattered practically to dust. The only way for the mechanics to heal properly—and the doctors had some doubts even then—was to clamp the thing shut and hope for the best. With any luck, he'd get his mouth back in full working order, although athletics were most definitely out of the question at least until next spring.

Joel had not taken the news well.

No more tongue, he realized, administered to or received from Molly DeVry. (Just moments away from being told that he had nearly been killed, and this was the first thought that crossed his mind. She was hot and fresh and eager; he was seventeen and sporting a pulse. One understands.)

Beer through a straw. *Food* through a straw! Christ, how was he going to keep his weight up, sipping soup for three months? How was he going to live without his Taco Bell #3s, hold the onions, extra cheese? Entire fast food empires might crumble now that he had been taken out of action.

And *shit!* how was he going to smoke? It had been killing him already, just the first day and a half he spent in the hospital, separated from his cigarettes.

He'd been lighting up since he was fourteen, since the summer between his freshman and sophomore years, when he realized that his acolytes were looking to him to lead the way into that illicit new world of disobedience and parent fucking.

He remembered that first purchase at the Happy Snack with the clarity reserved only for life's most meaningful events. He still felt the racing of his heart as he walked into the store, his minions—pubes freshly blossomed in their pants—lying low behind a dumpster, should the guy at the counter push the button and dispatch a SWAT team that would rappel down from a sleek black helicopter and whisk Joel Kasten away to a life of hard labor at a youth camp somewhere.

Joel had kind of resented it going in, having to put his ass on the line this way, particularly when *he* didn't want to smoke, didn't want to pollute the athletic body that was already taking him to heights of glory.

And even more, he was faintly aware of a distant call that wanted him to defy the cliché that led all teenagers to misbehave in such predictable fashion. His older sister smoked; his *parents* did at his age.

Surely there was some other way for a teenager to act up, thought a nervous Joel way back then as he broke the beam of the Happy Snack's electric eye. Surely there was a better way than to robotically indulge in the misbehavior so expected of him.

But like all outlaws and Christ figures worth a damn, he was a hero for delivering the goods. The only question asked of him by the Happy Snack guy was "Need matches?" (This was not, for the record, the grouchy swami guy who currently ran the Happy Snack; Joel Kasten was launched on his way toward excess phlegm production and a possible lingering cancer death by a "real" American.)

They hunkered down there behind the dumpster—Wad Wendell, Bobby Slopes, Zach Foley, poor, dead Dennis Stark—lighting up and sipping small, taking the first horrid taste of the smoke that would soon be their prop and best friend. Joel intended to fake it, particularly after that bitter inaugural puff, but he found almost immediately that he stood cooler, walked tougher, snarled fiercer with a butt in his mouth. It made complete the persona he was trying to carve for himself.

So what if he was betraying the few codes he had so far established? Here behind the trash bin, with his friends and their divvied-up Marlboros, they were *Bad-Asses: The Next Generation.*

— ◄ ▬ —

Lying in his hospital bed, Joel took a soda straw from his dinner tray and tried to simulate smoking, realizing instantly that while he would still be able to clamp his lips around a filter tip and force the smoke back through his clenched teeth, it was going to be about as satisfying as dry humping.

"Fuck," he cried, although, through his bolted-down jaw, it just sounded like a flush of angry air:

"*Fuuhhh…*"

"Hello?"

Peering through the door was Joel's Social Studies teacher, Mr. Kolak.

Joel immediately felt vulnerable, child-like. He had invested so much of himself forging an identity at school—superior, self-assured, *cool*—that it was a completely alien experience to find himself laid prostrate before a mere teacher.

Even Mr. Kolak, whom Joel liked.

The teenager pulled the flimsy hospital sheets up to his chest and tried to look manly. The purple-black bruise on the side of his face helped.

"Wow, did you get the number of the truck that hit you?"

Joel smiled weakly. When he was past forty, would every damned thing out of his mouth be a cliché, too?

Mr. Kolak squirmed self-consciously, taking Joel's silence to be typical teen sullenness, even though this was not a trait he tended to see in Joel.

He liked this kid, admired him even. He had smarter students, that was for sure, but he appreciated Joel for the fact that while he possessed that most sacred teenage tender—a handsome body, an athlete's grace, an effortless ability to lead—he nevertheless came to class willing, if not always quite able, to learn.

To a teacher, that was gold.

Frank had been teaching long enough to know the usual academic indifference and numbskulled omnipotence of the hallowed Jock King, getting by purely on his arrogance and the implicit school-wide imperative that such charmed boys were not to be trifled with.

Frank used to challenge such boys, routinely attempted to flunk them, maybe because he didn't want to pass them on to the next grade stupid—or maybe because it simply galled him that these loathsome young things were so inappropriately blessed with lives of hedonism and privilege.

But every year, the ruling powers—always led by a coach of some kind—told him to knock it off. His satisfaction would have to come later, at the reunions, which Mr. Kolak never failed to attend for the chance to see last year's Big Man on Campus, now doomed deliciously to fumble through life as a purposeless oaf, wondering where the worship went.

Frank would never wish this on Joel, nor did he worry that such was his fate. Joel was a good one—even as he stared a hole into his Social Studies teacher from his hospital bed.

"Um, I didn't know how long they were going to keep you, but they just told me you're being released Monday, so..." He awkwardly held up the manila folder he had brought with him. "I just thought you might like to see your grade on last week's take-home. That extra time you put in really made the difference."

The kid took the folder, still saying nothing. Mr. Kolak often cursed how a glowering teenager could make him feel so small.

"Well, I'll leave you alone. Sorry to…"

As his teacher turned to leave, Joel suddenly realized that he was hurting this man. Then figured out why.

"Nuuuu," he garbled through his clenched teeth. "Mah jahs wahred shuud. Ah cand tahk."

He pointed to his jaw and bared his teeth, cemented into a permanent smile.

"Doan go. Sid-dow."

He gestured to the chair beside the bed. Mr. Kolak, grateful to be welcome, sat.

"I was at the game Friday. You should know that the entire faculty intends to see that Hawthorne's coach is punished severely. That was a blatant shot you took."

Joel could only shrug. He wondered why he was hearing this from his Social Studies teacher and not his coach, but thus far Coach Timmonds had been a no-show at the hospital. Joel would learn later that Coach Timmonds blamed his star player for losing the finals, questioning why Joel wasn't anticipating a head shot when pitchers had been coming in tight on him all season. With so much on the line, how could Joel make such a mistake?

"Maybe because I just never figured a kid would try to kill me over a fucking trophy," Joel thought to himself at the time.

"But you guys had a great season," Mr. Kolak continued. "You have nothing to be ashamed of."

"Thaingsss."

The silence of the dank hospital room again pressed in on them. Joel fumbled idly with the homework folder that Mr. Kolak had brought.

"It's real improvement, Joel. You've really come a long way this year."

Joel flipped through the first couple pages, then he stopped uneasily. He held up the fourth page, which was flecked with blood. He looked to his teacher.

"Oh…"

Mr. Kolak flustered slightly, but surprised himself by not even considering a dodge. Maybe it was the vulnerability of the student laying before him. Or maybe he was ready to just stop caring.

"Sometimes I hurt myself," he said softly, holding up his bandaged hand. "Sometimes I think I'm not feeling things the way I used to, so…"

His voice trailed off, his confession hanging in the air like a knot of dark secrets.

Joel didn't know what to say. He was a teenager; he was not schooled in assessing the miserable contents of an adult's soul.

He fumbled through his homework folder, then looked again to his teacher. He wanted to relieve Mr. Kolak of this awkwardness.

"Uuu know," he began, fighting to be understood, "iff ah hat ben crotching down tree more intzes, like mah coatses ahways wahn-ned me to, tha ball woulda het me inda tempeh an ahd be det righ nah."

He looked to Mr. Kolak hopefully.

"I'm sorry. What?"

Joel sighed, frustrated but not angry. The fact was he liked the company. And this was important.

"Iff. *Ah*. Hat. Ben. *Crotching*…"

Allah by the Ding-Dongs

The oppressor always entered at the sound of a bell.

Whether in the middle of the day, while he shivered in the ice box, restocking the spectacular range of beers and sugary soda pops he sold, or hours before dawn, as he napped in the back room, dreaming of his family and friends so far away, they announced their presence with the muted, harassing *bong* of the electric eye.

Each chime of the bell was like the next round in a prize fight, each customer through the door an intruder to be wary of. If he was lucky, they would stroll his aisles, load up with the snack items and beverages he was pleased to believe were rotting Americans from the inside out, pay his audaciously inflated prices, and get the hell out.

If he was not so lucky, he would be shot dead, like his cousin Nadir in Baltimore just two weeks ago. And his uncle in June. And his brother's neighbor last year.

A marked man in a turban and a name tag, Daljit Singh took no chances, meeting every face that came through his door with a scowl so terrifying— usually further grizzled by a considerable lack of sleep—that many simply turned and ran. It was a scowl that said, "Feed your addictions. Deliver me your ill-gotten wealth. And flee into the night, you American bastards!"

(His name tag read "Jimmy." Some genius from the Happy Snack field office had determined early on, when the Sikhs and other brown-skinned races started taking over the franchise market, that a bright, thoroughly Caucasian name tag could actually counteract a portion of the trepidation and outright racism festering at the cash registers of most of their outlets, boosting sales in some sectors by some fraction of a point. In Daljit's case, however, nervous customers without fail kept their eyes on the transaction being negotiated, never lifting their gaze to Daljit's chest, and certainly never his eyes. His name tag may as well have read "Carol Channing."

Nobody would notice.)

On weekdays, when the high school was in session, his customers were invariably teenagers, the boys with their fancy cars and their muscled, bully boy swagger, and the girls dressed like whores. They stole from him, made fun of his accent and his inability to speak their awful, lying language. But they had a seemingly endless river of cash, free to spend it on whatever decadent wish they desired, so he endured their deceitful ways.

He sold them their beer, their condoms, and carton upon carton of cigarettes. For a long time, the only English he knew were the numerous brand names, and the accompanying discourse: "Give me the hard box." "Got any matches?"

The prices kept rising—two dollars, three dollars, four dollars a pack—and yet the pockets of this privileged devil spawn never emptied. He took the money from them happily, and he allowed them to congregate and smoke in his parking lot without hassle, so they wouldn't be encouraged to go spend it anywhere else. Happy Snack had suggested that, too.

Whatever they wanted, Daljit Singh would sell—even the vile, godless pornography that Happy Snack made him display behind the counter. Daljit could only imagine the hell that awaited these teenage boys—like Todd Noland, standing here before him—for the blasphemies within those pages they no doubt pleasured themselves with.

"Hey, Jimmy," Todd began, weary yet again to be going through this awkward ritual, just to have something new to masturbate to. He was, of course, well-traveled in all the dank corners of the internet, and had an endless array of perversions available to him at the click of a mouse, but he considered himself to be something of an old school chicken-choker. Besides, he had once ejaculated all over his keyboard, and nearly died of embarrassment trying to explain the accident to his parents so they'd replace it in time to get an extra credit project done in World History.

There was just no substitute for the slick, forbidden pages of an old-fashioned porno rag.

He always felt that a cool, familiar tone made this transaction go down the easiest; just a coupla men of the world here, Todd's brown-skinned friend probably just as interested as he was in this month's fifteen-page, full-color lesbo lickathon.

Hence: "Hey, Jimmy."

Daljit Singh simmered. To hell with the Happy Snack, no one should address him by that accursed name. And yet, because he was about to indulge in one of his favorite forms of amusement, he grunted back almost tolerantly.

"Okay, so I got a Coke here, two packs of gum, a Snickers," Todd began, seamlessly steering toward the promised land, "and I'll take one of those *Hustlers* back there."

Daljit turned and grabbed a phallic pickle-on-a-stick. He kept the display right next to the porno rack for just this purpose.

He forced it upon Todd and started ringing up the sale in one fluid motion.

"No, not the pickle. Next to it."

Daljit blinked dimly. Todd sighed. Holy *fuck*, could he not find just one girl who would sleep with him and deliver him from this horror?

"The magazine. There!"

Daljit growled, turned again, and came back with the current *Playgirl*. This was his favorite part; he'd flip through the pages, find a steely, circumcised penis waving out at him, and then utter some dark native curse at the homosexual standing before him.

"Blah blah *faggot* blah blah blah," the Sikh gibberish usually went.

Todd nearly whimpered as an old woman entered the store and headed toward the back. Now it was a race against time.

"No, *Hustler. There!!*"

Daljit glared at Todd, once again turning to the porno rack. He finally grabbed the *Hustler* and tossed it—cover up—onto the counter as he rang up the sale.

Todd quickly flipped it over, turning again toward the old lady. She was on her way.

Daljit saw her, too. If he timed this just right, he could make an extra $3.50 off this horny boy.

"Thirteen eighty-five."

Even knowing the gross mark-up of convenience store fare and pud-pulling accessories, Todd recognized that this was too high. He looked at the receipt.

"You charged me for the pickle."

Whatever English Daljit knew—and the truth was, he knew a lot—seemed suddenly to have left him.

"Eh?"

Todd squirmed. The old lady was almost upon them.

"There! You charged me for—Christ!"

He threw a ten and four ones on the counter, grabbed his goods, and skulked from the store.

Daljit was happy inside, the happiest he'd been all day.

"Do you sell thread?" the old lady asked.

Daljit trained lasers of hate upon her.

"Bread. Aisle two. No squeeze."

Birdland

"Five.

"Four.

"Three.

"Two.

"One."

"Hey! What-up? Casey Lattimer, rockin' on through the night, being on the rammer for the third—"

"Cut. From the top."

"*Whatever…*"

"Five.

"Four.

"Three.

"Two.

"One."

"What-up, y'all? Casey Lattimer, rockin' on here wit ya, being on the rammer for the third straight—"

"Cut!" the voice cried impatiently from the booth. "Christ, Casey, read the fucking line."

"Dude, I'm reading right off the fucking PrompTer."

"You said 'being on the rammer.' Twice. Does that make any sense to you?"

"It's on the fucking PrompTer, dude!"

This was not cool. With scores of dopey-eyed teens pressed against the glass, watching Casey Lattimer tape his "live" video intros in R²Rev's Manhattan studios, it would not do for the network's star veejay to betray the stoned, mellow-assed persona the creative team had spent so much time crafting.

Hutch watched from the shadows, curious to see how his newest star would handle himself, knowing it was just a matter of time before they had to free Casey from the safe-to-tape confines of the studio and set him loose as a functioning audience interactive. It was the flaw in Hutch's good fortune, the greasy spot on his high-wire, that so much of his success depended on the on-camera skills of borderline mongoloids.

"If it's on the fucking PrompTer, I say the fucking words. If you don't want the fucking words coming out of my fucking mouth, then get fucking someone to fix the fucking PrompTer!"

Hutch looked to the kids gathered outside the studio on this Tuesday afternoon. Intoxicated at being so close to an actual TV celebrity, they nevertheless were squirming uncomfortably at the hint that bad vibes were seeping into their fantasy world.

Everything was shiny on R²Rev; everybody was *down*. Hutch could practically read it on one chubby girl's anguished face: Are there bad vibes at R²Rev, just like out here in the real world? Do they hate each other here, just like my mom and dad?

Hutch stepped onto the heated studio floor, putting a supportive hand on Casey's shoulder as he squinted at his stage crew beyond the lights.

"How about it, Neal? Do we need to make some changes around here to make sure that the TelePrompTer is set properly for the talent?"

The disembodied voice of Neal, the long-suffering floor director, absorbed yet another loss in the battle of "talent" versus common-fucking-sense. "We're on it, Hutch. Won't happen again."

"Come here," Hutch said to his star, wanting to get him away from the scrutiny of the teens outside. But first, some damage control. "Give 'em one."

As programmed, Casey cast off his dark mood, turned to the throng with a taunting leer, and laid his trademark on them: both middle fingers, raised rigidly. Twin totems of maximum bad boy-ness.

"*Fuck you!*" his trademark said. "I'm in here, drawing a nice paycheck for selling you the darkest, most cynical load of crap we can come up with, while you're out there shivering in the cold instead of getting an education that might actually make you smart enough to see through this scam.

"But just in case you fail to grasp the true terms of our relationship, here's a genial '*FUCK YOU!*'"

(Somewhere tucked into a lightless corner of the control room was an NYU film school grad, whose sole job was to work within the 30-second tape delay to digitally blur any offending fingers before they were beamed to the world. Twice in the net's brief life, they had failed and the network had been fined. Hutch kept the toothless FCC complaints framed behind his desk.)

Thrilled and flattered, the gathered gumheads saluted back in kind, already looking forward to the envious looks on the faces of friends somewhere else when an actual TV personality told them to go fuck themselves.

"Fuck *you!*" their frozen middle fingers replied. "Fuck all of us! Goddamn, aren't we something, out here with our *attitudes* and our middle fingers all up in the air like this!"

Casey basked in their adoration, extending his arms to their limit, willing his middle fingers to reach even greater heights of outrageousness: Fuck *yoooouuuuuu!!!!!!!*

This could go on all day. Hutch finally led Casey to a dark corner of the studio.

"It still works, dude," Casey beamed.

"Look—"

"Hey, I saw Dr. Poon flippin' off his crew on 'Rap Slap' last night. Tell the nigger—"

"*Hey.*" Hutch almost never took a harsh tone with the talent. "How many times do I have to tell *you* that you can't call them 'niggers'? I can't, and you can't. That's *their* thing."

"Whatever. Tell the man that the flippin' off is *mine*. Grabbin' his dick, that works for him. He can grab all he wants, the fuck do I care? But I got to the finger first."

"Do you mind? We're on the clock here." Hutch softened his tone, knowing there were several mucky layers to penetrate here. "Look, you *have* to go over what's on the PrompTer before the tape rolls.

That's your job."

"Dude, I did! It said—"

"I know, I know. So you thought you were *supposed* to say 'being on the rammer'? What does that mean?"

"The fuck do I know? I don't know what half this shit you have me saying means. I see 'rammer,' I think 'fucking,' I figure: Rock and roll, bro!"

Hutch sighed. "Okay. From now on, I'll have an intern with you when you go over the scripts, in case you have any questions."

"Make it Roxanne. With the tits."

Neal's voice cut in from the studio. "We're ready, Hutch. We're backing up. We'd better keep moving."

Hutch offered Casey a fatherly pat on the back, then sent him back before the cameras. Upon seeing their hero again, the rabble outside started flipping him off to a fare-thee-well.

Casey, too dim to know much but savvy enough to not milk his signature, offered a weak, non-committal bird which, Hutch noted with some concern, was less of a "We're havin' a party here" *fuck you* and more of a, well, *fuck you.*

"Five.

"Four.

"Three.

"Two.

"One."

"Hey! What-up? Casey Lattimer, rockin' on through the night, bringing down the hammer for the third..." He squinted at the PrompTer and grinned stupidly. "Ahh, I get it..."

"Cut!"

Hutch grimaced and headed back to his office.

The Trajectory of Boys

On the fall day Joel's wires were to be cut, his mother had a staff meeting she couldn't miss.

His father's current girlfriend offered to take him to the doctor's office (his father was himself laid up, having water skied himself into a pontoon boat while attempting courtship with his 27-year-old lady love). But Joel had put her off in the hopes that her mother's second ex-boyfriend, whom Joel had actually come to like during the eight months he diddled his mother on the other side of his bedroom wall, would come through.

But by the time the ex-boyfriend reluctantly had to beg off due to "relationship concerns" (the woman he was hoping to move in with once her divorce went through found it troubling he was still seeing the children of a prior affair, especially when he seemed to be so miserable to her own kids), Joel's father's current girlfriend had made other plans.

"Fuck it," Joel had thought. He had his own wheels, he was practically out of the house and on his own anyway. And there wasn't a chance in hell he was going to reschedule the appointment, just so one of his parents and/or their respective sex partners could tag along to play all parent-like.

The X-rays were positive—the jaw had healed completely. It was time.

Still, he was glad to have Todd along that day. More than he would ever probably admit—although he had been thinking he might try, once he got the use of his mouth back—Joel had been grateful for all the help Todd had offered the past twelve weeks.

It had been the most surprising part of this whole experience, the way his perception of his friendships had shifted while waiting to undo the damage Kyle Hoffstetler had done.

— ⚾ —

When he first returned to school, less than a week after being hurt, Joel bathed in the attention that his apparent martyrdom had brought him.

Added to the long-familiar outpourings of adoration and blind faith was a genuine concern for his well-being, supplemented by the perception that Joel's wounds were *their* wounds.

He had bled for them. He had felt pain for them. To those rendered stupid by too deep a thought, there was profundity in their midst.

Until just about Thursday. After that, the pressing concerns of the classroom and the social meat grinder swung the spotlight away from Joel. And for the first time in his life, he could not swing it back.

Athletic practice was out of the question, given the tenuous state of his jaw, so his traditional star-making arenas were denied him. And because he could not speak, his ability to lead and coerce was stifled, even challenged!

After all, the discourse of a pack of grunting, testosterone-mutated teenage boys was nothing but a mullet-headed assault of endless improvisation—a foul-mouthed choir of crudities, insults, and boorish self-affirmations. To hold your own, you had to be able to talk the shit.

Joel was accustomed to standing at the center of these puberty scrums, orchestrating and modulating the nastiness with the effortless command of a master conductor:

"Fucking Atkinson, giving me another fucking D in Algebra!"

"Fuck right, we'll fucking take State!"

"Goddamned Stacy Barnes, I'd fucking do her in the ass if I had the fucking chance!"

"Fuck fuck fuck, fuck fuck fuck!"

Joel would oversee these invective free-for-alls with aplomb, making sure each of his tribesmen had his opportunity to howl, and yet always prepared to turn the conversation on a dime with a well-timed "Ah, fuck it." Next subject:

Cops busted up a rave on Saturday. "Fuck fuck fuck fuckin' fuck fuck fuck!"

But now, with Joel's voice stilled, the pack lost its center; the babble, its verve. Joel was grateful, but then alarmed, when Bobby Slopes took it upon himself to step into Joel's place as point man—a point man with none of Joel's panache and discretion.

Where Joel would've instinctively steered the hurtful bantering away from retarded Donna Vogel, who succumbed to a bout of diarrhea in the cafeteria, fucking Bobby Slopes worked the subject to howling heights of cruelty, with the poor girl cleaned up and still sitting just two tables away!

This was not teenage boys cutting up. This was just mean.

And Joel just had to sit there and *listen* to this crap, not even able to tell them to shut the fuck up. That is, if he would ever dare to judge them so harshly. Like an adult or something.

Still: Was this the way they always sounded, this foul-mouthed and vicious? Now peering in from a step outside, was this all his years of celebrity had brought him? To once have ruled over a pimpled mob of sadistic jerk-offs?

It had been the same with his girlfriend, the stunning and loose Molly DeVry, whom Joel had been seeing pretty much exclusively all senior year. Left to actually *hear* her, where before they vibrated blissfully to the resonant hum of two teenagers being better than everyone else, he began to not like her. Everything she said that wasn't bitchy nonsense had more and more to do with their future together beyond high school, a future Joel did not see being shared with her. He knew things were pretty much over for them. Maybe they had been for awhile, he was just too busy being wonderful to notice.

Shut up for a few minutes, and you can actually see what's going on around you. Who knew?

— ∎ —

By comparison, things just seemed so quiet, so gentle, down at Todd Noland's end of the table.

Joel and Todd had once been tight, back around third grade. Back before the wrong friendship could fuck you up for life.

They shared the usual fancies of eight-year-olds: clumsy first attempts at sports, collecting and obsessing over whichever hunk of crap Madison Avenue was mainlining them that year, playing boy-on-boy grab-ass on the playground with the sort of innocent abandon that would be looked upon as deeply troubling in another year or so.

Nothing special, merely the entire breadth and width of the universe. When you're eight.

Joel had already begun showing the coltish swagger of a world-beater; Todd, the contemplative melancholy of an over-informed, over-concerned mope.

They had first met in kindergarten when Joel, ripping around the room like a terror, trod upon Todd's little finger as he sat diligently on the floor, wondering if so much ripping around the room was really the best use of their time.

Todd complained meekly, referring to his smarting finger as a "pinkie." Joel, who had never heard the word before, was intrigued.

The wild child took the time to engage one of the room's presenceless boys, and was rewarded with a new word for his efforts.

They complemented each other.

The bond held for a while, with countless secrets and adventures shared during countless sleepovers and bike odysseys. But sixth grade brought new peer pressures and greater opportunities for Joel to cultivate an empire.

Sports started to mean something, and the simple fact that Joel could not be everywhere at once kept him from excelling at all that was possible.

And, of course, girls started to mean everything. The mysterious trouser yearnings of the healthy male buck began to announce themselves with an insistence awesome to behold. And while most eleven-year-olds were too clumsy and horrified to follow the fevered leash-tuggings of the puppy dog that was their penis, Joel—as he did in most things—ran ahead of the pack.

By the end of seventh grade, he had excitedly and repeatedly pinched a nipple, almost as if to inflate the breast to the pumpkinned proportions found in his father's poorly hidden collection of *Penthouses*.

By Christmas of the next year, he had found himself tingly-skinned naked with Nancy Stought, her parents' early return from a holiday party being the only thing preventing Joel from slipping into the promised land.

Still, he had stared down his first vagina, felt her hand, and—very briefly—her mouth on his hap-hap-happy boy thing. This would have to do until late that summer when, in Wad Wendell's parents' spare bedroom, Joel went to the mountaintop with Dee Dee Weir during a particularly fine party.

It was clumsier than he had anticipated, more to do with the fitting of parts, like building a model airplane. And, as near as he could tell, it was no fun for her whatsoever.

And yet, it was all heaven and earth needed to provide him for the rest of his natural born life and all that came after. He swore this to God or whomever could've squeezed into the room past the line of couples waiting just outside the door for their turn.

Unlike fractions, this was something Joel felt he'd like to spend a lot of time getting a handle on.

— ◄ ▬ —

Todd had been at that party, too.

Having carved a niche for himself that had him at least on the fringes of acceptance, being neither ugly enough nor fat enough nor effeminate enough nor dorky enough nor bland enough nor brainiac enough nor shy enough nor ethnic enough nor poor enough to earn the pro forma scorn of the in-crowd, Todd was allowed into the occasional party.

The goal at this age, after all, was simply to fill the house—so long as you didn't reek of the untouchables, what the hell, stop on by. The final measure of the party's success would be the number of kids who had to be flushed out of the house when the parents and/or cops arrived.

So Todd had been there that night, largely sticking to the margins and straying not at all from his own subset of borderline geeks. He watched, with an almost anthropological focus, the behavior of those who truly belonged here: the primal grunts and high-fives of the bully boys, and the giggly, teasing flitters of the girls. He envied their ease, their utter lack of reserve.

"*This* is how children should be," thought Todd, who was probably alone in the room in thinking that all of them were, at age thirteen, still "children." Life ahead was hard enough, so let loose *now*, for Christ's sake. Respect nothing. Celebrate the sheer wastefulness of youth.

At least make loud noises or break something.

So why had Todd felt, from the moment he entered the house, the vice-lock on his spine, the queasiness in his belly? Why was this minor league attempt at debauchery, staged by Wad Wendell's older sister while their parents were away at their grandfather's funeral, not catching Todd up in its hedonistic updraft? Why was he such a joyless pain-in-the-ass?

As he stood at the head of the short line for the bathroom, he pummeled himself with such self-loathing. Just behind him stood Cindy Becker, just about the most hellaciously fine piece of work the eighth grade had to offer. Hovering around her was Sue DeAngelus, whose reputation for indiscriminate sluttiness more than made up for a horsy face and a stickpin body.

Such girls were never alone, Todd noted, not even in line to use the can. They were always, as now, with their leering, peacockish boyfriends—a jock or a sociopath or whatever it was girls that age fancied. He knew they never fancied him.

"Jesus," he thought, the need to pee reaching critical stages. "With three-quarters of a beer in me, I might even be bold enough to chat a girl up if there was one here without a guy putting his hands all over her."

If everybody in this line wasn't in fact paired up, waiting to get into the…

Todd figured it out in the exact instant the door opened and Joel Kasten emerged, Dee Dee Weir trailing behind. Both were adjusting their clothes.

Joel looked flushed, slightly dazed, as he stumbled into Todd, next in line.

"Oh," Joel said, surprised and then impressed to find Todd Noland here. "Hey. It's all yours…"

Joel looked around, trying to see who Todd had scored as a sex mate. No one was there, as Todd—and the rest of the room—painfully realized.

"Better get out of his way, dude," Barry Patton guffawed, a couple gallons of beer already in him. A large group—mostly juniors, and all smelling blood—crowed, "This kid needs the room to himself!"

Barry made the universal sign for jerking off as Todd went pale, realizing that his blunder had been a source of sniggering fun for the past several minutes.

Todd looked past Joel into what he had thought was the bathroom, and saw the knotted sheets upon the bed, the wadded tissues and rubber wrappers on the nightstand. On the wall above the bed, Todd noted, was an embroidered rendering of two teddy bears hugging, with big cartoon hearts over their heads.

"Hugs 'n' kisses!" it said.

Todd looked to Joel, wondering if his old friend might save him.

"Jesus, dude," Joel said. His minions, having laid bare the underbelly, breathlessly awaited the plunging of the knife. "Go jack off someplace else. The fuck's the matter with you?"

Off Joel's razor blade sneer, the boys in the rec room fell into hoots and snorts, singeing his skin. The embarrassed, emasculating giggles of the girls drove him toward the stairway leading up and out.

He sat on the curb for an hour and a half until his dad came to take him home.

Todd Says "Fuck"

From the doctor's office, it was a natural straight shot to the Happy Snack. Beyond Joel's fierce desire for a cigarette, he knew that gathered in the store's parking lot would be a fair sampling of his constituency, sucking their smokes, swigging their beers, striking their poses.

While Joel had never physically left them, his true essence had been denied them for going on three months. He longed to be among them again, their silenced king restored!

Only as Joel crawled from his car and noticed the scruffy knot of teenaged ennui that awaited him did it occur to him that he was about to make his triumphant Happy Snack return with Todd Noland at his side. It was an instinctive thing, this automatic style-gauge that hovered above his head and constantly cast back pictures of the precise attitude he was conveying in that moment, allowing him to make unconscious alterations—whether subtle or pronounced—which would make him conform perfectly to the image he sought to project. Cool people are born with these things.

The gauge had never failed him before, and now the alarms were going off: Todd Noland, a tolerable drone when he knew to stick to the corners, was about to be recast as someone vital to Joel's recovery.

A line would be crossed. Todd would now be offered to the A-crowd as someone worthy of Joel's company, and thus a new member of the team.

Joel did not anoint outsiders casually. Did Todd Noland—who never wore the right clothes, who played no sport, who leaked insecurity and awkwardness like a watery fart—truly have the Right Stuff?

"Fuck it," Joel thought. He made the rules; he could break the rules. Maybe the finest privilege of mass acclaim was to do something unexpected, just to watch the others follow behind.

This would be his thank-you gift to Todd. For helping him.

"See ya," Todd said, already half a block toward school as Joel came around the back of the car. Todd pulled on his invisible body armor as the school building—the repository of the Right Thing To Do, no matter how viciously it scraped the essence from the soul—pulled him closer.

"Hey," Joel shouted through his tender but joyously revived jaw. "Where're you going?" A storm was predicted for later in the day. The cooling air felt marvelous on his face.

Todd turned, walked backward as he spoke. The Right Thing To Do would not be denied.

"Got Trig. Gonna be late."

Joel ran to catch up.

"No, come on. Hang with me for a while. I want you to."

Todd scrunched up his face and looked to the Happy Snack parking lot, where a dense, sticky cloud of smoke and teen punk swagger clung to the air. Not only was that the Wrong Thing To Do, it was also kind of a joke.

"Nah."

Todd obviously didn't get it. "Come on," Joel said, a little sternly. "You're with me now."

Todd looked again to the parking lot as Bobby Slopes hawked up a huge ball of snot and spat it onto the side of a Honda.

"So you skip a class," Joel crooned. "I'll fix it with Webber. I'll tell him you were helping me. He won't touch you. Besides, I don't have any money. You gotta buy me some cigarettes."

"I'm not buying cigarettes!" Todd squeaked, instantly ashamed for his timidness, but at the same time proud of his stance. He thought cigarettes were for assholes.

"Then I'll just take your cash. Come on."

It was so odd, yet not unfamiliar, to have Joel Kasten *begging* for Todd's companionship. Back when they were eight—back when there was parity—they would switch off luring the other into adventures.

Todd looked back toward school.

"Go with him," it whispered. "I'll just swallow you whole tomorrow."

Todd shrugged. Inside his head, where his thoughts were always allowed to pool and gather potency before being sent forth, he said:

"What the fuck."

(Unlike his peers, Todd didn't swear that often, believing that the indiscriminate spraying of an expletive as glorious and wicked as "fuck" simply diluted its sting. Time was, not that long ago, when a "fuck" introduced into everyday conversation meant something, could even guarantee a response most definitely provoked. It was a word grenade, he thought, to be employed sparingly. When it mattered.)

And so he said: "Yeah. What the fuck."

Joel smiled, his jaw—still being road-tested—smarting from the workout.

— ◄ ▬ —

"Fucker!" Wad Wendell howled upon noting Joel's arrival, high-fiving him heartily and throwing a forearm into his shoulder. Todd always noticed how dim people invariably greeted each other with strenuous over-exaggeration, as if to celebrate the fact that neither had been struck dead by their staggering stupidity since last they met.

Joel threw his head back and let out a wolfish "Whoooo!"

"Hey," Wad continued. "Fucking Slopes has VD!"

"Shut the fuck up, I do not!" Bobby protested as the coterie of parking lot sluts stirred uncomfortably.

"His piss hurts!"

Joel was confused. *This* was the reception he was getting?

Slopes drew nearer, deep dread in his voice. "Dude, it burns when I piss, like razor blades. That don't mean it's VD, right? Could just be like a dick virus, right?"

"Hey!" Joel protested. "I'm just back from the doctor, you fucks. Anybody notice I'm talking for the first time in two fucking months?"

"Dude, you're talking!" Wad smiled, winding up to pretend to sock Joel right in his still fragile jaw. "Now you can tell Slopes his dick is gonna fall off!"

Joel glowered. "Just shut the fuck up. Who's got a cigarette?"

Wad didn't. Wad never had any. Wad was a first-class mooch.

Slopes had just lit his last and thrown the empty pack to the ground, where garbage was already nearly ankle deep. On this precise spot, in the middle of the night, while these degenerate teens dreamed their foul, musky dreams, a broom-bearing Daljit Singh would be uttering dark curses at them all.

"Here," Rod Broyals offered. It looked like a joint, but Joel knew it was a bidi, one of those dopey Indian imports that somehow had become fashionable. Joel deeply resented any fad that ignited without his endorsement. "It's cinnamon," Broyals boasted.

"Get that the fuck away from me," Joel barked. "I haven't had a smoke in two months, and my first is gonna be some gay foreign thing?"

He looked to his men, his top lieutenants. They had nothing for him.

"You guys are fucking useless. Come on," he turned to Todd, who had been rendered invisible up to this point. As Todd followed Joel through the crowd toward the store, Wad and the others looked on with surprised sneers.

A foul mood was draping itself over Joel. There were the usual high-fives and dead-eyed offerings of genuflection, but nobody seemed to realize the significance of this day. It's not like there was a memo released, alerting them to the trip to the doctor. But in the past, word just got around when something key happened to Joel Kasten.

Back in the second grade, Joel had seen a video of Eskimos honoring one of their own by standing in a circle, holding an animal skin taut, and trampolining their hero high into the air, his body flung heavenward by the love of his people.

He couldn't quite envision how this would translate to his present reality, but Joel really kind of thought that by now he'd have been thrown into the air like an Eskimo.

"Give me one of those," he growled upon seeing the first pack of Marlboros in the crowd. He didn't even know the girl he took it from, just knew that if he didn't get a smoke soon, this piss-poor morning was going to really bottom out.

He held the cigarette between his fingers, and felt the raw smoothness of its paper. Its time had come. Its skin would now be set ablaze, its fertile contents glowing gloriously as it transmogrified from scratchy tobacco to smooth, smooth smoke, set free to caress the hungry passageways of Joel

Kasten's respiratory system.

From the centuries-old tobacco fields of America's proud South to this diagonally-striped parking lot in a strip mall, a holy communion would now commence.

Joel engaged the flint of his child-proof disposable lighter, and touched the flame to the tip of the Marlboro, welcoming the smoke into his lungs.

And coughed. Not dramatically—no hacking or gagging. But still: not cool.

"Shit!" he barked, throwing the cigarette to the ground. "How the fuck old are these?!" His jaw raged as he ground his teeth.

Darlene Foster, from whom Joel had swiped the cigarette, panicked. She had never once been addressed by Joel Kasten, not in the thirteen years they had gone to the same schools.

She was an ugly girl. She had no business being here.

"I just…"

"Christ!" Joel sneered, pushing his way toward the store.

Todd followed behind, turning to give a sympathetic nod to Darlene as he passed. He understood.

Home

The swelling would go down; she'd stop in a minute to get some ice for it. Annie McCullough wished she hadn't yelled at them so viciously but, dammit! she had to get this work done.

She could hear them rustling shyly outside the door, too afraid to knock, but desperately curious to know what she was doing in there.

What she did, not just in her old bedroom but with her career, her *life*, baffled them. They knew she lived in Manhattan. They knew she worked for that company that shows the rock and roll videos. And they knew she had become so very brittle, harsh, and gaunt since leaving home. By all accounts she was flourishing, at whatever it was she did.

And, lord, how she smoked. It had been the big issue, after her mother had convinced her to come home for a full week to celebrate her father's fiftieth birthday. Did she have to smoke in the house?

It was the worst possible time for Annie who, as VP of Special Projects at R²Rev, had quickly learned that her sole special project was finding a way out of this joke of a position that Hutch Posner had stuck her with.

Over the course of a couple years, the network had taken off, just as Hutch had promised, its scabrous blend of well-faked societal contempt and lowbrow irreverence sparking a chemical charge in the lustily-sought-after teen male demo. The cross promotions with World Wrestling Entertainment, the hiring of porn princess Mimi SoWett as veejay for the vital ten p.m. to two a.m. daypart, special programming like *Bowel Cloud Theatre* (Roger Viner's smash idea to air things like the State of the Union Address mixed with fart noises)—they all spoke to the very special entertainment needs of the average American male teenager. The fact that post-adolescent tastemakers and trend-definers on both coasts were also tuning in and getting their rocks off was just a validation that R²Rev worked.

And watching it all from the sidelines was Annie McCullough, who simmered and stewed every time she saw the R²Rev logo cast in gold and dangling from a rapper's neck, or tattooed over the scabby sores on a thrash metaller's biceps, or driving a marked-up goldmine at every mall boutique in the country.

Having done no less than name the goddamned enterprise, Annie had then fallen back on her Midwestern naiveté, foolishly assuming that the R²Rev tidal wave would sweep her along and deposit her in a position that rightfully acknowledged her role in the network's success. Only after weeks stretched into months, only after she began to realize that the skin-searing misogyny that would come to fuel R²Rev's programming also defined the well-sculpted go-go boys who were driving it, did Annie realize she had been screwed.

She had expected more of Hutch Posner, who had been a decent boss prior to the birth of the network, and with whom she had actually shared her bed several times in the dizzying early days of pre-production. She had admired the way Hutch had nurtured his germ of an idea into a potential industry, and in the early going she had thrilled at his eager acceptance of her ideas and concepts. She felt that they could very well go forward as partners, in business, though definitely not as lovers. ("Too long to raise the flag and then nothing to salute," as her dotty Aunt Felicia used to say.)

But as the network rocketed toward reality and the bully boys began elbowing for titles and corner offices and positions on comp lists all over Manhattan, Annie realized that nothing of note would be given to her. She took her complaints to Hutch—regrettably, *after* she had drawn shut her legs—and only through persistent badgering and well-placed guilt did Hutch come up with VP of Special Projects.

Which, for the past year, had translated into just one thing: Casey Lattimer.

— ◆ —

It wasn't that Casey wasn't popular. True, Mimi SoWett got most of the press in the early days, particularly once enterprising teens figured out that with a picture-in-picture television they could simultaneously watch

Mimi interviewing Snoop Dogg while being gang-banged on DVD. Even *Newsweek* ran a "What has the world come to?" piece about this internet-fueled phenomenon.

The zeitgeist was strummed; the conquest drew nearer.

But Casey was hanging in there, holding down the early evening shift when latchkey kids were home from school and able to hook into R²Rev before their parents got home. Hanging with Casey Lattimer was like being left in the care of the dopiest, most degenerate outlaw at school—the kind of kid who would've been Ritalin-ed down or booted out for spouting the kind of idiocy that flowed from his mouth. And yet, here he was, set loose before a TV camera four hours a day to bust things up between videos.

The problem was that Casey was stupid—book stupid, life stupid, *hygienically* stupid. Hutch knew Casey was stupid when he plucked him out of the open casting call, which drew every aspiring actor, musician, and miscreant within a 1,000 mile radius of Manhattan.

It had been both the most exhilarating and depressing day of Hutch's life—this horrid stew of narcissistic kids, each raised with the promise that somehow celebrity was owed them, all looking to ride R²Rev to a life of fortune and mass adulation. Hutch needed just a handful of the perfectly tattooed, pierced, and sneer-laden to populate his world. The rest would have to be sent away to suckle their delusions somewhere else.

Casey had stood out because he really didn't care, kept insisting that he was there to audition for *Wheel of Fortune*, which, the staff kept telling him, was taped in Los Angeles and, regardless, would turn a hose on him before allowing him within 100 yards of Vanna White.

"Vanna White," he crooned. "Vanna *Wet*. Heh heh heh. I gotta buy me a vowel, Pat!"

From the observation suite next door, Hutch watched Casey over the live feed and detected something fresh and raw in the kid. Every other auditioner had some kind of shtick—wizened club slut, rap-sheeted rap slinger, white boy slacker. But few were able to ape the demographic as effortlessly as Casey. If R²Rev was to mirror its intended audience, then this was precisely the kind of kid who could deliver a daypart.

Casey was brought back for a series of interviews, during which he entertained Hutch's selection team with a mortifying lack of candor and a reasonable knowledge of current pop culture. His prime negative was that he stank—literally—to the extent that the interviews were finally moved out of doors, where the dank and gritty winds of 52nd Street could blow Casey's less favorable qualities in someone else's direction.

Hutch observed it all—the interview sessions, the mock video links that Casey taped with goggle-eyed wonder—and began to sense that this was his man. It would be a gamble, throwing someone this unstable before a live camera, but Hutch knew that victory would come only from walking that razor's edge between canned, demo-stroking anarchy, and actual garbage.

— ◉ —

After insisting that someone steer Casey toward a shower and a bar of soap, Hutch met with his future star for a one-on-one.

"Can I get you anything?" Hutch asked as he relaxed casually in a chair across from Casey. He noticed immediately that the kid's stench was only slightly bettered by a summery waft of apricot shampoo.

"Know what I'd like?" Casey began. "I'd like to be inside a bomb when it goes off, right? But in slow motion. Right? It's, like, black inside there, all quiet and nice, and then—boom!—I'm flyin' out. Flyin' *up*. I'm lookin' down at the hole I've made and the people I've fucked up, but I'm flyin', right alongside all the dirt and rock and shit. And I'm getting higher and higher, and it's getting quieter and quieter. It's beautiful, dude.

"And then I'm falling, but it's cool because I'm light, like a feather, right? I'm floatin' and I'm fallin'. And I touch down, and it's peaceful there, too. I'm miles away from what I've done. But nothing's the same anymore. Something blew up, dude. Blew up bad. You don't never put things right after that."

"Something to drink, maybe? Water? A Coke?"

"I'd *like* a beer."

"Mm, not cool, really. You know, we're trying to run a business here."

"Yeah," Casey rolled his eyes and snorted disdainfully. "I get it."

"Christ," Hutch thought. "It only took fifteen seconds for this kid to bust *me* as the Establishment. And I'm barely thirty-five!"

He pressed on. "You've got a great look, very street. Ever done any modeling?"

"Nope."

"Any acting experience?"

"Nope."

"Been in a band? Been before an audience for any reason?"

"Nope."

"Given a speech in a speech class?"

"Nope."

"Played around with a home video camera? Maybe done some goofing around on camera?"

"Nope."

"Any store surveillance tape we could get our hands on?"

Casey just stared at him. For all his proclamations of ballsiness, Hutch hadn't had to make any nervy calls yet in the network's young life. If he were to go with this hunch, give this skanky, silly young man a potentially global platform with which to do God knows what, *that* would be ballsy. That would be R²Rev.

Establishment, my ass.

Hutch studied Casey, trying to picture him bouncing off a multi-million dollar satellite, into homes with doors locked to protect themselves from just such street trash.

Point man for a revolution.

It got very quiet.

"*Boom!!!*" Casey screamed, then cackled delightedly. Once again, he was a feather, freed from a bomb.

So Casey Lattimer had been there when R²Rev made its debut three years back, part of the veejay team that also included Mimi SoWett and Dr. Poon, the hip-hop firebrand whose profane hit albums and string of felonies brought much street cred to the new net.

Keeping Casey on a short leash—meaning on tape—Hutch packaged the kid brilliantly, sending him out into the street for engagements with the fans, unleashing him, Howard Stern-style, at stuffy gatherings, and setting him up with the occasional celebrity interview, during which Casey would invariably try to score drugs. Hutch now had over seven minutes of video trims, offering nothing but his young star trying to mooch dope off famous people. He imagined such encounters going out live, and he shuddered.

After several months of study, Hutch knew that Casey simply could not serve R²Rev as a live entity. True, there was something scintillating and scary about letting him loose on-air. Early on he did an entire four-hour block built around stepping in dog shit and trying to get it off his shoe. It was, in a train wreck kind of way, terribly compelling television. (The fetching NYU grad riding the tape delay that day didn't let a single "shit" get through and was honored accordingly. If Annie McCullough had thought to look, she'd have seen that this kid was nearly on the same salary track she was.)

No, Casey was to be caged on tape for the life of his involvement with the network.

Finding venues for his very special talents, however—*that* became Annie's problem. Manhattan and the surrounding boroughs were quickly ruled out, both by the fact that Casey's antics had half the city wanting to throw his scrawny little ass in jail, and the fact that Letterman and all the other TV wise-asses had been milking New York backdrops for decades.

Hutch didn't want his network confined to the coasts, where trends have such a short shelf life. He wanted to take R²Rev straight into the heartland, where lives were dull and teens less inclined to notice that their latest Shiny New Thing had become a joke out in the real world.

"Swear to God," Hutch would laugh, "they've still got Farrah Fawcett hair out there!"

So it was decided that Casey Lattimer would be the network's emissary, spreading his special magic at inappropriate gatherings like state fairs and Shriner parades, where he could be parachuted in and then yanked out before some good ol' boy snapped his neck.

The rubes in the sticks, at least until they came to hate him, could goggle at the celebrity in their midst and maybe even get themselves on the tee-vee. The sophisticates in the major markets could dine on Casey's oafish debasement of small-town institutions and beliefs. Everybody wins!

Annie's job—her Special Project—was to find new canvases on which Casey could smear his genius.

It was best, she decided, to send Casey into cornball events in nowhere burgs that drew the town's most easily offended residents: all-you-can-eat pancake fundraisers, statue dedications, Junior Farm Queen pageants, and the like. The announcement and coverage of such events were the lifeblood of small-town newspapers across the country, but—no surprise—such papers often had neither the reason nor the sophistication for establishing themselves on the internet. That meant Annie had to gather her information the old-fashioned way: poring over out-of-state phone directories, making cold calls, and building a network of young volunteer stringers across the country who would make her aware of potential "Casey environments" in exchange for R²Rev hats and T-shirts.

And so there she was, the week of her father's fiftieth birthday, holed up in her old bedroom in suburban Ann Arbor, tying up the family's phone line for hours on end, trying to schedule Casey's next six months. The sense at the network was that they were under-utilizing their star, and that his act was starting to take on a troubling sameness. The pressure was on Annie to subtly reconceptualize Casey Lattimer while leaving his engaging abrasiveness intact.

She had told her mother it was a bad time, and apologized to her father as best she could for her preoccupation. She hoped he would appreciate that she was as committed to her career as he was to his (her father was a cop, earning only slightly more than his daughter after 25 years of service; she spent sixteen hours a day trying to find trusting people who could be humiliated on TV for sport).

But she was in the home stretch. Her father's birthday dinner was on the table, and they were all waiting. All she had to do was hear back from one more stringer and her October was set. Her cell phone had died, and her little brother had been on the landline for what seemed like hours. She had spent the late afternoon pacing, burning through a pack and a half of cigarettes while telepathically begging her brother to hang the hell up.

Finally, the call made it through: Casey and the guerilla video crew would be welcome at a hog breeding exhibition in Baraboo, Wisconsin, on the fourteenth. Annie's heart sang. Farmers! Animal sex! Pig shit to accidentally step in! She could already envision the smirking promo spots as she proudly typed the specifics into her laptop and emailed them off to New York.

She stood with satisfaction, exhausted but happy to finally be able to devote some attention to her family. It was never easy to explain what she did or why it mattered, but tonight she would try. While pretty much everything she had Casey doing was offensive and embarrassing, she was a linchpin in the programming pipeline of the hottest cable channel in the country. Surely they could see beyond Casey being thrown in jail for trying to give a wedgie to the mayor of Mederville, Iowa, and understand her vital role at R²Rev.

She stubbed out her cigarette and felt a sincere wave of pride and enthusiasm carry her through the bedroom door, only to have her feet tangle in a dense pile of towels that her mother had laid on the floor to contain her cigarette smoke.

Annie spilled out into the hallway in a belch of smoke, her forehead colliding sharply with the linen closet doorknob as she fell. It really, really hurt.

"*Jesus fucking Christ!*"

Her family, gathered Waltons-like around the dinner table, heard the thud and her voice rumbling down the hallway, and braced themselves. Her father, fifty today, winced.

"God*damn!*" Annie screamed, coming at her mother with a fistful of towels. "I mean… Dammit, Mother!"

She hurled the towels across the room. Equal parts furious, wounded, and embarrassed, she whinnied like a demented horse and instinctively stomped back to her room and her work.

"Christ!"

She slammed the door behind her, immediately understanding that she had just done an awful thing. Her heart sank. Her career concerns paled next to her regret at what had just happened. All they wanted was to see their little girl again, to try and re-create, if only for one week, life as it used to be. And she was being such a bitch.

She would cool down, make things right—after a smoke, and maybe just a little more work.

There was still November to book.

Lost before the Levee

Rain was due. And Frank Kolak felt it. He always felt it. It was when his blue moods took hold, laid him low until the weather passed. In a life tending toward the melancholy, clouds blowing in invariably brought almost more sadness than he could bear.

His father had died in the rain.

It was a South Carolina summer, and Frank was nine years old. Every year the little town of Beckett got too much rain—houses flooded, sewers overflowed, Hard Tar Road filled up like a soup bowl, clean up to the 6th Street bridge. But what was coming that summer day was being called a disaster—a once in a lifetime kind of thing.

Maybe he remembered things differently after it happened, trying to project some kind of ominous portent on the days leading up to the storm, but Frank recalled his father spending a great deal of time charting the path of the weather system bearing down on them. On that first morning, when the paper first gave word that something horrible seemed to be coming together over the Gulf of Mexico, Walter Kolak sat at the breakfast table and sullenly read the story over and over. He was so entranced by the news that he was late getting to the shop, a first for him. Long after customers stopped coming around, Walter still prided himself on opening his doors on time.

Back then, it wasn't so easy to see bad weather coming. In the first couple days, it actually looked like the storm wouldn't hit as far north as Beckett. But just in case, a special service was held at church to wish the disaster away, and Walter Kolak insisted that he and his family be there. Frank remembers how intensely his father closed his eyes and prayed. This was when the boy first understood how serious this all was.

When the storm fixed upon its course, when the assault became inevitable, Walter bore down. Even in the mildest summer storm, the Kolak house took on some water, but now Walter seemed determined to beat it back. He was a slight man, as Frank would grow up to be, but he took on astonishing strength from somewhere. His hands were worn raw as he tore dirt from the back yard to build a steep grade around the perimeter of the house. To the irritation of his neighbors, he dug trenches with which to funnel the tide away. He cleaned out the gutters, cemented over cracks in the foundation, and boarded up the first floor windows should the waters rise that high. He ripped apart the shed out back, which housed his sad little repair business, for plywood.

And then, should all that fail, he dragged anything of worth up to the attic, starting with the important papers, including the bankruptcy records and the will that he and Lucille had cobbled together. Her wedding dress, his jazz records, a small freezer that only worked half the time—they were all moved upstairs. With not all that much time to spare, Frank marveled at how much deliberation his father gave each item. He ran his hand slowly over everything that had been sitting long-neglected in their moldy old cellar, as if to find a memory that would earn it a passage to safety.

Meanwhile, he ordered his wife Lucille to take every bit of cash they had and stock up on canned goods and necessities—huge amounts, more than the family of three could use in a year. "Empty out the bank account," he had insisted. "What's not used will keep. Best to have it on hand, just in case."

For eighteen hours straight, Frank watched as his father worked without rest, listening obsessively to the radio and watching the purpling sky. Frank did what he could to help, hoping that, by joining his father in this almost messianic quest, there might be a bond, finally, between the two. But mostly he just stayed out of the old man's way.

When the waters recede, Frank figured, *then* they could see what they had accomplished together.

No one slept that night, what with the pounding and the shouting and the unrelenting hiss of the radio, its forecasters growing ever more dire as the storm took shape over Alabama and started heading northeast.

Just past four in the morning, the South Fork river rose up and swallowed whole the nearby town of Kitchings Mill, rain falling at a rate of almost three inches in just over an hour. Entire city blocks were being swept away. Folks who hadn't obeyed the order to head to higher ground—"Well," the grim-voiced man on the radio said into the night, "God have mercy on 'em."

With the morning sun cloaked behind matted black clouds, unable to accept its responsibility for the day, Frank's neighborhood lost power at dawn. Frank's mother broke into the carton of batteries she had brought home from the market the night before and fired up the flashlights and the transistor radio, just in time to hear that the heart of the storm could be expected within the half hour.

Already it was raining—Frank's father soaked to the bone as he put the finishing touches on a final berm—but this was just a prelude. The ground, already saturated, had no hope of accepting what was to come.

Finally, Walter Kolak put down his shovel and dragged himself into the kitchen as his wife broke open the refrigerator and served up everything inside, lest it spoil anyway. Tired and scared, Frank nevertheless rejoiced at this turn of events, piling his plate up with ice cream and bologna and hardboiled eggs. Never before daring to be playful with his father, Frank took advantage of the lull before God-knew–what, and urged his old man to pull up a seat and help himself to the damnedest breakfast he'd ever seen.

Walter just grunted wearily beneath a sad half-grin and poured himself the last bitter cup of the night's coffee.

"The levee's gonna need shoring up. I'd better get over there."

Beckett was that kind of small town—when Walter's shoe repair shop was about to go broke, and his hardware store before that, neighbors instinctively came around, spending what they could to keep his doors open. What was destined to happen anyway happened a little later, thanks to good people Walter didn't really know.

So when the town itself was at risk, when the Congaree took on more water than it could hold and threatened to jump its banks, the townsfolk instinctively grabbed shovels and met at the levee. The river always won, but there was never any thought of not putting up a fight. Walter, knowing a debt was owed to these people, would be the last to surrender to the waterline.

All of nine years old, Frank felt halfway grown up already, and begged to come along and help. But Walter solemnly told his son that his place was with his mother, to see to it that the house and everyone inside got through this as best they could. On the other side of the storm, he said, he'd want to hear that Frank stood up like a man.

Walter refused breakfast, said he'd packed something in a knapsack, if he needed the strength. He said a terse goodbye to his family and headed down to the river. With the rainy gray dawn casting a bleak, despairing light, Frank and his mother watched as, all along the block, men with their shovels went off to battle.

The flood wall quickly dissolved away, just as everyone knew it would, and all the men of the neighborhood raced home just ahead of the deluge.

All, that is, except Walter. As the great fist of water hit, Frank and his mother watched hopefully in the direction he had last traveled. Down the road, now a river, came tires, furniture—tangles of this and that torn loose from countless lives. But still no Walter.

With a fury that sliced shingles from rooftops and punched holes clean through, the tempest pummeled the neighborhood. Some of the older homes on the block, built cheaply by people who couldn't afford better and who never knew how long before they'd be ridden out to live somewhere else, simply melted into the turbulence. Whole families were flushed out into the street, only to be fished out by neighbors whose homes were faring better.

As agonizingly slow as the rains had come, they moved on in under a half-hour. Almost immediately, the sun started earning its way back through the clouds, the people of the neighborhood descending from high ground and upper stories to wade through water that rose to the chest in some spots. Many homes would ultimately have to be torn down, their aged wooden structures infected by the rot caused by such an assault of mud and water. But Walter Kolak's house stood firm—six inches of river left to stagnate in his cellar—but otherwise Walter had won. When he finally turned up, he'd have rare reason to celebrate.

Just past two that afternoon, the Congaree crested. Tadpoles, freshly introduced to life in lower middle-class living rooms, began to feel the gentle tug of the tide that would return them to their top-flight river homes, and to their futures as frogs.

With an agonizing stillness that belied any movement whatsoever, the hot, fetid waters slowly began to recede. If not tomorrow then the next day, Beckett would have order restored—and a fresh tragedy to deal with.

Surely Walter Kolak was dead, presumably swept downstream before he even reached the levee. In the aftermath of the flood, no one could say for sure that Walter and his shovel had actually made it to the flood wall. Truth be told, more than one man had scowled angrily at Walter's absence at such a desperate time. The man never fit into the neighborhood, they thought, with his skittish ways and his pathetic ability to foul up even the most simple-minded business. When this crisis passed, some men on the levee had said, Walter Kolak would have to answer for his inaction.

The police were called, and authorities downstream promised to start dragging the river once the silt stopped churning. Goaded on by the sight of Walter's timidly frantic wife and poor, fragile Frank, the men of Beckett attempted to retrace his last known steps, poking through the tangles of reeds and branches lining the river to see if his body had never actually made it out of town.

It was a half-hearted search, the decent gesture to make, despite the fact that they all had flooded homes needing their immediate attention. The fact was that Walter Kolak barely seemed to occupy space while living. His remains would probably prove just as hard to get a fix on.

— ◆———◁ —

The pond that filled Hard Tar Road after every flood was always the gift, the temporary swimming hole that the children of Beckett could splash away in while their parents tended to the back-breaking business of shoveling water and sludge out of their cellars. They weren't supposed to, but sometimes they jumped right off the 6th Street bridge into the gritty, torpid water below, ignoring the fact that, as the waters receded, the submerged surface of the flooded road drew nearer and nearer.

At dusk on the day after the flood, Jeffy Kind dove into the Hard Tar from the overpass, and there was Walter, tangled in something and swelled up dead from having sat at the bottom of the makeshift swimming hole for the last day and a half. Police sent to feel their way down to the bottom of the boggy pool and pull him loose had to give up until the waters went away. Whatever Walter had got himself snagged onto didn't want to let him go.

Frank and his mother sat vigil by the side of the flooded road all night, traffic on the 6th Street bridge howling over their heads. It didn't *have* to be Walter down there, both thought as they watched the water recede inch by inch. But most likely it was.

It was past noon the next day before authorities knew the water was low enough to retrieve Walter. All along Hard Tar, all along the overpass, people gathered to watch, until the police had sense enough to close off the area.

Lucille, too quiet to ever let on how close she was to losing her mind over the past couple days, recognized that this was not the place for Frank. They would return to the house. "Could someone please send word once the job is done?"

The water was soon only knee deep, and Walter's swollen body met the air once again. Officer Jack Pouter, who had been known to watch out for Walter when life rose up time and again to send things spiraling, took it upon himself to get in close and set Walter free. What he found broke his heart. Made him mad. Haunted him forever.

Walter Kolak wasn't stuck at all. Instead, he had been chained and padlocked to a sewer grate. As the flood began to batter the town and as the waters rushed down the Hard Tar, he had been alive, had fought for air as the deluge quickly rose above his head. Then, when he was dead, the rampaging river tore at his body, held in place by the heaviest gauge chain link available, the kind that Frank used to marvel at in Walter's hardware store—the kind Walter used to tell his five-year-old son was the very same used to hold down King Kong.

In his breast pocket, in a plastic sandwich bag meticulously taped shut to keep its contents dry, was a note:

"I did it."

This was not the work of an exceptionally sadistic killer wandering the land, nor an example of the sort of racial viciousness that still thrived in the South of the mid-sixties. Walter did this, by his own hand; he had needed to make that clear. Even in death, he didn't want to cause anyone any trouble.

When word got to young Frank, however, the boy heard the same words form a different message. Years later, an adult Frank would explain away those words in a more benign light, but in that nightmarish instant in which the nine-year-old boy was told of the circumstances of his father's death, when a freshly assaulted mind can hear truths that are too harsh to consider later on, Frank found an air of triumph in Walter's note:

"I *did* it. I accomplished this! I am free."

He pictured his old man settling in under the bridge, snapping shut the padlock, dropping the key down the sewer, and waiting patiently for his pain to be washed away—and hoping, this time, that things would work out.

When the rains came, and low roads took on water—these were the days Frank Kolak smoked.

Driving to school that morning, he desperately wanted to stop at the Happy Snack for cigarettes, but he could never bear to wade through the knot of teenagers perpetually stationed in the parking lot. They smoked and drank and did God knows what else there, sullenly flagrant in their disregard for laws and consequences. For Frank to walk among them would require him either to condone their behavior, which he could not, or stop it, which he also could not.

As he drove past, he looked longingly at the teenagers lighting up so freely. Hopefully, he could bum a smoke from someone in the teacher's lounge. When the rain started and the students scattered, he would sneak out to the Happy Snack during his sixth hour free time and stock up.

Stand

The sign on the Happy Snack's front door read "No More Than Two Students During School Hours." At ten o'clock this morning, more than twenty students were inside. Daljit Singh couldn't possibly monitor them all, and knew for a fact that inventory was being stolen all around him, while he basked in the glow of the market at work.

He had once seen the tightly-guarded formula with which the Happy Snack corporate office folded estimated theft losses into the skyrocketing mark-up of shelf prices, leading to record-high company earnings despite the fact that seemingly a third of its stock was being shop-lifted.

It was an artful exercise in supply-and-demand hijacking, the bean-counters at corporate gauging with fascination the point at which cash-flush consumers would balk at the high prices. Like the proverbial frog in the pot of water, blissfully boiling to death as the temperature rises degree by subtle degree, the secret was to bone the customer a penny at a time.

They hadn't caught on yet. Not even close.

Daljit Singh understood that the more that was stolen, the higher he could raise his prices. The more children he allowed in, the more inventory went out.

There went a pack of Oreos—over there, a bag of rubber bands. Could a six dollar hotdog (wholesale cost: 43 cents) be far behind? Daljit thought so, maybe in his lifetime. If he was not shot dead behind the register.

Not all kids stole, of course, because that would interfere with their spending. So they lined up five-deep at the counter, these moneyed young jackals who took for granted the privilege of education, which they rejected at the school down the street. This was what Daljit Singh hated about them most of all: that they should be offered so much of substance, only to throw it away in favor of squalor and frivolity.

The money changed hands skillfully, smooth, uncalloused white palms emerging from pockets and wallets laden with cash, to be deposited into the brown, needy palm of the humble storeowner.

Sometimes these children, aiming for a show of defiance and disdain in front of their friends, threw the money down onto the counter rather than into Daljit's hand. He liked this fine—liked to see the cash spread out before him. To these hate-laden toughs, he always offered a timid bow and a slight tremor to the hand as he quickly, fearfully, made their change. He wanted them to know how inferior he felt to their American swagger. He knew they'd come back two or three times during the day to buy more, just for the chance to sneer at a foreigner.

Oh, the ways to make a dollar in this wondrous, wondrous land.

— ❧ —

Joel rocked on his feet, almost preferring to be in class than endure this wait.

"The fuck's the problem up there?" he grumbled.

Todd stood beside him with a one-liter bottle—a vat, really—of Coke. Somewhere in Todd's brief lifespan, the twelve-ounce can had become a kiddie thing, like training wheels or a hand held crossing the street. Children begged quarters off their mommies to buy *cans* from a vending machine; teenagers demanded vastly more to satisfy their needs.

Now that he was seventeen, Todd just wanted *heft* for his dollar. Coke in a twelve-ounce can was just as sweet, its simple, classic red-and-white packaging just as seductive and fine. But look here: *feel* the weight of the one-liter bottle. Note how its bulk announces itself to your arm, your wrist. *This* is a purchase. Look through the clearness of the plastic (can you see through the can? No!): There's *more* Coke in there. The red and white label? It's *bigger*. There's more bright color. Maybe the eye shouldn't even see this much red; the optic nerve just might burst from such an intense rush of *red*. Red like a fire truck, like a bouncy ball. Red can be like a friend, sometimes.

If the only reason to choose less over more is money—and there's always more money—why would anyone buy less? Even if all you really want is twelve ounces of Coke?

That's what Todd thought. Empires depended on it.

— 🌀 —

Kurt Berger farted—a dry, spiky one. Berger beamed. His friends—no one Joel recognized and thus no one worth knowing—nodded appreciatively, like an earlier generation might have for the second act curtain of a Noel Coward play.

Joel, next in line and just wanting to get out of this goddamned store, was appalled.

"Berger, you suck."

Todd smirked at Joel. "Hanging out with you is great."

"Shut up."

Berger finished his transaction and left; his gassy accomplishment did not. Daljit Singh sniffed the air and gave Joel the hairy eyeball.

"It wasn't me! Just…" He trailed off bitterly, not feeling like an Eskimo at all.

Todd plopped his magnum of Coke on the counter. He handed the storekeeper a twenty, Daljit rang up the sale with a dead-eyed grimace, and Todd gave Joel a five from the change.

Joel took the money without a word of thanks and stepped to the counter, his pack of Marlboros already waiting for him. The cash register pealed.

"Four-twenty-two." Daljit's hand was outstretched, the exchange of cash merely a formality at this point.

Joel fumed: What fucking nerve, this guy knowing from memory what he smoked. He looked at the pack of cigarettes, the stark but familiar label stroking a pleasure node deep inside his subconscious. At this point, the purchase, the zipping off of the cellophane, the tightly-packed set of twenty, straight and white and ready—it all came automatically.

Joel's throat was still raw from the drag he took in the parking lot. There was nothing wrong with that cigarette. He had just forgotten what it felt like.

Students were growing restless behind him. Daljit Singh repeated what was due him.

"Four-twenty-two."

Joel set his spine.

"No. You know what? Forget it."

Todd, still there, sensed something brewing. Joel stuffed the five back into Todd's hand.

Daljit noted the merchandise on the counter, its conversion into currency forestalled.

"You buy something." It wasn't an order. It was a statement of fact, along the lines of "You. Bird. Fly."

"No. I not buy something," He turned to Todd. "Let's go."

Daljit looked to the line of cash-bearing customers who had gone unplucked while Joel wasted these precious moments. He hadn't slept in 37 hours.

"You *buy* something!"

"Get bent."

"You look!" Daljit barked, pointing to the sign near the front door. "'No loitering'!!"

Joel bore down. "*You* look!" He pointed to a small placard next to the register, a laughable remnant of some long-forgotten legal settlement against the tobacco companies. The one in which they agreed to stop selling cigarettes to kids.

"I'm seventeen years old! You're not supposed to be selling me this shit!" He jabbed at the pack of Marlboros, inadvertently causing it to slide across the counter and onto the floor.

Daljit's eyes went wide with outrage. Stealing the inventory—*this* he had been trained to allow. But do it no harm.

"You go!" Daljit cried, causing the customers in line to squirm warily. "You get out of my store. You do not come back until you be buying something!!"

"Fine, you dick!" Joel sneered, running on adrenaline now. He took a swipe at the beef jerky carousel, causing it to spin merrily. The tangy delightfulness of spiced, dried meat wafted into the air.

Reflexively, through his rage, an order was issued from some intricate part of Joel's machinery long beyond his control:

"Buy beef jerky."

He'd be butt-fucked before he'd spend a nickel in this guy's store right now. And yet, even at the height of his defiance, as he sought to deprive this greedy bastard of his coin, his brain was instinctively going for his wallet:

"Package colorful. Smell good. Rack spinning, like toy.

"Buy beef jerky."

This was a fractionated second. Joel didn't consciously register anything here.

He just wanted out. He pushed past Todd for the door. Todd, who *did* understand, looked to his friend with admiration, then to the simmering storeowner, who was already fixing his contempt on the next customer.

"You know what?" Todd said softly, surprising himself. "I've changed my mind." He held up the bottle of Coke.

"I'd like my money back."

Daljit Singh couldn't believe how his morning was going. "What?"

"I'd like my money back. Please."

"No refunds."

Now Joel was watching. Which emboldened Todd.

"I've got my receipt right here. I haven't opened the bottle yet. You can just return it to the cooler. I'm pretty sure you have to give me my money back."

The students in line began to groan. If Daljit didn't deal with this quickly, business was going to flee out the door.

He grabbed a dust-caked pad of forms with the Happy Snack logo printed jauntily across the top.

"Fill this out. Check will be mailed, four to six weeks."

"It's a dollar sixty-nine!"

"Company policy."

"You have to give me my money back."

"Don't know how."

"Look, it's easy." Todd boldly leaned into the cash register. "We have registers just like this at the video store. You push this button here."

The register chirped an alien, menacing new chirp—the sound of money, once collected, being freed.

The cash drawer popped open compliantly. In complete surrender.

"And that negates the transaction. When you do your audit at the end of your shift, it'll show up as a cash refund. *We* have to initial them on the tape, so the corporate office doesn't think we're stealing."

He smiled at Daljit Singh pleasantly. He was being somewhat of a smart-ass, but he was also just trying to help.

The merchant dug his hand into the cash, eyeballing the exact count of paper and coin that would get this terrible, terrible boy out of his store.

"You, too, get out of my store! Don't come back until you will be buying something!!!"

"Okay. Thank you!" Todd said brightly. Now he was just being a smart-ass.

He met Joel at the door, each supremely proud of themselves. They were blocking the electric eye, causing it to "bong" incessantly.

"Go!" Daljit shrieked.

They burst through to the parking lot to discover that it was raining in sheets, the gathered teens flushed away like rats from a crawl space. Todd and Joel were equal parts annoyed and entertained as they squeezed together under the building's narrow overhang. Joel's car was a long half-block away.

The boys laughed. "Shit!"

At the curb, a nearly perfect cigarette had been thrown down as the sky let loose. It was still lit, and its ash snapped with an illicit sizzle as rain dropped from the gutter.

Joel eyed it longingly. Todd knew the look.

"Come on!"

He leapt into the torrential rain, sprinting with a crazy laugh toward Joel's car. If Joel didn't follow with his keys, Todd would get drenched.

Joel giggled boyishly and jumped into the rain after him.

"Motherfucker!!!"

The two created a wake sloshing across the parking lot, getting soaked to the skin but not minding much. This felt familiar, from when they were small.

"You're splashing me!" Joel howled. "Quit!"

"*You* quit!"

Keepin' It Real (Underpants)

The issue at hand was the impending release of the new album from something called ScroatM.

A spindly white rapper with acne scars, a sunken chest, and a catch-all societal rage which could be dialed up effortlessly to ape whichever hateful stance would move the most units, ScroatM went six-times platinum with his previous release, *Right White Nigga*, and in the process, transformed a sniveling canker of a human being into an industry.

The album's leering success (6.5 million units sold in the U.S. alone), combined with a sold-out eighteen-month tour and ancillary product, had made the skeevy, chalk-toned rapper a millionaire several times over, and had single-handedly turned the fledgling Tok$ic label into an industry player.

Bottom-feeders who had cashed in their mob-supported restaurant supply empire in Jersey in order to crash the glamorous world of entertainment, the Tok$ic brain trust had spent the past two years building to this event, the debut of *Freakal Matter*, ScroatM's sophomore effort. The street date wasn't until mid-April, but the rumble in the recording industry was already taking for granted that the album would break the rarefied million unit mark its first week, and in order to ensure that, promotional work had to begin several months out. Everyone with a piece of ScroatM's magic—either directly or as a media conduit—stood to score riches beyond their imagination.

It had been a heady couple of years for Scroat. He had entered the studio to record *Nigga* just days after beating a charge that he had caused a girlfriend's kidney to fail by kicking her repeatedly in the back, and had lived as a pop star prince ever since.

Born Ronald Gerber, a fact not known until the first lawsuit was filed against him, Scroat started as a deejay at clubs in his native Pittsburgh, and then came up through the properly funked-up boroughs of New York, crafting for himself a bile-hissing persona that laid suitably obscene rhymes over samples and phat beats provided by uncredited, soon-to-be-litigious friends.

Without even breaking a sweat, he could rhyme "diarrhea" with "try to see ya" and "die next year (*yee-ah*)" in "Ass Cancer," his legendary, never-to-be-recorded contemplation on the AIDS crisis in the gay community. He broke new ground with the introduction of "gash" as a rhyme-rich alternative to the over-worked sobriquets "bitch" and "ho" (cash, rash, stash, flash, hash, trash, bash, crash, mash, dash, thrash, moustache—all by himself, he thought of words that rhymed with "gash").

He had many fine tattoos. He loved his mama.

He was money.

The disorienting success of *Right White Nigga* had brought problems along with the millions, keeping Scroat busy the past two years with a series of lawsuits filed by leeches from back in the day, a pro forma child abandonment charge brought by the kidney-kicked mother of his three-year-old daughter, and one nightclub assault that had caught Scroat a cred-enhancing night in jail (the final words of Scroat's victim before being hit across the head with a Corona bottle: "You *do* realize you're not black, don't you?").

The most serious of his legal hassles, though, were the seven sexual assaults stretching across the country, all of which grew out of his massively popular track, "Hey, Baldy." A frolicsome little tune about diddling prepubescent girls, the song culminated in Scroat's exhortation to his listeners that they use tweezers to pluck and collect a little girl's first pubic hair as a trophy. "Hey, Baldy" had inspired a leering video that remained in R²Rev's heavy rotation for weeks, featuring a smirking ScroatM rolling around in a sea of unclothed Kewpie dolls, slathered up with K-Y jelly. Merely adding to the fun was the video smear Hutch Posner had deemed necessary when the artist was given to licking and rubbing the plastic baby doll genitalia.

Not having all that much fun, however, were the 11- and 12-year-old girls who found themselves stripped naked in rec rooms and backs of vans, getting crude gynecological exams from rap-frenzied, tweezer-bearing teenaged boys out to party the ScroatM way. The attackers were all white, all caricatured suburban trash.

And they were "child molesters," Scroat declared in the contrite, legalese-laden statement that Tok$ic's bank of attorneys had drafted for him to read in a frail, troubled voice. He "wasn't down with" any of his fans who would act upon his lyrics in such a deplorable fashion.

But should there be any confusion, ScroatM—it turned out—was merely a character through which Ronald Gerber portrayed, with high levels of satire, a crude barbarian rendered immoral by the influences of the world around him. You could no more blame Ronald Gerber for ScroatM as you would Robert DeNiro for Travis Bickle.

Still, a civil suit was mounted against Gerber (aka ScroatM); Tok$ic Records; Soundstream, the monolithic parent company of Tok$ic that had just recently been bought out by the British distillery Fine Geneva; R²Rev Industries; and MediaTrust—the latter two entities having been dragged into the action by R²Rev's incessant playing of the "Hey, Baldy" video.

The case fell apart almost from the beginning, the ACLU and the recording industry's raft of lawyers falling all over themselves to assert ScroatM's First Amendment right to give a wise-ass thumbs-up to fingering seventh-graders. Another suit, filed by the parents of the molesters, who were determined to blame someone other than themselves for the depravity living down the hall in their ranch houses, never got out of the gate.

Still, the trial was an embarrassment for all concerned. Figureheads at Fine Geneva and MediaTrust made appropriate noises approximating a commitment to clean up the acts of revenue-generating tentacles they not only could not control but without help couldn't even find on the flow chart of company holdings.

Dragged to the stand to defend himself, Ronald Gerber—sporting a suit he appeared to have bought from Wal-Mart and scowling like a petulant ten-year-old—was momentarily discomfited when required to give a deadpan recitation of his lyrics in order to have them read into the record:

"Gonna slap you silly 'til you show me your twat/Beggin' on your daddy to show you what's what/When I'm finished on the topside, gonna work on yo butt…"

A song for a twelve-year-old.

This is how men made money in the early 21st century.

— ━●━ —

"S'bout keepin' it real," ScroatM sulked into his Froot Loops.

R²Rev interns, rattled at the high-level stakes surrounding this strategy meeting, had been charged with having fifteen different breakfasts at the ready for the star, nine of them sugary cereals designed for first-graders. Orange juice (pulped and unpulped), toast, bagels, donuts, eggs, pancakes, waffles, and French toast were all standing by in an area just outside the plush R²Rev conference room, despite the very real chance that the talent might not make the meeting at all. It was scheduled for very early in the morning, and Scroat was more and more inclined to let his handlers take care of business. Their nut was banked on Scroat cleaning up. They'd see to it that his fortunes remained stoked.

But he understood what was on the line. *Nigga* had been a scary success, begging for a backlash. There had always been a cruel, bloodless tradition of eviscerating a pop titan for making them care the first time around, but each generation of fans had gotten progressively more vicious. That earlier album—the one that had fused itself to their core being like an opiate-secreting parasite—had spackled in the pock marks of their universe, providing a caricature on which they could base their pose. Their sludgy, lord-don't-make-me-work-too-hard-for-this search for rebellion, preordained to fall in behind *some* cynical play for their hearts and wallets, had randomly lighted on ScroatM.

The zeitgeist, in its maddeningly indiscriminate way, had pissed him golden.

And now, here he came again, bearing new tracks that would be expected to somehow mesh organically with the ScroatM oeuvre that had long ago passed into halfwit hagiography. Tracks that would now be peddled by an artist barely able to hide his contempt for his audience the first time around—he had done everything but pick them up by their ankles and shaken them to get their every last dime. Tracks that were being forged and market-tested with the icy efficiency of a NASA launch, by middle-aged men trying to perpetuate the ScroatM gravy train for an ever-broadening stable of trophy wives. Tracks that would have no choice but to compete with the

Scroat clones who had risen in his wake and eclipsed him in the pantheon of moneyed sociopaths you can dance to.

Tracks that sought to do no less than engender the same zombified loyalty that the ScroatM demographic had succumbed to two years ago—a lifetime in pop fandom.

Oh, and by the way, ScroatM is a *character* portrayed by Ronald Gerber who, with a high degree of satire, blah blah blah…

Teen consumers could always surprise you, which is why R²Rev was prepared to give over hours of its programming to hyping the CD's release. But Hutch Posner sensed that ScroatM was over.

He had seen it countless times before in the net's young life, could almost offer up a formula designed to estimate the half-life of a pop star: divide the number in the entourage by the number of lawsuits filed by friends or family members, add in the number of times his breakthrough album had gone platinum, and multiply that by the number of times he or his posse had been arrested.

If you could do the math—any math, really—you were probably smart enough to see that you had been had. And you moved on.

Still, ScroatM had been a mainstay in R²Rev's formative years. He and his handlers had nurtured a mutually beneficial relationship back when his career took off, using R²Rev as Scroat's base of fan maintenance when he could've gone to one of the other nets.

Many of the acts who had been red hot when R²Rev debuted were already over or in their death throes. Hutch had begun to worry that there were no evergreens, no acts that could stand the test of time and remain a constant supplier of content for his empire. It seemed like every week R²Rev had to grease the skids for the *new* Biggest Act Ever, dealing with another set of freshly morphed egos, dead-eyed coteries of managers and label thugs, and a blandly embraced escalation in the debasement of "popular entertainment."

As he sat across the sleekly polished conference table, Hutch found himself growing almost nostalgic for ScroatM, who had changed very little over the years: same backwards baseball hat, same underpants hanging out of his baggies. Better pimp jewelry, more tattoos. But the fact that ScroatM couldn't even be bothered to change his look as he prepared to reengage the marketplace, maybe *that* was bad-ass.

Or maybe he just didn't care.

"S'bout keepin' it real."

That was about the extent of Scroat's contribution to the meeting, along with *"Yo"* (a dated, non-specific assertion of street credibility, often employed at random moments by white artists trying to pass), *"Knowuddumsayin?"* (a lazy-tongued slur heard whenever those encountering ScroatM found themselves staring at him blankly), and—of course—*"Whatever... ,"* the rebel yell of a generation, delivered with a cocky shrug of surrender and the clear message of: "I'll be damned. I *can* care even less."

And thus it was agreed: ScroatM would flood the R²Rev airwaves starting in mid-February, world-premiering his first video from the new album at a heavily hyped release party, performing and presenting at the vitally important *VideoYear* Awards, contributing celebrity flatulence to *Bowel Cloud Theatre*, and showing up merely to chill with the R²Rev veejays, but only during Mimi SoWett's shift.

Hutch had secured assurances that ScroatM's videos, with guaranteed heavy rotation on the net, would engender the R²Rev gestalt of posed violence and hatred with, perhaps, a little less of the jaunty pedophilia of "Hey, Baldy." ScroatM's management team agreed that everyone was now on the same page, revealing that the video for the album's first single— "Dingleberry"—would be a straight concert clip taken from a three-date shakedown tour ScroatM had gone on the month before.

Again, Hutch wondered what image ScroatM sought to project. A low-tech concert piece, in an age when music videos routinely cost hundreds of thousands of dollars, frequently directed by slumming movie directors and awash with state-of-the-art digital imagery, felt like a step backward, particularly with the visual potential of a song called "Dingleberry."

Maybe this was ScroatM's statement, that he was disavowing the over-produced flash that had come to define hip-hop and was returning to the simpler, rougher stance of his roots.

Or, again, maybe he just didn't care.

Technology simply did not exist to gauge the subtle shades of difference between feigned soullessness and the real deal.

Designated for Air

Who knew a sixty-year-old could fight like this?

"Come on! Ow! Mister, OW! I'm sorry!! I'm sorry!! Shit! *OW!!*"

Casey Lattimer lay curled on the ground, manure-crusted boots kicking him in the ribs. He knew this experience from when he was a kid growing up in Hollywood, Florida, forced to play football in school and perpetually finding himself ground into the sod by big, mean kids who hated him for being so weird.

But this wasn't playing. This man, old enough to be his grandpa, had veins bulging out of his neck, had gone purple in the face, and had begun to try to beat Casey to death. Only Annie and her three-man video crew kept him from succeeding.

"That's it! That's it! That's *it!* Please!" Annie shouted into the chest of Carl Jubel, the old man straining to get past her and get another shot in.

"What the hell's the matter with him?" Mr. Jubel yelled, pointing down at the long-haired boy who was shrieking and weeping on the ground.

"He's on TV," Annie offered as explanation. Provoked by what he took to be her wise-ass response, Mr. Jubel shoved past Annie and drove another kick into Casey's ass.

"*Please!!!*" Casey cried.

John, the buff and handsome camera guy, took Annie by the elbow and flung her from the center of the fray. This was turning really ugly, and somebody had to assert some control. Carl Jubel was merely the man who had been *specifically* offended by Casey. Dozens of others—muscled, leather-skinned, and supremely pissed off—were coiled to get in their licks.

Something elemental had been inflamed here.

"We were just trying to have some fun," John said.

"This isn't funny!" strafed Mrs. Ruth Bender, stocky and hag-like.

"Your cow is constipated. That's kinda funny."

"This is our life! If these animals get sick, if they *die*, we could lose everything!"

There was a rustle among the knot of angry farmers as Annie pushed her way through and reasserted herself at the heart of the storm. She did not at all appreciate being pushed aside by John. They would talk later.

"And all we were trying to do was educate our viewers about how you deal with these situations," she insisted soberly. "This could be a learning tool."

"That little faggot wanted to stick his hand up my cow's ass!" Carl Jubel spit. Casey, still on the ground and intending never to stand again, whimpered at being mentioned.

"*You* were going to!" Annie argued.

"It is a medical procedure. If something's impacted up there, it has to come out somehow. But it's serious business. It's not some goddamned game!"

The time felt right to stand down.

"I'm sorry. We misunderstood," soothed the VP of Special Projects. "We'll go."

"You'd better go!" sneered Ruth Bender. "Get offa this farm, and get outta this town! We ain't gonna be part of your tee-vee show!"

Annie stood in the middle of this boggy field somewhere in Indiana and absorbed the woman's fury. Annie grew up around women like this in Michigan: big-boned, formless, scary-ass ugly. Proud, but at the end of the day really just peasant stock with pickup trucks.

If they had cable out here, she told herself, they'd know that this was a big deal. Instead, the farmers snarled one last snarl and headed back to work, Carl Jubel pulling on a thick rubber glove that stretched clear past his elbow. He had a job to do.

Annie watched them recede into the farmland, then turned to her crew, her heart still racing. It was all John, Kenny, and Carlos could do to not bust out laughing.

"Look at that glove! He's really going up a cow's ass!" Carlos marveled. The others stifled laughs as another farmer looked over his shoulder to make sure they weren't being mocked.

Kenny goofed through ventriloquist lips. "Man, I wasted my time in film school. I want *that* job."

"Shut up!" Annie hissed. She bore down on John. "Don't you ever show me up on a location! You do that again and you'll—"

"What? Never work in this town again?" John cracked, gesturing to the small burg they had just vandalized and would soon flee.

Annie was set to explode when her phone blurbled.

"What?!"

Hutch had just been brought a cup of Starbucks mocha grandé. The heat radiated a fine white haze across the top of his spare and flawless desk.

He jumped at the harshness of Annie's voice. "Annie? Jesus, it's Hutch. What's going on?"

Everything Annie wanted—not just Hutch's hiply restrained office with the icy-fine view of Manhattan, but all that was shiny and exhilarating and *clean* about this new media age—congealed in the cosmos and hurled itself at her through her state-of-the-art phone. It took everything she had to not grind it into the slime beneath her feet.

"Nothing. Casey just got roughed up by some locals."

Hutch instinctively sat upright and looked to a framed one-sheet, part of a collection of posters Marketing had put together for the very first NATPE show where R²Rev had had a presence. It featured Casey in rubber gloves and surgical scrubs drenched in blood. Hutch couldn't remember the piece exactly, but it was some kind of skit that had Casey traveling back in time and aborting Ricky Martin. Ricky Martin's mother had put up a real fight, and Casey had to sic the INS on her. Hutch remembered it was funny as hell.

There was real panic in his voice. "Is he all right?"

Annie looked to the ground, where R²Rev's prime asset was finally sitting up, snot running down his face as he picked hay and cow shit out of his long, greasy hair. She regretted finding this sight so satisfying.

"He's fine. Old MacDonald just took offense at him trying to sodomize his cow."

Hutch tittered like an 11-year-old. "Oooo. Sounds wild."

"Yeah, well. I'll throw the tape in tonight's pouch for you. No one else is ever going to see it."

A red flag went up. "What? Why?"

"Because we're not going to get releases from any of these people. We're lucky we weren't lynched."

"So we'll face-smear. It'll be funny, all these farmers with their faces electronically scrambled, like they're felons or something."

"Forget it," Annie said. "This one's a wash. It wasn't funny. It was just… really bad."

John, Kenny, and Carlos stood in a semi-circle around Casey, nursing bottled water and moving not an inch to tend to their bedraggled star. Casey had his hand down his pants, soothing his ass.

Hutch bore down on the phone. He shouldn't have to lecture Annie at this point. "Annie, we're not sponsoring a tour of America for you. We're spending thousands of dollars a day to keep you out there. Your job is to come back with video we can use.

"Casey pushes buttons. That's what he does. If you're telling me somebody finally went off on him, and you got it on tape, Jesus, that's gold. Geraldo got his nose busted on-air by a skinhead a hundred years ago and that dickwad is *still* milking it."

"Hutch…"

He grew firm. "You gotta get releases. Face smear won't cut it. These farmers, they're like really ugly, right?" Hutch laughed again just thinking about it. "Oh, man…"

Annie ground her teeth. "There's no way they're—"

"Have Carlos do it. Those rubes will see that big Puerto Rican coming at them and they'll sign anything he's got. Tell him I'll double today's per diem if he can pull it off."

Annie, surprisingly, unforgivably, found herself wanting to cry. But maybe it was this hardscrabble Midwestern backdrop—the simple, determined Middle American ethos bred into her whether she cared to admit it or not—that inspired her instead to dig in.

"Hutch, I don't want to do this anymore."

"Do what?"

"The Casey thing, the tweak-a-hick thing. You have to find something else for me."

Hutch squirmed a bit. But he made sure he sounded offended.

"I made you a VP. I didn't have to do that, Annie."

"Hutch," she began. Right on the spot, right in the middle of a mucky cow pasture twelve light years away from where she belonged, she summoned up the silky coo of a beautiful young woman who would ordinarily get her way simply based on that, but who—is it right that one should be so blessed?— also possessed blackmail material. "You know I deserve more than this."

He thought she might, or at least that's what the lawyer had said. Back when she started to make noises, right after she said she wouldn't sleep with him anymore, Hutch had consulted one of the company attorneys, just to determine what his exposure was.

The lawyer had concerns. All it would take is one person from that meeting who recalled Annie leaning in to help her boss after his *arrr-arrr-arrrrrr* manifesto went down in flames to suddenly call into question Hutch's authorship of the celebrated R²Rev logo. That initial sketch had been framed and put on display in the lobby of the net's suite of offices. It wouldn't take an expert to determine that Hutch hadn't drawn it.

The inevitable protests by feminist groups over the net's scabrous content had been picking up potency since R²Rev first went on the air. Wait until they heard that a man had stolen its ubiquitous logo from a subordinate young woman he was sleeping with.

"Don't offer her the world," the lawyer had said. "Determine the lowest possible threshold for her happiness—and give her a little less. When she becomes dissatisfied with *that*, upgrade her to 'happy.' By the time she's dissatisfied with that, a cushion of deniability will have been established. Her contract will be up and she won't be your problem anymore."

"I just want you to be happy, Annie," Hutch spun into the phone. It made him feel good, saying nice words.

She smiled, ready to cry again, but from a different place. "It's just that...

I'm out here on the road, and I like it. I think I can do good work from here. But there has to be something more important I can bring to the net. You know? There are stories out here that maybe aren't—"

"Annie, look," Hutch interrupted. If he could keep cutting her off midvision, he could string this along for months. "You need to sit down with yourself and really figure out what it is you want to do. When you've got it, when you can articulate it, my door is open to you, any time, any place. You bring me something that resonates with the R²Rev philosophy, and I'll make it happen. *We'll* make it happen."

"Okay," she smiled softly, now contented and hopeful. "Thank you, Hutch."

"But you might have to sleep with me again," Hutch thought.

"Thank *you*, Annie," he said. "And get me those releases."

He hopped off.

Annie slipped the phone into her pocket, a whole new world awaiting her. She fought every urge to look skyward, feeling almost as if a helicopter would descend within the instant to whisk her away to a better place. She'd just leave Casey and the crew there to figure out who to assault next.

She sidled over to her boys, sad at the notion of leaving them but pleased for them because they would never run out of victims of their asshollery. They'd see each other again when the crew passed through Manhattan, share a laugh at the Christmas party over the trouble they caused. Much of this, Annie told herself, would seem a lot less despicable with the passage of time.

The crew was gathered around a small monitor, watching the playback of the day's fun, and Casey was up now, eager to critique his work. Annie grimaced at the prospect of reliving this, but she could tell by the tone of Hutch's voice that this material would be designated for air. It was her job—at least for now—to assess its potential.

On the screen, Casey and Mr. Jubel stood at the ass-end of a cow, the other farm folk trying to squeeze into the frame. They were still in what Annie had come to think of as "the nice place," that convivial, doomed period in which Casey was on his best behavior, all the better to trick the hayseeds into not anticipating the knife to the gut.

They had no cable, you see? They couldn't have known.

"Huh…" Casey said, wide-eyed and eager to learn as he considered the cow's anus. It was his gift, really, to turn his dimwittedness into a charming, child-like innocence. With his scrawny, scarecrow frame and his knotty mess of hair, the locals invariably took a liking to him, intent on having a little harmless fun with this odd-looking waif from the big city.

"That's right," Mr. Jubel said, never thinking he'd find a televised forum on which to share his expertise on bovine bowel obstructions. "Sometimes, the bowel itself gets twisted. Now *that* can be a mess."

Mr. Jubel shared a sly wink with his farmer friends as the fellah from the tee-vee blanched.

A long rubber glove and a big sloppy can of lubricant were suddenly in the frame. Mr. Jubel prepared to suit up.

"Hey, you know what?"

(It always began with "Hey, you know what?" Annie wished she could make it stop.)

"How about if I do it?" Casey offered, just as eager and well-intentioned as you please. Mr. Jubel actually seemed to consider this for about a fifth of a second, until he got that first vague whiff of trouble.

"Well, now, I 'ppreciate your interest, but I don't think—"

"Look! My hand's smaller than yours. I'm just thinking of the cow's comfort."

The farmer's mind began to race. Things were getting confused, all the more so with that camera trained on him.

"The boy really does seem sincere," he thought to himself, "but I wonder if maybe this whole thing was a bad idea. Guess it'd be rude to back out now."

"And I've seen this in gay porno," Casey went on. "You work the hand in, a finger at a time, right?"

Oh God, oh God, oh God. When air was wrenched from a scene this violently, oxygen masks should fall from the ceiling. Or cyanide pills.

Annie felt that familiar queasiness as the farm folk on the screen stood dumbstruck, all of them hazily convinced that they couldn't possibly have heard what they just heard. They blinked reflexively, and smiled hopefully.

Into this stunned void, there was always plenty of time to tee up the kill shot. Casey never failed to play it perfectly.

"I mean, you get to do it all the time. Right, Mrs. Jubel?"

Annie had to turn away. Casey and the crew marveled at this car wreck of their own making as she listened to working men, just trying to eke out a living, having given up an afternoon to indulge this pretty gal and her friends from New York City, set to beating the snot out of her star.

There was lots of swearing, she was trained to note. Hutch would approve. Bleeped-out profanity, together with digitally-scrambled faces, genitals, and breasts, meant that R²Rev was delivering on its promise to the viewer.

Pushing the envelope. Burying the needle. Coloring outside the lines.

Balls-out extreme.

There had to be a place in there for Annie somewhere.

Recalling the Yahtzee Compact

"For the first one hundred and twenty years, it was comprised primarily but not exclusively of totems and oligarchies informed by the practices and beliefs shared most commonly by Teeters and similar mindsets established in the Yahtzee compact of 1643. Noonan, Burgher, and Tet, first among the Ablers, established as their mandate the notion of equal balance before the law. First among these—and this will be on the test—were numbers, non-numbers, and subsets thereof."

Joel's skin ached. His head grew heavy from the tinfoil twang of a migraine. The sky outside had gone pure black as rain painted the windows of the classroom.

And Mr. Kolak droned on with his typically arid discourse on ancient bullshit which nobody could've possibly cared about even while they were living it, let alone a happening teenager in America of the 21st century who felt confident that things were going to break pretty spiffily, future-wise, without having to commit to memory the purposeless facts and figures apparently crucial to the forward progress of lesser humans.

Usually Mr. Kolak's enthusiasm for whatever the hell he was talking about kept Joel alert, if not actually educated. But today, Mr. Kolak seemed just as pained as his student.

"Primarily through the largesse of the lesser colonies, the government's purview almost exclusively was incumbent upon—and this will be on the test—1812, 1813, and 1808."

Joel looked at his notes: "*Teeters?*" Did he say "Teeters?"

His careless hand-writing, combined with the fact that he really, truly didn't need to know any of this, had left a non-committal scrawl of words and word approximations, all of which added up to nothing but the certainty that he was going to be caught bare-assed on the quarter exam scheduled for the end of the month.

God, he needed a cigarette.

He extended an eyeball across the aisle to Todd's desk, where the insufferably able teenager was transcribing everything the teacher said. Todd knew he was being observed—had an unerring detector for the unlikely moment in which he was the focus of anyone else's attention—and he discreetly cloaked his writings behind his hand.

Joel scowled. Todd turned and shrugged sheepishly, his hands coiled protectively over the knowledge he had written down, as if the words were butterflies captured in a jar.

"This is all I have," the look said. "You have so much. Can't I keep this?"

Joel let it go. Todd was changing, growing some balls, like when he stood up to that swami dick at the Happy Snack. Joel wondered where *that* came from.

Joel was circling the drain, academically speaking. He had to do something.

To his own surprise, and that of his classmates, he raised his hand. Mr. Kolak, who had drifted off and was caught staring into the rain, didn't see it.

"A'hem," Joel said. The teacher turned and blinked doubtfully, as if a leprechaun had just appeared before him.

"Mr. Kasten?"

"Yeah," he said grimly, as if about to launch the first question on *Meet the Press*. "Is this gonna be on the test?"

The room snickered. Most times Joel was revered for his charisma and athleticism. Sometimes it was because he was just the right kind of dumb.

Mr. Kolak noted the boy's freshly undone jaw. "You speak. And yet you say nothing."

There was a tired, embittered tone to Mr. Kolak's voice. Todd noticed that the teacher, now glowering at Joel, was holding his white board marker like a cigarette.

Usually Mr. Kolak seemed to give Joel a pass.

"I'm just…" Joel fumbled. "Look, I'm not getting this. I'm not needing this. Nobody here needs this. We're outta here in a few months. We need to know how to get jobs and stuff. *Your* job is to get us ready for what's out there, and all you do is drill us with ancient crap that has nothing to do with the way the world is *now*."

The room rustled approvingly. Mr. Kolak, as ever, felt out-numbered. He stared at the back wall, contemplating something.

"The past is all I've got to work with," Mr. Kolak shrugged, resigned but not without pride. "I mean, I can't interest you in the present. None of you read newspapers, watch the news… pay attention.

"You all stare at me and want the *future* from me—'Which job should I pursue?' 'Which fact will I have to call upon ten years from now?'—but I can't give you that. Wouldn't if I could. It'd take all the fun out of it.

"So I got this." He shook his textbook limply, like a filling but dull bag lunch. "Things go wrong. Societies fall apart. That's what they *do*. You want to know the future? There's a great, big foot hovering up there somewhere, heading straight for our little anthill here.

"Wanna see it coming?" he asked, punctuating the question by slamming his open palm into the cover of the book. "So did they. They were going to get around to paying attention."

The sound of the book startled Bobby Slopes out of his nap. He wasn't sure, but he thought Mr. Kolak had just said that they'd be studying ants.

"Ants are messed up!" he giggled to himself.

Mr. Kolak began retreating to his desk. "It's like the man said: Those who don't learn from history… must've copied off Joel Kasten's notes."

It took a couple seconds for the gag to penetrate the gathered apathy, but then the class chuckled appreciatively. Mr. Kolak, his back to his charges, smiled shyly.

"Hey!" Joel barked in protest just as the bell rang. Todd stifled a derisive laugh as he rumbled out of the room along with the others. In a matter of seconds, it was just Joel and his teacher.

Joel held up his page of notes. "Are *any* of these words anything you actually said?"

Mr. Kolak had already gathered his coat and was heading out the door.

He grabbed Joel's paper as he passed.

"'The.' I definitely said 'the.'" He zeroed in on another word transcribed. "If I said *that*, I'd be arrested."

He let Joel's paper flutter back to the desk as he hustled for the door. He didn't care who was gathered in the Happy Snack's parking lot. He needed a cigarette.

But he looked back at Joel before he left, and noted his genuine despair.

"You'll pull it out, Joel. Just like you always do." There was envy in Mr. Kolak's voice. And disapproval. "But time is running out."

Then, Joel was alone in the classroom. Education, abandoned by generations of students, hung in the air.

He remembered a movie he'd seen. After a disastrous accident that left them with no way home, astronauts walked for the first time on the surface of a new planet. The team leader, refusing to concede that all was lost, slowly removed his helmet. He hesitated for a profound beat or two, then breathed in deeply, not knowing if the atmosphere would kill him but knowing he had no choice but to find out.

He lived. They made it home in the lame-ass sequel.

Joel looked up to the smudgy corners of the classroom, and wondered if he shouldn't just inhale greedily, accept into his body whatever was contained here.

Absorb it. See what would take, and where it would take him.

He double-checked that he was all alone, and heard only distant voices and rumbles down the hallway. Then, sitting statue-like, knowing that even in isolation his style gauge was diligently monitoring him for behavior that betrayed his coolness, he delicately sipped at the air. He pretended that his brain tingled when welcoming fresh knowledge, felt the kind of icy rush he thrilled to that summer he worked stocking the freezer case at Piggly Wiggly. It was invigorating, almost illicitly so, to subject the body to such a violent shift in attitude.

A Neanderthal shout came echoing up the hallway. It was no one in particular, but just enough to shake Joel out of his reverie, to force him to note, with chilling clarity, how *gay* it was to be sitting here like this.

He gathered up his things and bolted. Like a haunted house, there were vibrations here that you wouldn't want to be left alone with.

The End of Jimmy the Swami?

"Fuck you," Joel sneered as he tore from the parking lot.

"I'm just saying…"

"Who are you, my mother?"

Todd sank into the worn embrace of the passenger's seat. This was already beginning to feel like his spot, Robin to Joel's Batman.

"Forget it."

"You know, if you're gonna hang with me, this holy-ass shit has gotta go. The fuck you doing, keeping me from seeing your notes?"

"I was doing you a favor. You have to figure this stuff out for yourself."

"Hey, thanks," Joel said. "Next time you're takin' a dump, I'll drop on by and kiss your ass for being so good to me. I'll wipe while I'm back there, too."

Todd smiled. Joel smiled off Todd's smile. Their riffs were falling into a groove. They could hang.

Todd prepared to provoke. "So, how 'bout it? Just say you *don't* go buy cigarettes?"

"You're such a fag!"

"Whatever." Todd feigned hurt feelings. He looked away until Joel bit.

"Dude!" Joel exploded, laughing at the fact that his newly anointed sidekick was so freely busting his balls. "I haven't had a decent cigarette in six weeks! You don't know! You don't smoke! You don't just all of a sudden not smoke!"

"You did, for six weeks."

"I had no choice!"

Todd shook his head. "Dunno. All of a sudden, there you were not smoking. You lived."

"Yeah, and I fucking hated it."

"So what happened this morning? You finally get your mouth working again, you finally get a smoke all fired up, and you're coughin' and gaggin' like a girl or something."

"That cigarette was wack! It tasted like shit!"

"They all taste like shit. Just after six weeks, you forgot."

Joel watched the road. This new alliance with Todd was going to be a problem if he kept knowing stuff.

"Maybe."

"Yeah, maybe," Todd mimicked. "'Hey, here's a plan: I'm gonna set some weeds on fire and suck the smoke into my lungs, because that's just *got* to be tasty. *And* I'm gonna pay a ton of money to do it, and I'll stink afterwards, and it maybe might kill me.'" Todd shook his head. "Geniuses."

Joel hit the brakes hard at the curb. The Happy Snack lay just ahead.

"You know what? Get the fuck outta here. Go lay this gay shit on the Boy Scouts. I can't be seen with this."

"Look at them!" Todd jabbed toward the parking lot, where America's future had re-congealed in the aftermath of the storm. Wad Wendell had found a Baby Ruth wrapper with melted chocolate all over it. He was pretending to wipe his ass. "What is *that?*"

"We hang out. It pisses people off," Joel said. "What's the problem?"

"You're not pissing off Jimmy the Swami. Everything you smoke, everything you eat, everything you drink—that's money in that dick's pocket! He's in there giving us grief, jerking us around, and meanwhile he's just loving the fact that we keep coming back for more."

"Maybe."

"What 'maybe'?! He makes a living because we can't stop buying his shit. You don't even really *want* a cigarette, but he's in there right now, just waiting for you: 'He'll be back. He's got money for me, that little shit. He'll be back. All his friends will be back. Before long, I can afford to buy *three* camels!'"

Joel stifled a laugh. "You're crazy."

"And his bosses, Happy Snack Incorporated? And the rich, white, country club assholes that make the cigarettes and the Doritos and the Mountain fucking Dew? Millionaires, every damned one of 'em. From picking our pockets. If we grew a brain, they'd all be eating outta dumpsters."

Joel looked at Todd, guardedly awed. Todd was swaggering, armed with nothing but words.

Something floating here felt best shot down. "Yeah, right."

"Don't think so? Wanna mess Jimmy up? Just stop coming here, all of us. You couldn't hurt him more if you burned the place to the ground. And it's legal."

Joel watched the sun flare off the store's endlessly opening front door. No one walked out empty-handed.

"Huh…" Joel said thoughtfully. Todd saw something take hold.

"A pack of cigarettes is over four bucks a pop. How much money did you save, not buying cigarettes the past six weeks?"

"I don't know. Seventy, eighty bucks."

"Jesus!" Todd marveled. "And no munchies, no Cokes. Right?"

Joel tried to calculate. "Yeah. That's probably another forty right there. Christ…"

"Think Jimmy didn't miss you?"

Joel glowered. "Fucker sure didn't show it this morning."

"Sure he did. He had your smokes right there ready for you, he was so happy to see you. He was your buddy, ready to give you what you wanted. You sure as hell had what *he* wanted."

Joel's car continued to rumble at the curb. Todd knew how much it cost to keep this wreck on the road, knew that Joel's various athletic commitments kept him from holding down a part-time job.

"So, just don't give him your money, at least not today," Todd said. "See how you feel tomorrow."

Joel felt Todd trying to empower him. He squirmed with both anticipation and unease as Todd sought to expand his understanding of how he moved through the world.

And yet…

"Dude, I really need a cigarette!" Joel laughed. "You don't understand how hard it is to stop!"

"You *have* stopped. Just don't start again."

Joel grimaced and rubbed his jaw. He looked longingly at the smokers in the parking lot.

"Dude," Todd bore down. "You took a fastball in the face. You coulda died. And *now* you're gonna act like a pussy?"

Joel stared at Todd. He could kick Todd's ass for such a taunt, or worse still, simply throw him from the car and from his inner circle back into the colorless nothing in which he previously wallowed.

What must be at stake here, for Todd to risk smashing this new camaraderie he had allowed to take root?

Joel threw his car into gear with a wet, metallic thunk, his wheels spinning free of the rain-washed asphalt as he sped away from the Happy Snack.

He eyed Todd quizzically as he shook his head. "Too numerous."

Boys on a Field

"That's fucked up." Bobby Slopes smiled uneasily.

There were sixteen of them there: Joel's key disciples and five or six others who had earned the right to hang because they were on the team. Practice had just finished, and a chilled, mid-fall dusk was beginning to tether itself to the football field for the night. The strapping, preening starters—all juniors and seniors—draped themselves on and around the rusted out blocking sled.

Todd hung around the perimeter, pretending to round up gear.

Slopes still had his arm outstretched, an open pack of Marlboros in his hand. He let it fall limply.

"Just don't want one," Joel growled. "What's the big fucking deal?"

Wad crowed oafishly. "You got busted! Marty and Lucille caught you lightin' up and now you're eatin' shit!"

"Nobody busted me," Joel sneered, eyeing Wad's cigarette hungrily. "I'm just not using anymore. It's fucking up my game. And I'm tired of wasting my money on this shit."

Slopes was back with his Marlboros. For some reason, he thought it was important for him to close this transaction. "I'm *giving* you a smoke. Won't cost you nothing."

Joel looked to Todd hopefully. Todd shrugged: Do what you gotta do.

Joel held strong. "Yeah, so then you'll come up short, and that'll send you back to the Happy Snack even sooner. You have any idea how much money we spend there?"

"The fuck do I care?" Jeff Regan stretched languorously. "I'm workin' twenty hours a week. My parents are paying me a hundred bucks a month just to keep a C average. I got money comin' outta my ass."

"Yeah," Slopes concurred. "We gotta spend it somewhere."

Joel looked to his team. Less than half the players smoked, but all were nestled among liter bottles of soda, shredded bags of chips, and an array of candy bars. In their lockers hung Abercrombie, J. Crew, and Gap wear, and Nikes lay unlaced, ready to accept their feet. In almost every pocket was a cell phone, should they need to check in on the pointlessness going on in a friend's life.

They stank from consumption.

"You don't *gotta* spend it anywhere! Jesus Christ, look at this." Joel reached into his athletic bag and pulled out nearly two hundred bucks in cash, mostly fives and tens. At the end of all this, this might've been Todd's shrewdest move, steering Joel to an ATM to make a withdrawal.

The football team sat up and took notice.

"Jesus," Slopes ogled. "Where the fuck did that come from?"

"This is what I didn't spend at the Happy Snack while my mouth was fucked up." Joel fanned it out. "This is *my* money now. Mine, not that fucking towelhead's."

Wad simmered. "That dude's fucked up. Christ, you go into that store and he treats you like a fuckin' criminal."

"Fuck yeah," Jeff said. "Somebody oughta mess him up."

Joel felt something click into place. He looked into the darkness for Todd, who remained outside the circle. The onset of night prevented their eyes from meeting. Joel pressed on, trying to fuse his effortless charisma with the rant that Todd had laid on him the day before.

What Todd had said, it stuck.

"So stop giving him your money! Fuck him if he's not going to show us respect!"

The team fell silent. They had been blindly following Joel Kasten since they were children. All of a sudden, he seemed to be asking something of them.

Wad Wendell spoke doubtfully. "Dude, I gotta smoke."

"You gotta smoke because you're addicted. You're addicted because rich old fucks somewhere, who are even bigger assholes than your old man, made sure you got addicted. They knew you'd light up the first time because that's what fuckin' kids do when they're trying to be bad-asses, and they built something into the cigarette to make sure you kept coming back. You're a *kid*, and they did this to you.

"These things will fucking *kill* you, for all they care. They just need your cash. They're living fat-ass large offa you!"

Slopes considered his smoke, and took another drag.

Joel bent over and grabbed a fistful of cigarette and junk food wrappers. He tossed them into the air and watched them float to earth.

"This is all money we don't have anymore. This is all cash we paid into the machine. Every dime we spend, *they* win."

Ted Starkey, a cigarette virgin, washed down a Ding Dong with a swig of day-glo purple sports drink.

"Gotta eat, bro," he belched. "Kinda key to my not dyin'."

Joel's rant was waning, and this crowd seemed hard-wired to get chumped—which was just what the market required of them.

"Yeah, well," he slumped back onto the blocking sled. "You don't gotta eat what they expect you to eat. I mean, fuck, we're teenagers. We're supposed to tell 'em to fuck off when they're trying to get us to do something, and what they mostly want us to do is buy stuff.

"We're making it too easy for them, that's all."

The night absorbed whatever contemplation was to occur here. Wad looked at Joel with a wry grin, trying to find the joke in all this.

"You are just too numerous, baby," he chuckled.

The smokers smoked; the scarfers scarfed. Todd found his way to Joel, unsettled but proud to see his influence impressed upon the biggest fucking deal in the senior class.

"Yeah, that's me," Joel drawled. "Too numerous, stretched long."

Christ, he wanted a cigarette.

The Dream Defined

"*Ple-e-e-e-e-z!* I have diarrhea!"

Casey kept pounding on the front door of the bank, dancing from foot to foot and contorting his face in anguish. John, Kenny, and Carlos huddled behind the two-way mirror on the side of the van. They were in Frankfort, Indiana. They were doing their jobs.

This had become a staple of the Casey show, when no one could be bothered to come up with something new. They'd pull up in front of a bank or some other impregnable institution in some Middle American town, push Casey out with instructions to pretend like he was about to make a dump in his pants, and see if anyone could be persuaded to open their doors for him off-hours.

Carlos yawned behind the camera. John skimmed through *Variety* while Kenny tried to catch up on his sleep. They had done this often enough to know that no one was going to let Casey in. The humor came from the screamed encounters through the glass. Early on, Kenny thought it'd be cool to rig up some radio-controlled colostomy bag type thing that could blow inside Casey's pants for additional effect, but so far no one in New York would sign off on it.

Annie was a block away on a bench in the middle of the town square, squeezing her cell phone until she thought it would break.

"Are you sure he's been receiving my messages?"

Hutch hadn't gotten back to her for over a week, since the day she had attempted to share with him her vision of what she could bring to the network. During this freeze-out, she had convinced herself that she was on to something.

Almost as an accidental sideline, Annie had found herself meeting real teenagers as she forced Casey upon America. The stringers who provided her with so many of her story ideas were all high school students, all brighter-than-average kids, most of them toiling away at their school paper. All of a sudden, here was this girl, sounding not much older than themselves, calling from R²Rev in New York City, talking to them almost as colleagues as she asked them to keep an ear to the ground and relay to her any community events at which Casey Lattimer's presence might instigate some fun.

These kids all sounded like Annie did only a few years earlier. When they pressed her for exciting details about life working for America's hottest cable network, she felt honor-bound to make it all sound as scintillating as possible. She remembered how easily fantasies died when she was young, and she couldn't bear to nick any arteries of hope with the truth.

Touching down in cities like Milwaukee, Tulsa, Fort Wayne and Flint, Annie never failed to find herself surrounded with fresh-faced teenagers desperate to make her brief stay as fruitful as possible. They were often pale and spotty and lump-like, almost never as dynamic or beautiful as the teen-ish models in the ads that paid Annie's salary, but their simple desire to help and be appreciated was what made Annie's job doable at all. The fact that they tended to treat her as a celebrity in her own right also never failed to boost her ego.

Everywhere she went, Annie could see the infection spread by R²Rev, but it was chiefly around the edges: the slackers in the high school parking lot, the gangstas lurking in the malls, the cap-backward skate punks dodging cars near the McDonald's drive-thru. It was alternately hilarious and heartbreaking, these hopelessly malleable children—literally farm kids, some of them—costumed and contaminated by the dank, cynical caricatures that had been provided a rocket sled into teen consciousness by Hutch Posner's basic cable snot party.

It was this gap—between the basically normal kids Annie worked with and the net-deformed poseurs who swaggered and sulked within her view—that caught Annie's attention. Clearly a fair number of her stringers were avid R²Rev fans. The net's astronomical ratings and broad demographics confirmed that. But these kids weren't buying into the whole package. They were cherry-picking what they needed from the programming without allowing it to define them.

These kids, Annie noted, weren't truly represented in the R²Rev universe. Because they had no visual appeal or behavioral toxicity, the net's "regular" fans weren't getting their due. Since her own studies in the field found that the vast majority of R²Rev's viewers skewed normal, wouldn't the net be broadening its appeal by giving them some attention?

Her reports would be cutting edge, would still root themselves in teens sticking it to convention, but be free of piercings, tattoos, gangsta armor, and sneering contempt. Just for variety.

This was the pitch Annie had breathlessly begun to lay on Hutch earlier in the week, just as he was being called into a meeting. She hadn't heard from him since.

"Annie, hi!" Gwen had chirped with a flat-toned peppiness. Annie hated Gwen, knew that she had been sleeping with Hutch for the past several months. Way beyond that, Annie also knew that despite the fact that Gwen was merely a ten-dollar-an-hour assistant, she was *there*, in Manhattan, at the core of the R²Rev dynamo, while Annie—VP In Charge of Extracting Casey Lattimer's Head From His Ass—was interminably, inextricably elsewhere.

"You know what? You just missed him. He just went into his nine o'clock."

Annie simmered. Grinding her teeth, she glanced toward the bank and saw an ancient-looking and very skittish guard actually opening the door in response to Casey's diarrhea dance. She figured she was obligated to keep half an eye on this to see if it led anywhere.

"Since when has Hutch had a nine o'clock?"

"It's actually yesterday's three o'clock. He's a very busy boy, you know. So how *are* you?"

"Gwen, look. I need to talk to him. I want you to tell him I do not appreciate being ignored like this."

"Annie," Gwen said in a disapproving tone, not as an assistant protecting her boss but like a spouse defending her man. "Hutch gets all of his messages. Who he chooses to return is his business. I'm sure you'll be hearing from him when he finds the time."

Annie heard the bleat of Gwen's other line. "Sweetie, I have to—"

Annie jabbed dead her cell, refusing Gwen the satisfaction of casting her back into oblivion. In a jarring paranoid flash, she pictured Hutch dialing in on the other line from his office fifteen feet away, conspiring with Gwen in this bit of theatre to keep Annie and her dream away from him.

The bank guard had now detected something hinky in this ridiculous young man begging to use his toilet. He was trying to pull the door shut, but Casey—God love him—had jammed his foot in the way.

Yeah, this'll play in the package somewhere, Annie noted.

She hit the speed dial for her stringer in Elmwood Park, Ill., a Chicago suburb a day's drive away. In addition to scouring for Casey environments, Annie had begun to ask her stringers to come back to her with story ideas that fed into her vision of profiling less odious members of the net's audience. Look beyond the rote delinquency and easy posturing. What were kids *really* pissed off about?

Karen Dix—16 and plain, anorexic but fighting back—picked up.

"Karen, hey. It's Annie McCullough with—"

The sound of the gunshot stilled the town square. Annie remained unmoved for a millisecond, programmed from birth to know that the sound of a bullet was merely entertainment fodder on her TV: carnage had now commenced, to be pantomimed for your viewing pleasure.

But then she turned with a jerk toward the bank.

Casey was balled up on the ground, clutching his side and gasping violently for air. The doddering old guard stood frozen in confusion, the gun still in his hand, as Annie's crew leapt from the van.

In a subsequent unguarded millisecond, during the thin slice of reality in which a person's response is unchecked and pure as ether, Annie caught herself thinking eagerly:

"Wait'll New York sees *this!*"

Tender Denied

History would show that it was a boy named Wad who bit first.

He was gathered there at the Happy Snack with Joel and Slopes and the rest of the tribe, luxuriating on a brilliant, biting fall afternoon. The hoods and side panels of their cars, heated by the sun, provided a womb-like embrace as the boys pressed against their vehicles for warmth.

There was the usual flow in and out of the store, Joel's fading declaration of a consumer boycott having impressed pretty much no one. Joel himself seemed ready to crack, his nicotine jones perhaps behind him, but the relentless need to buy something sweet or salty or crunchy or bubbly or gooey pressing in on him like a thumb against an artery.

Already Todd had seen him sneak a drag off someone else's cigarette and a fistful of Cheetos from someone else's bag, after which he looked to Todd with a shrug that was both defiance and self-loathing.

"Dude, this is *hard*," the look said.

Everyone was waiting for the moment that came every afternoon when Daljit Singh emptied the trash cans and lugged the bags to the dumpster. His wife—sullen and scared and seemingly three feet tall—would be brought down from their apartment above the store to grimly man the cash register, at which time the day's prime shoplifting would commence. Before departing the store every afternoon, Daljit moved over-stock items to prominent shelf positions in hopes that the thieves would rid him of merchandise cluttering up his miniscule storage closet. He would write them into that night's lost inventory report, and the store's mark-up would rise another fraction of a cent. The day of the six dollar hotdog drew even closer.

The throng stirred as the simmering brown man made his exit, fumbling beneath the squishy bulk of several slick bags of garbage, just from inside the store. By this time of day, the four trash cans in the parking lot would be overflowing and in need of relief.

It was like leaves from a tree or skin from a snake—the debris left behind by the endless banquet.

Daljit always had to elbow his way through the mob to get to the trash cans, the teenagers leaning against the receptacles as if they would crumple to the ground from sheer lack of will if not for the support. Again, there was a glowering strand of racism that some of the more brutish boys laid upon the dark-toned shopkeeper in order to keep their testosterone percolating. Daljit sucked it up and bowed timidly, praying that such boys would continue to patronize him in whatever manner they found pleasing.

Wad Wendell watched Daljit through a slit-eyed sneer. "You know, my grandpa died in World War II tryin' to *kill* people like that."

A happy snort escaped from Todd's lips. "Yeah, parachuting into India and shooting up the place pretty much turned the war around. I hear Spielberg's about to start production on *Saving Wad's Grandpa.*"

Elemental in this wise-ass remark was at least a passing grasp of world history, which left Wad completely unarmed. All he could do in rebuttal was grunt and spit toward Todd's feet.

Wad lit his last smoke and threw the empty pack to the ground. Slopes was already in movement, headed for the store. He put out his hand to Wad.

"Lend me five bucks. I'll buy you another pack while I'm in there."

Wad instinctively jabbed his hand into his pocket to comply, but when it returned with a balled up twenty, he unfurled it and studied it with new purpose. He looked again toward Daljit Singh, barking at a couple of sophomores for ignoring the freshly emptied trash can and throwing their refuse at his feet.

He considered his twenty again, eyeing it meaningfully as if about to send it on a long journey, then returned his disapproving glare to Daljit Singh.

"Nah," he said to Slopes while looking to Joel for approval. "Think I'll pass."

Wad took the top corners of the bill between his thumb and forefingers and idly let it air out.

Slopes redirected his open palm to Joel. "Five bucks."

Joel went into his pocket and found a ten. He smiled at Slopes as if prepared to comply, but then smoothed the bill out against the muscled contour of his leg. "Sorry. Got other plans for this."

A cloak of solidarity seemed to be falling over the gang. Slopes grew pissed and slightly panicked as everyone looked away, intent on jerking him around.

He finally descended on Todd, parked on the hood of Ted Starkey's Camry. Slopes was a starting defensive lineman—he could easily beat the shit out of Todd Noland, which he did once when they were in the eighth grade.

"I want you to think very carefully before answering this question: Five bucks."

Todd knew the eyes of Joel and the others were upon him, but to enlist them in his defense would be pussy. He looked past Slopes and saw Daljit Singh working his way toward them. They had stationed themselves alongside one of the trash cans.

Events were coalescing. If this was to be about taking stands, here was his.

"Nah," Todd drawled boldly.

Slopes bore down. "Asswipe, you want I should—"

"Yo, Jimmy," Wad suddenly said, trying to throw some muscle into his voice. "You lookin' for this?"

Everyone turned as Wad continued to brandish the twenty dollar bill like a banner. Daljit, who was legitimately scared of the burly senior boys towering over him, forced himself to look up from his garbage duty.

Wad stared him down cockily. "Thinkin' I might just hang onto this. What do you think about that? Thinkin' you might not be taking any more money offa me. Ever. That be okay by you?"

Daljit could've fallen back on his usual shtick of pretending not to understand English, but he felt something menacing bubbling up. His wife was alone in the store. He needed to eat whatever shit was required here and get back to his post.

He looked from Wad to Joel and the others. Joel, his ten spot still in hand, understood. He unfurled his money in the same fashion as Wad and displayed it to Daljit with a thin smile.

The others saw that something was happening and proceeded to fish through their pockets. The stand being taken was lost on most. All that mattered was that they follow the lead, just like always.

Todd watched the defiance flow slowly through the group. There was no taunting, no harsh words, as they stared down Daljit Singh. Just a small regalia of paper money, like flags of a united nation, blowing in the breeze.

Awed, Todd almost missed the chance to take part. He quickly burrowed into his jacket pocket and unearthed a single damned dollar bill. He had to laugh to himself. Once again, Todd Noland comes up small.

But denomination wasn't the point. He staked his dollar alongside the others: The front was complete.

The parking lot crowd was aware of what was happening. The freshmen and sophomores, ever-mindful of trends set by the upper classmen that would trigger which lemming-like behavior they would be obliged to indulge in, paid close attention.

"We're tired of you taking all our money and treating us like shit," Wad said with a swagger. "Till you start showing us some respect, this all stays with us."

As he watched his livelihood disappear back into the pockets of those accursed loose-fitting khakis, Daljit suddenly understood what was being threatened. This was food taken from his children's mouths, dollars that one day would stretch end to end to carry him and his family back to his beloved India.

He was outnumbered, but war had been declared.

"This parking lot is all for customers," he hissed. "You be buying something, or I call police!"

Joel stood up and drew closer. As always, he would see this through.

"You really wanna do that?" he asked. "'Cause once you're through, we'll tell 'em how you've been selling cigarettes to fifteen-year-olds by the case. You couldn't even *begin* to pay the fine they'd lay on you."

It always led back to money: How much could you take off this mob? How much could *that* mob take off you?

Daljit saw nowhere to go. He spit angrily and went back to struggling with the full trash receptacle, an incensed stream of foreign curses billowing from his clenched teeth. "American fuckers" was the sole English phrase that could be understood by the crowd.

The trash bag was stuck, it was so full of paper and plastic and cardboard. He fought with it furiously as the teens watched in amusement.

Then a small, nearly weightless object bounced off his pant cuff and jangled to the cement. The penny danced in a weak circle for a second or two before lying down flat.

Joel stood over Daljit, smiling coldly. "A little something for you."

Wad, never one to miss a chance to piss on someone, found a penny in his pocket and lofted it in a lazy arc toward the shopkeeper. Some of the guys in the gang did, too, followed by a junior none of them recognized.

Pennies started falling all around Daljit's feet. Feeling the mocking sting as each hit the pavement, he pulled the full trash bag from its container with one mighty tug, quickly replaced it with an empty, and began pushing his way back toward his store.

One kid, a truly dangerous sophomore named Dan Kilby, whipped a penny at Daljit with full force, catching the man in the neck. Skin was broken.

Joel saw this and jumped up on the hood of his car.

"Hey!" he shouted.

Everyone turned. He could convey it with a look: This wasn't about physically hurting anyone.

Daljit rubbed his stung neck, confused why this boy had come to his defense.

A few more pennies were flung lazily, but by this time Daljit had reached the front door and disappeared back inside. He passed teenagers emerging empty-handed—word had already spread that a boycott was on. When the crowd saw that they had refrained from buying, some applauded.

A sludgy lack of purpose fell over the parking lot. Not everyone understood that a movement had begun in their midst. Many just found it fun to throw objects at a foreigner. And, besides, most had bought their cigarettes and junk food before the boycott began. For the short term anyway, how hard was it to protest when you weren't actually giving up anything?

But Joel and Todd understood what had just happened, and truth be told, so did Wad and Slopes and the others—you didn't hang with the likes of Joel Kasten since grade school and not gain some grasp of the potential that was there for anyone who paid attention.

Still: "Hey, where're you going?"

Slopes was heading to the mini-mart across the street. Todd couldn't believe their front was collapsing already.

"Berger gave me five bucks. I gotta suck him off later," Slopes smiled, waving the five spot cheerfully. "Anybody want anything?"

"But... You can't!" Todd cried, a little more shrilly than he had intended. "What's the point if you just go buy the same crap somewhere else?"

Slopes was walking backwards with no intention of being diverted. "Dude. I gotta smoke."

Something was within their grasp here, although even Todd couldn't articulate it. Still, he was certain Joel felt it, too.

He turned to hand the protest off to Joel, who just waved Slopes off with a sneer.

"The fuck do I care?" he said, playing Slopes like a beef-witted Stradivarius. "The pussy can't control his urges like a man, let him go."

Slopes stopped dead. He couldn't stand it when Joel turned on him.

"Hey," he whimpered. "Come on."

"So, Slopes," Joel continued, "when you let that tackle from East get through the line Saturday night, damned near took my fucking head off, maybe you were too busy thinking of sneaking out for a smoke then, too, huh?"

Slopes was wounded, but he was nonetheless being drawn back to the pack. "Hey, fuck you."

"Fuck yourself. I just need to know where your head's at. I just need to know you're with the team."

They *were* a team, gathered on and around their cars. It was the only constant Slopes had ever known—that easy, non-judgmental hold of his guys. If he went across the street right now, they might all be gone when he got back.

Or worse, they'd still be there... but not for him.

"Shit," he whined, rejoining the group.

His addiction was thrumming. He wasn't going to be able to fight this forever, but for now it meant everything that he try. Everyone recognized the struggle he was facing, but no one was gay enough to actually commend him for his efforts.

"Um. Hey."

It was Ted Eliot. Ted Eliot was a Todd Noland, maybe a notch or two below. He was always just hanging around, not so tragic as to be abused, but far from worthy enough to ever warrant attention.

Now he was standing at his open trunk, an unopened carton of Marlboros in each hand. Slopes pounced, followed by the others.

"Jesus!" Slopes marveled. "Where did you—?"

"My stepfather kicks ass on my birthday!" Ted beamed. In seventeen years, he had never felt more popular.

"Fuckin' crack 'em open, dude," Slopes squirmed. To Todd, this looked like one of those Nature Channel shows where a pack of lions sets to ripping apart a gazelle.

"Wait!" The crowd parted and Joel stepped up. "You're giving these away?"

"Well, yeah. I guess," Ted said shyly. "I mean, I thought maybe I could..."

Slopes started pawing at one of the cartons. Joel elbowed him away.

"All right, then here's the plan. We'll take these, and give them out only when somebody absolutely, positively, *has* to smoke."

Slopes whimpered. Joel tore open the first pack and jammed a single cigarette into Slopes' hand. "Get the fuck away from me."

He turned to the crowd. "Anybody else got a stash, hand 'em over. Know where your parents keep theirs?" He shrugged slyly, like a Mafia don silently ordering a hit. "I ain't sayin', I'm just sayin'.

He was being swept up in it now. This was like all sorts of movies and TV shows he had seen, in which the leader talks fast, talks hard, and gets the troops in line.

"Anybody thinking of quitting? Do it. Anybody thinking of starting? Do it and I'll kick your ass—freshmen, this means you. You're too young to smoke anyway.

"We're gonna need every cigarette we can get. We can do this."

He looked toward the Happy Snack, where Daljit Singh was just a silhouette behind the counter—an angry silhouette, alone with his merchandise.

Joel held the two cartons of Marlboros over his head and stared down Daljit defiantly, then lowered the cartons with some ceremony into the back of Jeff Regan's pickup truck. Additional packs were tossed in by joiners to the cause, along with some loose cigarettes. It made for a pretty pathetic collection, but the point was made.

Here were teenagers choosing to do without, to give when keeping was their nature—all in the name of a cause.

Ted Eliot, who donated the first two cartons to the campaign, was quickly elbowed back out to the periphery. Within the week, Wad Wendell would blame a truly rank fart on him in Biology, right there in front of Julie Doling, for whom Ted yearned with a crush that bordered on dementia. Thus he was marked with ridicule that would linger right up to graduation.

He didn't come around much after that. And he never got his cigarettes back.

Sick-Ass TV

Casey Lattimer would live. The security guard's bullet had nicked his lung, but passed right through him without causing any hard damage.

He spent the night in the Frankfort hospital, Annie McCullough at his side the whole time so as to thwart any ideas he had of foraging for morphine. By the time he was ready to be released the next day, he was proudly showing off the hole in his body, offering to stick the eraser end of a pencil into it for the camera if Annie thought that might make for some "sick-ass TV." Given the legal mess that their latest stunt had caused, Annie thought not.

Lawyers for R²Rev and MediaTrust were on a plane for Indiana practically before Casey made it to the emergency room. Frankfort, a town of about 15,000 people, *did* have cable, so any initial attempt to pass off Casey's claims of critical bowel distress as legit were quickly shot down. Even if the adults who treated Casey and those who would soon file charges against him were oblivious to the celebrity in their midst, the town's teenagers quickly blew his cover. The elders were forced to take it on faith that Casey Lattimer drew a paycheck by feigning diarrhea in cities all over Middle America.

This was serious business, Annie was quick to realize. Small towns took their institutions seriously. Moreover, Ernie Stanz, the elderly bank guard, was in intensive care right down the hall from Casey, suffering from the trauma of being forced to discharge his weapon for the first time in his career. It was touch-and-go during the early stages, doctors afraid that the old man had succumbed to a stroke.

And all for some revolting stunt, pulled off by a bunch of punk New Yorkers, out to have fun at the expense of the good people of Frankfort?

Until the lawyers arrived, it fell on Annie's shoulder to endure the town's wrath.

"It's a TV show?" asked an incredulous Randy Tupper, a 56-year-old police sergeant with a flattop and a veiny, bulbous nose. "About going to the bathroom?"

"It's not *about* going to the bathroom," Annie said weakly. "Casey gets into situations with everyday people, and sometimes it turns out to be funny."

"My nephew says your friend—" Sgt. Tupper squinted to read his notes, then stared over his half-glasses at Annie. —"farts on people."

She coughed. "He might, for instance, go into a shoe store, and he'll sit there trying on shoes, with the employee of the shoe store kneeling there in front of him, and he'll… emit gas.

"It's… Our viewers just think it's funny."

"Like *Candid Camera*?"

"Yes!"

He grunted wearily, reminded for the umpteenth time how everything that used to be innocent had been bastardized and perverted to conform to a world that was certainly rocketing straight to hell.

"You get a permit to film here?"

"Yes!" Annie offered eagerly. Permits were a hit-or-miss thing. Mercifully, in this case, she had attempted to go by the book. "We went straight to your City Hall to find out which ordinances we needed to be aware of. I think you'll find that everything was done to code."

"And you alerted them to the fact that there might be… farting involved?"

"We told them we were gathering material for a television program, which, in fact, we were. We would've been happy to offer specifics if we had been asked."

"I guess they trusted you."

"I guess so."

He put down his notepad and stared at her. She was so young, so pretty—and wired in a way that was completely alien to him. He felt oddly protective of her, at the same time that he wanted to wring her neck. And this was a *girl*.

"How old are you?"

"I'm twenty-six."

"And you're a…" He consulted his notes again. "…*vice president?*"

"Vice President of Special Projects, yes." She cleared her throat and sat up straighter. "I know it seems unlikely to you, but what I do is actually kind of important to the people I work for."

"My brother-in-law was just made vice president down at the bank. He's forty-eight."

"Well, these are completely different environments," Annie said, trying to sound like an adult. "I'm sure he has completely different responsibilities than I do."

"I'd imagine." Sgt. Tupper flipped through his pad. "Heard from the airport about a half-hour ago. They got a call asking if they had runway enough to handle some kind of private jet out of New York. I assume they're with you?"

"My superiors wanted to send out a team in order to hopefully resolve this as quickly as possible."

"Any more vice presidents?"

"Pretty much all of them."

She smiled hopefully, brushing a wisp of hair from her face and tracing circles on the knee of her jeans. The cop couldn't figure her out.

"*How* old are you?" the cop asked again.

— —

The lawyers made quick work of the case. MediaTrust, whose vast network of cable systems nationwide included a chokehold on Frankfort, was able to placate the town fathers by shaving a few cents off the city's cable rates. The savings were then routed into municipal coffers for new public works projects that would make the Common Council appear proactive and competent when the next set of elections rolled around.

The district attorney, who had responded to public outrage by railing long and hard about his intent to extract vengeance from the Big City demons, was able to wriggle out of his hard-line stance thanks entirely to the efforts of the Big City defendant.

It turned out that when struck by the bullet, Casey Lattimer had excreted approximately twelve milliliters of fecal matter—not an uncommon reaction to sudden, blunt trauma, a local doctor testified. With this remarkably good bit of evidence in hand, R²Rev's lawyers were then able to argue that despite the defendant's established pattern of inciting confrontation by faking an urgent need to defecate, it was conceivable that, in the specific instance before the court, Mr. Lattimer was sincere in his frenetic requests for a bathroom.

The district attorney and the judge, most interested in quickly resolving the case and expelling these people from their town, punted. The R²Rev attorney who happened upon what shortly became known as the "doodie defense," sparing his employers an expensive and embarrassing court case, returned to New York a hero.

And Casey Lattimer found himself out of a job, Hutch Posner having finally been forced to concede that Casey simply embodied the R²Rev philosophy too enthusiastically to be contained. It was one thing to promulgate—from a safe distance—a lifestyle steeped in debauchery and culture defamation, but it was quite another to claim *responsibility* for such a lifestyle, almost like a parent. While R²Rev⁴Films, the company's motion picture arm, still coveted Casey for what was being referred to as the *Dumb Ass* series (*Dumb Ass Goes To College, Dumb Ass Joins the Navy, Hey! Dumb Ass!*), Hutch determined that it was best to simply sever all ties.

It was a melancholy decision for Hutch. In his way, the kid had served the net well, and had made himself a nice chunk of change in the process. Hutch hoped he could comfortably go back to a life of farting on an amateur basis, purely for the love of it.

On the night the video of his shooting debuted in a prime, maniacally-promoted Saturday night slot, Casey received a new pair of underpants—and a firm boot back to obscurity. Mimi SoWett, slow to realize that Casey thought his sacking was merely an on-air goof, told the viewers that their Casey was leaving R²Rev for bigger and better things. Within three years, he was driving a school bus. Then he probably died young or something.

— ◼—

Annie McCullough, meanwhile, was finally given her break.

In the aftermath of the Casey incident, with Hutch no more interested in indulging Annie's career fantasies, she and the boys were ordered to stay on the road and roll tape on anything they found that rocked the R²Rev way. Whatever they sent back to New York would be used as B-roll, or maybe incorporated into the net's farcical "news" packages, which were almost entirely devoted to thinly-disguised promotions of new CDs and ongoing court appearances by R²Rev's brightest stars.

That, of course, had essentially been Annie's own proposal to Hutch, which he had stolen and returned to her stamped with the de rigueur stamp of the Hutch Posner Genius. But where his intent was for the crew to simply document skateboard dipshits and rhyme-silly gangstas flaunting their pimp hands, all with the requisite snarling and smarm, Annie was primed to look elsewhere. She had a camera crew, an expense account, and very little interest in keeping this job much longer.

She was dangerous.

Destroyer

They sat there at the table, the two of them: Joel and Marty Kasten. It must've been a Saturday, two weeks after their previous Saturday, because these were the only times father and son ate breakfast together.

The custody agreement was actually more generous to Marty, but Marty told Joel a long time ago that Joel's mom was "busting his balls on the whole visitation thing just to fuck with me." If Joel had ever doubted his father, or if he had ever had the courage to prove his doubts, his mother would've been delighted to tell him that his father just wasn't all that interested in seeing him more than a couple times a month.

"Welcome to the club," she would've enjoyed saying.

It was a big day, this Saturday, because it was the first time Joel had escaped the sports page. Practically since tee-ball, Joel Kasten had been a fixture in the box scores and game summaries of the local paper, which expended buckets of ink documenting the on-field excellence of this kid who made winning seem so effortless.

When Kyle Hoffstetler's fastball had connected with Joel Kasten's face, it was above-the-fold, front-of-the-section news, the paper's lead sports columnist wringing his hands at length about the cutthroat nature of high school sports that had led to this near-homicidal attack on the town's finest young athlete. The day after Hawthorne East collected their trophies for winning State, the paper, in tribute to Joel, gave it scant notice.

But now, here he was on the front page of the Metro section, all for having instigated a protest of some kind down at the Happy Snack. According to the story, a group of Dickinson High seniors had declared war on the popular mini-mart, and on the manufacturers of the products sold there. The reporter and photographer, who were familiar with Joel from his athletic achievements, instinctively knew whom to speak to.

"We're just tired of the adults, who make this stuff and sell this stuff, assuming that we're going to keep them rich by giving them all our money," he was quoted as saying. "We turn on the TV, or we open a magazine, and all we see is billions of dollars being spent on advertising trying to trick us into buying stuff. And we're not so stupid that we don't know that they wouldn't spend billions if they weren't pocketing fifty times that much. Off of *us.*"

This was all Todd's initial rant, rendered far less dogmatic by the simpler mind of Joel Kasten.

"We're just shutting the faucet off for a while to tell them we know what's what."

The arrival of the newspaper team, followed quickly by crews from all four local TV news outlets, had solidified the boycott. For the first few days, it wasn't always easy to distinguish the protest action from the general milling about that would've taken place in the parking lot anyway. Joel and his lieutenants put in more time than usual, trying to intimidate the younger students from spending, in part by doling out provisions from the stockpile collected. But the front had begun to spring leaks almost as soon as it was mounted. Handfuls of students—particularly those not at all impressed by the dynamism of Joel Kasten—continued to spend freely at the Happy Snack, enduring the taunts of the true-believers as they passed.

But the appearance of the TV cameras focused things nicely. After all, these were children raised on media scrums, the chaotic, live-as-it-happens news rodeos that had been running on cable seemingly non-stop since the day they were born: O.J., Lady Di, Monicagate, Michael Jackson. Every day, at every hour, there seemed to be something going on somewhere which compelled TV cameras to suck up the images of gathered simpletons and blast them live to the entire world.

It had begun to feel almost like a birthright, this sense that eventually everyone would find themselves in a crisis worthy of saturation media coverage. Unconsciously, people would rehearse their man-on-the-street responses to questions posed to them, even picture in their minds the precise text and font of the witty, provocative placards that would single them out from the pack and bring them on-air glory.

And now, like a dust devil rising from nothing in the New Mexico desert, here was a news frenzy all their own, right in the middle of the Happy Snack parking lot, all because Joel and his friends had decided to stick it to Daljit Singh.

The cause and effect couldn't have been more stark: Make some noise, get on TV. Make more noise, *stay* on TV. You could actually step through your television screen and become programming. You could scratch your ass on mini-mart asphalt, and folks throughout the land would watch.

Lives there a person strong enough to resist such temptation?

— ◖▬▬● —

Early on, though, when the story was confined to the newspaper and therefore not yet an officially sanctioned hullabaloo, Marty Kasten wasn't impressed.

"What are you doing?" he asked his son over the breakfast table.

"What?"

"*This.*"

Marty jabbed at the story in the paper. Joel was secretly thrilled with himself, but he was seventeen and therefore obligated to offer only minutely shaded displays of disregard.

"Dunno."

"Your mother know about this?"

"Yeah, I guess."

"She *let* you do this?"

"Yeah. I guess."

Here it came. Marty grunted, and contained within the grunt was this: If *I* had a hold of you, this kind of shit wouldn't be happening. If your mother had done better by me, if I had married better, if life hadn't gutted me from my balls to my throat and screwed me out of what I had coming to me, *you'd* still have a father who could keep you in line. You caught a break the day I decided I wanted out, son of mine.

It carried a punch, this grunt. Joel felt a sick, dull ache in his stomach every time he heard it. He wondered if maybe he was getting an ulcer.

"Some of the men who own some of these stores that share this parking lot—I know them," said Marty. "They don't need this."

"We're just trying to make a point."

Marty clucked derisively. "Yeah, I know. When you're seventeen, everybody all of a sudden has a point."

"Did you have a point when you were seventeen, Dad?" Joel was being sincere. He really wanted to know.

"Yeah, my point was keep on the right side of my parents, do the work I was told to do, and shut the hell up. You get out into the real world, and you learn really fast that nobody much cares what your *point* is. Do your job, do it well, everything else will take care of itself."

Joel looked around his father's sterile, two-bedroom apartment, and noticed for the first time how much of his expensive furniture was given over to chrome and hard corners. Every time Marty found a new girlfriend, she contributed something to the decor, since Marty couldn't have cared less about such things. But even though he had a steady stream of young women doing his interior design—Joel's good looks were definitely a product of his father's genes—the apartment always looked empty to Joel.

Marty chuckled as he quoted his son from the paper.

"'Teenagers spend one hundred billion dollars a year on stuff, and their parents spend another fifty billion dollars on them. If we all of a sudden went away, all these companies would be screwed. Maybe they need to start thinking about that.'"

Marty looked at his son skeptically. "Where're you getting this?"

The implication—that Joel was too dim to form an opinion of his own—smarted. "It's something I heard," he said quietly.

"Well, I want this to stop. Are you even going to football practice anymore?"

"Yes." But not as much.

"This is the time, you know. This is when college recruiters show up at your games to have a look at you."

"Dad, I'm not gonna get a scholarship for football. I'm not that good. It's gonna be baseball or nothing."

"Yeah. We saw how that worked out."

"I had three schools interested in me! All I had to do was pick one."

"I did not put all my time and all my money into your baseball career to have you playing for some second-tier college in the middle of some farm town. The Majors are signing prospects right out of high school."

"Dad. I'm a really good ballplayer, for here. Maybe compared to kids from other towns, bigger towns, I'm just... okay. You know?"

Marty waved it away. "When spring training opens, teams are gonna see the holes on their bench. They'll take another look at you, wonder how they got so lucky to find you still available, and we'll let them fight over you. Meanwhile, football will keep you focused, keep you in shape. I do not want you missing any more practices."

Joel finished his cereal. They were waiting for him down at the Happy Snack. "Whatever."

Marty started straightening up the table. He took the morning's paper—including the Metro section—and threw it in the trash.

It was not a hostile gesture. It just didn't matter.

"I have to go into the office for a few hours today. This friend of mine really wants to see a movie, so I figured she could join us. I'll buy you both dinner."

Joel grimaced: "This friend of mine," like they were Tom Sawyer and Huck Finn or something. When Joel had been up late the night before, channel surfing, he had found a twelve-inch vibrator in the cushions of his father's buttery leather sofa.

"You know," said Joel, "maybe just the two of you should go. I kinda made plans."

Marty tensed. "*We* had plans."

"Yeah, *we* did, and then..." Joel trailed off. There was no point. If he had to act the asshole teenager in order for both of them to get what they really wanted for the evening... *whatever.* "I just wouldn't count on me tonight."

This was great! This was better than Christmas: Marty Kasten got to act wounded. He was 42 years old, and he got to take an emotional jab at his teenage son to start his day.

Hoozah!!

"Fine," he said frostily, grabbing his briefcase with an accentuated crispness and heading for the door. "Make sure I know where you are."

"I'll draw you a map."

Marty stopped angrily. He thought he might have just been slighted. "*What?*"

"Nothing. Bye."

Teacher

He stepped from his car, wary but intrigued. Under normal circumstances, he would've driven elsewhere to buy his cigarettes more discreetly. But not today.

"Hey, Mr. Kolak," Joel said brightly. He and his crew had seemingly taken up permanent residence in a full quarter of the parking lot. If the protest stretched out much longer, Frank knew the city and the Happy Snack people would challenge their right to congregate on private property to push such a flagrant political agenda. Now *that* would be interesting.

"How goes the battle?"

Joel nodded toward the Channel Six news team, interviewing a grim-faced Bobby Slopes. "That makes all four stations. Channel Fifteen sent over Debbie Fedder. She's *hot.*"

Wad Wendell stood behind Slopes, pretending to pick his nose for the camera. Joel sighed: these were his foot soldiers.

"They saw a lot of that at the Boston Tea Party, too," Mr. Kolak said wryly. Joel processed this, then chuckled. It killed him when adults joked with him like he actually had a clue.

Joel's laugh made Mr. Kolak grin shyly.

The news crew stirred as the front door of the Happy Snack opened and Daljit Singh emerged. It was dumpster time.

Fueled by the cameras, the crowd of teens began hooting derisively and lobbing pennies at Daljit, who put this chore off to later and later in the day, hoping he could do his job unassailed. Word was making it back to the parking lot that merchants at other markets around town were experiencing the same thing—kids sticking their heads into stores just long enough to chuck some pennies, then laughing and running off without making a purchase. It was becoming the Thing to Do.

"You know, he's just trying to earn a living," Frank said with more than a bit of empathy for the little man trying to run the gauntlet from trash can to trash can, his tiny wife waiting nervously inside.

"Yeah, selling crap nobody needs."

"Oh, I know, I know," Frank soothed. "I just think you need to figure out who your beef is really with. If it's the companies that make and market that crap, then maybe Mr. Happy Snack over there is just caught in the crossfire."

"Hey, towelhead!" Joel and Frank turned. A thick-necked senior, a genuine punk whom Frank had never seen in an actual classroom, whipped a fistful of pennies at Daljit. Really hard.

"Go back to Vietnam!"

Frank winced. Joel did, too. His teacher looked to him with disapproval.

"It's not... We're not about that," Joel said quickly. He didn't know a whole lot about black people, but he knew racism was a problem.

Frank spoke directly. "You can't control everything that's going on here, Joel. But you made yourself a leader, and these kids look to you for direction. If you see something going on here you don't approve of, you have it in you to change it."

Joel gulped. "Okay."

Frank smiled, not meaning to make too much of the events. He sat down beside Joel on the hood of his car and reflexively produced a pack of cigarettes. He shook out the last one as Joel eyed it hungrily.

Frank thought the look was merely the face of a student catching his teacher doing something taboo. He bridled a bit, but lit up anyway.

"What can I say? It's a bad, bad habit. Don't ever start."

"Yeah, well..."

Frank could tell by Joel's guilty look it was too late for that. He shook his head with a tolerant frown, but was actually, genuinely disappointed.

"Joel... You're an athlete!"

"I know! I was never that heavy into smoking. And now I don't do it at all." He waved defensively to the throng. "Pretty much nobody does. Today, anyway."

Frank looked darkly to Daljit as he heaved his bags into the dumpster. "But he'd sell them to you, even though you're underage?"

"Shit, yeah," Joel said, then blushing when he remembered he was conversing with a teacher. "Sorry. I mean, every couple months, cops show up and make some noise, and then for like a week we have to go back to copping them off our parents or finding a machine that'll sell to us. But we know we can come back eventually. He'll sell you beer, too, if you look old enough. But the people that run this stupid town never seem all that concerned about any of it."

Frank looked to his shoes. He'd known for years what was going on in this store, and had never done anything about it, either. To fill the silence, he took a drag.

Joel continued to watch the cigarette intently. The longing remained.

Frank finally got it. In sympathy, he snuffed out the perfectly good smoke and crushed the empty pack in his fist.

Joel nodded toward the store, more than a little envious. "This is *our* thing. Guess there's nothing keeping you from going in there and buying yourself a fresh pack."

Frank watched Daljit scurry back into the store in another shower of pennies. Frank's compassion for him was fleeting. His curiosity as to why the town never moved to slap him down was stoked.

"Nah." He took the balled-up cigarette pack and lofted it expertly into a trash can more than ten feet away. He was 44-years-old—this was precisely the eighth time in his entire life he had sunk such a shot. In college, when his black friends mercilessly ridiculed his lack of grace, he used to practice alone in his dorm room.

"It's time I quit, too," he said.

"All right!" Joel reached into his jacket pocket, offering up a sheet of nicotine gum. "Here, I bought some at the grocery store on the way over."

Frank declined with a wizened shake of the head.

"So then *they* win."

Joel, uncomprehending: "Huh?"

"Cigarette sales go down, but nicotine gum sales go up. Every time you and your friends buy this stuff, a computer sends word to the store's distribution warehouse: There's a run on nicotine gum, send more. Word goes from the warehouse to the production plant: We're running out of nicotine gum. *Make* more. Word finally gets back to all those rich old men you guys got a bug up your butt about. They're all clearing more space in the bank vault because now they see there's money to be made off your withdrawal from the addiction they left you with.

"Next thing you know, you're picking up the new issue of *Maxim*, and there's a big color ad with ScroatM or whichever idiot they've been able to buy off, saying 'Don't buy *their* nicotine gum, buy our nicotine gum. We're the *happenin'* nicotine gum! Fork over the cash, punk.'"

Joel's head spun. He knew where this was going.

"You look close enough," Frank continued, now on a roll, "you'll probably see that the cigarette companies and the nicotine gum companies are owned by the same conglomeration. You guys hit them on the cigarette side, but they just make it up somewhere else."

He laid a sympathetic nod on Joel. "If you guys are really gonna do this, you gotta understand what you're up against."

Joel looked at the sheet of gum—eight cleanly-crafted squares of relief, laid out in a futuristic-looking containment module of foil and plastic. It was no accident that these things were packaged so as to engage a simple mind.

It all just sucked.

"Dude…" he moaned.

He took the brand new pack of gum and painfully stuffed it into the trash can. He had barely withdrawn his arm before a cold-turkeying sophomore tried to pluck the gum back out.

Joel laid a menacing glare on him. "Forget about it."

He grabbed the sophomore's half-gallon-sized slushy—contraband, after all—and poured it in on top of the gum in order to render it garbage.

The kid seemed to almost weep, then went back to rocking gently, waiting for his turn on a lone cigarette being passed among his friends as if they were soldiers in a foxhole. The image was pathetic.

Joel returned to Frank, who could've hugged this kid if not for fear of a molestation suit.

"You're going to be fine."

"Yeah. Sure." Joel reached through the open window of his car and dipped his hand into the box of provisions. He hesitated, kicked himself, then withdrew his hand with a cigarette between his fingers.

"Joel!" Frank cried, half in mock alarm at the kid's genial audaciousness.

"I know, I know," he pleaded. "I'm down to like none. This is my first one of the day, swear to God."

Not at all thwarted by his teacher's disapproval, Joel sparked it up and took a deep, milk-every-moment drag. He hated himself for this, but it was beyond his control.

"You know," Frank said, "I'm supposed to take that away from you. You shouldn't be doing this."

Joel waved to the parking lot throng. "I shouldn't be doing any of this. But it's kinda sweet."

Frank had to concede that.

Next thing he knew, Joel was offering him a drag. The teacher stopped, checked to see if anyone was paying attention, then shrugged and took a brief, clandestine hit. It was kind of exciting.

The pair sat side by side on Joel's hood and watched the milling crowd. A genuine party mood was in the air. Kids with video cameras darted about to record it all.

A stringy Oriental kid—a sophomore, Joel believed—ignored the razzing and elbowed his way into the store, like a fallen woman breaching an abortion clinic protest. He flipped off his classmates as he disappeared inside.

"Kid's got no respect," Joel said sadly.

Frank shrugged. "This is hard. You're gonna see more and more of that the longer this goes on."

"Yeah. Then we'll be done," Joel sighed wistfully. "But, you know, we do have a point."

Connection

Todd saw her first, emerging from an expensive-looking van, a three-man video crew trailing behind her. This was obviously not the local news. The local news did not pack lightweight, state-of-the-art gear like this. The local news was, without fail, staffed by young, pasty geek types with freshly minted communications degrees and aspirations of becoming the next Spielberg.

This group, from the van, were scruffed up and dressed down meticulously. They had all the right piercings, all the right casual-at-a-cost clothing. They looked like they could have their own show on the WB.

And the girl, she was… She was…

"Hi. I'm Annie McCullough with R²Rev, in New York."

Giggling, Todd realized as he giggled, was probably not the way to go here. "W-what?"

"R²Rev? New York? You do have cable here, don't you?"

"Yeah. And maps. So we've heard of R²Rev *and* New York."

When you're thrown off a bridge, you can merely fall, or you can flap your arms while falling, just so someone might say you at least went down with panache. Todd, when talking to girls, especially cute girls (and this was easily the cutest he'd ever found himself addressing), learned long ago that if he was going to strike out, *someone* was going to be entertained—even if it always ended up just being him.

Annie smiled at his shy sarcasm. She could instantly spot a kid who, whether he realized it or not, defied the stereotypes. And this one could help her.

"My crew and I are traveling the country, documenting events and opinions that matter to our viewers. Someone at the school paper at Longfellow High told us what you guys were up to here, so we made a detour to check it out."

Carlos was already panning his camera across the crowd. This was a relatively light turnout—school was in session and a lot of prep work was going on for quarter exams—but mercifully those on hand were a telegenic bunch, ably conveying a caricatured tableau of fussy teenage rabble.

When the boycott had made it a full week and Channel Twelve sent a crew out a second time to commemorate the occasion, Todd had had the foresight to supply a few signs to enhance the visuals. He used crude penmanship and blunt sloganeering in order to fairly portray the mindset of the crowd ("We're Not 4 Sale!"), then slipped the signs to the scrawniest freshmen. He knew that elder classmen, always looking for an advantage that would get them on TV, would wrench them away from the weaklings and brandish them obnoxiously. Before long, everyone would have to have one.

Soon, the more creative students showed up with proclamations of their own. On Tuesday, the slogan emerged. It was, Todd immediately recognized, exquisite:

"We're not buying this shit!"

It was rude. It was funny. It was dead-on apt. It could not appear on air because of the profanity, but by the time Todd scrawled it out on a couple dozen more signs and flung them to the protesters, it could not be ignored. News channels and photographers would have to digitally smear the "shit," giving the campaign an outlaw sheen.

This was a pirate operation, an up-your-ass show of teenage disrespect.

The pose was fed masterfully.

By the end of the day that Tuesday, "We're not buying this shit!" was spray-painted on Daljit Singh's dumpster. The next morning, it was scratched dementedly across a T-shirt.

Todd, who knew things, got on the internet and learned how to trademark a phrase.

"What exactly is going on here?" Annie asked doubtfully.

She had expected more of a scene. She was from the Midwest and knew that a gangly knot of actual American teenagers was often not a pretty picture. But what she had been told was an "uprising" turned out to be just thirty or so blandly rebellious kids loitering in a strip mall parking lot.

Todd watched her watching the crowd. She was not dolled up. She had just spent six hours stuck in a van with her three intellectually retarded crewmen and their daily flatulence showdown. She stank of stale cigarettes and morning mouth.

But... "My god," Todd gawked to himself.

My god...

"Umm. We're taking a stand against the corporations that use manipulation and addiction to make themselves rich off of us. They need us to keep buying, so we're not, just to see what happens."

He was sounding like a dick! He was sounding like Frank Guiden in ninth grade Public Speaking class, right before he pissed his pants and his family had to send him off to a special school. All of a sudden, there's a camera crew from New York and this babe from R²Rev asking him questions and his input was important AND HE WAS SOUNDING LIKE A DICK!!!

Where the hell was Joel?

He begged off. "I'm really not—"

She'd stopped listening. Todd had said enough. The simplicity of it made Annie smile, almost in awe.

"Corporate disobedience," she marveled.

She watched two skanked-out freshmen girls getting harassed for emerging from the store with cigarettes. The girls reveled in the derision— it had become popular among the freaks to score points of their own by boycotting the boycott, not letting preppy jack-offs like Joel Kasten dictate their delinquency—but the anger of the crowd was raw and legit.

Here were teenagers taking sides, taking positions, on an issue— unabashed youth-targeted consumerism—which had heretofore flourished promiscuously by the sheer grace of the target market's apathy.

This was something.

And yet... *corporate disobedience?*

"Well..." Todd recoiled at the loftiness of the phrase, but then realized with a start that that was exactly what they had here. "Yeah."

"You're throwing bombs, just by refusing to get played."

"We're not buying this shit."

She turned excitedly. "Kenny. Get a mike on…"

Her eyes met Todd's. He went liquid. "Todd. But… Wait."

He was engaged, he saw the whole picture. He would saw off a thumb to keep this girl's attention, but he knew that if anything here was going to stick, it needed a face. And it wasn't going to be his.

"You have to meet Joel Kasten. This was all his idea. He's really the guy you want to interview."

Her eyes searched the crowd. "We'll talk to him, too. Where is he?"

"He's at school right now. You know, we still have to be in class and stuff."

In fact, Joel hadn't come around yesterday, and might not today. His commitment was fading. That morning Todd saw Joel in the school parking lot with a full pack of cigarettes. He was buying somewhere.

"But he's got a free hour after lunch. He'll—"

Kenny had already handed Annie a lapel mike. With a brazenness that would've kicked off some great porn if he weren't surrounded by several dozens of his classmates, Annie stuck her hand up inside the bottom of Todd's shirt and started snaking the mike up toward his collar.

It tickled. There was way too much giggling going on here.

"Hey!" Todd protested, both at the intrusion and the predictable stirring in his shorts. Her fingers—her New York fingers—were cold against his skin.

"You want to be heard, don't you?"

"No, I don't," he lied, yanking on the mike cable.

"Hey, kid," Kenny growled darkly from beside the camera, "don't fuck with that."

Annie fussed with the mike, pinning it to Todd's collar, then primping him as if she were his mother sending him off to Sunday school. His perimeter was *way* penetrated.

"Okay, so tell me about—"

"Look," he protested, "I know how this works. This is all just entertainment for you guys. It's all just crap to run between the commercials. If it doesn't have the right angle, if it doesn't look like everything else on

R²Rev, it's never going to see the light of day. Right?"

Annie studied him hard. Who *was* this kid? And how quickly would the Hutch Posners of the world seize up and die if there were too many more like him?

"Well, yeah."

"Well, I think this is a good story. I think what we're talking about here is important. But nobody at all would've bought into it if it wasn't for Joel. He made the difference. So maybe you oughta take my word for it and give him a chance to tell you what this is all about. He'll give you what you need."

She could tell that this kid was the brains behind the movement. She understood the bargain being struck here. "And," she said, "I'll give *you* what you need."

Todd shrugged. "I think people should hear what we've got to say. If R²Rev doesn't want to run it… whatever. But I'm not doing this."

He yanked the mike off. Annie was impressed. Here was a kid who didn't want to mug for the camera, who obviously had a message, but was savvy enough to know that he didn't have the charisma to pull it off. He obviously understood the medium. If he had found a face to sell the product, who was Annie to argue?

"Okay. We'll wait."

"Okay," Todd said, more than a little spent. Here was this gorgeous older woman, from only the hottest channel in the country, with a video crew that could clearly kick his ass, and little Todd Noland had stood his ground. He was that sure he was onto something.

"So," he wheezed, suddenly charged with occupying her until Joel turned up, "why didn't you get somebody to shoot Casey Lattimer a long time ago?"

Too Numerous

"Come on, dude. Let it go."

Todd had pounced on Joel the moment he left his Spanish class. He breathlessly told him about this total piece of ass from R²Rev who was waiting for him down at the Happy Snack, eager to put him on camera and possibly before a national audience, espousing his views on the boycott.

But this girl and her crew were headed out of town. They had to go *now*.

Joel wasn't impressed.

"It's kind of stale, isn't it?"

"It's stale because there hasn't been anybody new to bring into this. Everybody we know paid attention for a couple weeks, and now it's like 'Yeah, yeah… whatever.' What we cared about when this started hasn't changed. We just needed fresh ears to hear about it. This is our chance!"

Todd's enthusiasm wasn't working on Joel. The average teenager was conditioned to pull away from anything suggesting sincerity or ambition. And, besides, who could be expected to stay passionate about something for more than a couple weeks anyway?

"I don't know…"

"She's killer, I'm telling you, dude. And she really cares about what we're saying. Christ, she was actually interested in *me*. Wait'll she gets a look at you."

This Todd, he was good. Joel scrunched up his face with contemplation, then generously surrendered.

"Okay, but look, if I miss another practice, Coach is gonna call my old man, and I don't need that kind of drama. Tell her if she'll come to the field—"

"No! It has to be at the Happy Snack. They need to do you there, for the visuals."

Joel studied him hard. It was like there was software downloaded into this kid that no one else his age had access to.

"Where do you get this stuff?"

"Because I've ruled Video Club since seventh grade," he pleaded without embarrassment. "Because the whole time you've been out winning trophies and bagging the honeys and being Big Chief Jockstrap, I've been home watching television. Really *watching* television. This is stuff I know about."

Joel hadn't really noted Todd's intensity on this whole thing until now. And, for the first time, it seemed like too much.

"Look," he withdrew. "I think I just want to—"

"Dude, you have no clue what it's like to not have anything going on, *ever*. Since kindergarten, you've had all of us kissing your ass and making your life pretty damned sweet. Everything you do, somebody notices.

"This thing down at the Happy Snack, *I* did that. You're the one everybody's listening to, but who put you up to it? I wanted to see what would happen and, dude, *something happened.*"

Joel instinctively wanted to rebut this, wanted to challenge Todd's assertion that Joel was anything other than the true instigator of their little protest. But there was no getting around the fact that when Todd first started yammering about money and cigarettes and sticking it to Jimmy the Swami, Joel didn't know what the hell he was talking about.

"I just want to see this through to the end. I just want to find out if I really got this figured out. You know?"

Joel felt his longing. They had been best friends way back when—virtual strangers in the middle bit, Joel actually pretty shitty to him when their paths crossed—but here they were: older, more filled in. And good friends once again.

That thing that had brought them together as five-year-olds—who knew it was still living there? Surely anything that innocent should've been ground down and excreted years ago.

But there it was.

Joel looked at Todd with a bemused shake of the head. "You are too numerous," he said with a crooked grin. "Maybe the most. The most numerous."

Todd was already leading Joel down the hallway. He whipped out a legal pad full of notes. Talking points.

"Okay, I don't know how much time she's gonna give you, so I think you should start with this…"

— ▪ ▬ —

He was gorgeous. Annie had to give Todd that. When he delivered Joel to her, the parking lot crowd parted reverently to let him pass, like he was Jesus come to say whatever it was that Jesus had to say that day, and she instantly saw that he had It. Whatever quality it was that made celluloid and pixels resonate *just so* for those who find fortune with their good looks, this Joel Kasten kid splashed it around more than a little.

He might open his mouth and she'd be in the van and gone before he got to his first "dude," but just to look at him? That thing you wanted to have twanged? Annie's got twanged.

"Christ, he's my little brother's age," Annie thought as she sized him up.

Introductions were made, and Annie's hand went up Joel's shirt with the mike. There was absolutely nothing appropriate about the way she noted how taut and hairless his stomach was.

The throng, given almost two hours to turn out at word of R²Rev's presence, had grown to a gratifying size. And they all hooted derisively as Joel got felt up by this honey from New York.

He preened and flashed his goofy smile. Annie blushed, withdrew her hand, and composed herself for her first question. Carlos was already taping. He wanted to get the hell out of this hick burg.

"All right. Joel Kasten, seventeen. Senior, Dickinson High School. Berline, Illinois. Tell me what's going on here."

Joel centered himself. Todd had put a lot of pressure on him on the way over, and all of a sudden everything was on him. It was going to take a little time to ramp up.

"Okay. Well, you know… Like, when did you start smoking?"

"Who says I—?"

126

"You reek," he said, beaming guiltily. There was nothing better than knocking a pretty girl down a peg or two.

Annie maintained a professional non-reaction as the boys in the crew stifled laughs.

"I started smoking when I was fifteen."

"And you knew cigarettes could kill you. You *still* know cigarettes could kill you, right? Cancer will pretty much kick your ass if it gets hold of you. Right?"

"Okay…"

"And the companies that make the cigarettes, they know this. Right?"

"They say—"

"These companies *know* that a few hundred thousand people a year die from cigarettes, and they *know* that almost all of them started smoking when they were young and stupid and easy to fool, just like us. Right? And once you start, it's almost impossible to stop. They *know* this."

"Sure."

"The laws, which are a joke, tell them they can't be selling to us, but they'd have no business without us. Okay?"

"Okay."

"So, and maybe I'm just talking outta my ass, but—can I say 'ass'?"

"Yes," Annie said, perturbed at Joel for continually breaking his flow. She was already seeing the edit. "We like 'ass'."

"So maybe I'm talking outta my ass, but it seems pretty obvious to me that these companies are okay with killing teenagers by the thousands just to make a buck. And I don't know why we're not pissed off about that. Christ, if these same old farts were up in the water tower shooting us down in those kinds of numbers, we'd kick their asses.

"I mean, I know we're supposed to smoke because we're *not* supposed to smoke, know what I'm saying? And, yeah, it'll piss off our parents and make us look like hard-asses and, anyway, if the cancer's gonna get us, it's not like it's gonna get us *today*.

"So, we all—everybody who smokes—we think we're getting away with something all sneaky and cool, and meanwhile we're doing just what the cigarette companies are banking on us doing.

"We're getting played, maybe to death," Joel summed up with a genuine sense of bafflement. "Just seems like a hell of a price to pay for a pose."

Annie listened, transfixed. This was great stuff.

"So... ?"

"So we figured it out," he shrugged cockily. "And we're not buying this shit."

"Does this mean—?"

"And you know what else I found out?" Joel was getting revved up. "The clothes and shoes and crap we all spend way too much money on, the stuff that they spend about twelve billion dollars advertising to drill it into our heads that we ain't happening unless we're wearing their shit. You know who makes that stuff? Little kids! Poor little tiny kids, making like two nickels a day in some smelly-ass country, for stuff that we're spending hundreds, *thousands* of dollars on. What's up with that?"

Todd grew uneasy, wondering if he should find a way to cut Joel off—this wasn't from the talking points. Joel was tapping into his own storehouse of knowledge. That couldn't be good.

And yet Joel was now sounding his most impassioned, and it was coming through. Annie hung on his every word.

"I mean, hey, *we're* teenagers. We're obnoxious and lazy and stupid. If you want to see us suffer, who could blame you? But..." He fumbled for a second, honestly offended by the thought. "Little kids, eight- and nine-year-old kids, not getting to play, just working all the time for like no money, all so we can look fine down at the mall and maybe get some nookie?

"We're supposed to be cool with that? I don't think so."

The moment presented itself. He went for it.

He was wearing a J. Crew collared shirt, one of his favorites. And he impulsively yanked at it, ripping off buttons as it tore. His lapel mike flew off with the shirt; Annie, with remarkable agility, grabbed it in mid-air and trained it on Joel, who now stood before the camera shirtless, his chiseled chest and sculpted biceps rendering him nearly god-like.

A great, silly, 17-year-old god.

The crowd, already pumped by the presence of R²Rev, hooted at his theatrics. It was early November. The cold sting of the air against his skin just accentuated the statement.

"We. Are not. Buying. This. *Shit*," Joel proclaimed, winningly guileless in his half-naked state. Tossing the shreds of his shirt to the mob, he was just a really cool character in a TV show they were watching.

"Deal with it," he pronounced into the camera.

The crowd cheered. One kid ripped his shirt off in tribute. Another kicked off his $120 Nikes and threw them up in the air.

For the tenth time, Annie made sure Carlos was capturing all this. Then she found Todd in the crowd.

He had delivered, just as he promised. His heart was racing, because Joel had hit it out of the park—and because Annie McCullough, from R²Rev in New York, was looking at him, with admiration and gratitude.

There, in the Happy Snack parking lot, agendas were fused.

They had something here.

A Sweetie-P Christmas

The suggested infinity of the stark white backdrop enhanced the dark, dark chocolate of his skin to an absolute matte black. He sat on a throne, draped in Italian leather and thirty thousand dollars' worth of jewelry, with a floppy Santa hat on his head.

A nine-month-old baby girl named Shanté cooed lovingly on his knee, and a three-year-old boy named Bryce darted in and out from under the throne. Their mothers—his girlfriends (one ex, one on the bubble)—and a posse of eleven juggled the administration of ass kisses as R²Rev crew members cooled their heels and waited.

He was Sweetie-P, hip-hop mogul, empire builder, one-time crack dealer, and—for today's purpose anyway—doting father.

R²Rev had persuaded the industry titan to cut some promotional spots for a *Year In Review* special (Sweetie had a greatest hits package—*Da Hitz!*—coming out for Christmas and could use the added exposure), and part of the sell had been giving him free rein to script the ads.

Sweetie and the Sweetie machine had spent the past year trying to transition into the mainstream, playing down his gangsta affiliations and emphasizing his more legitimate pursuits, like his new clothing line and his motion picture company. It had occurred to the artist—via a memo from an image consultant to whom it occurred first—that showing off his gentler, domestic side would "be the shit."

A Christmas theme was arrived upon—"so long as I ain't lookin' like a faggot," Sweetie had warned. For weeks, the Santa hat was the source of tense negotiations, until one of his handlers convinced Sweetie that white people might find him less scary if he wore it.

Showing his kids off would work wonders, too. To that, Sweetie chuckled, "Oh, yeah. White folks always like to know we're makin' more of us."

So they had gathered here at R²Rev's Manhattan soundstage, Sweetie-P to be seen coddling his offspring in his Santa hat, set against a limitless white backdrop. Sweetie didn't want candy canes and Christmas trees and reindeer ("Fuck the reindeers!"). He had already agreed to the hat.

He was keepin' it real. Or whatever.

The problem was that his *other* child—two-year-old D'Monte—was stuck in traffic. Or, to be more precise, his mother—another ex—was trapped in a limo somewhere up on the Brooklyn Bridge, trying to make her way out of Bed-Stuy. She had been more than an hour late just making it to the car, and now she had kept everyone on the soundstage waiting pretty much all morning.

Sweetie had initially welcomed the opportunity to snuggle up with the two kids who *had* shown up, but the burden of fatherhood was beginning to make him cranky as the wait dragged on under the hot studio lights.

Meanwhile, the respective mothers of his progeny stood tensely just feet apart, shooting daggers at each other and silently counting the minutes that Sweetie showered affection on one child over the other. Kept in high style by the Sweetie gravy train, each mother had her own mini-posse, members of which spent the time flirting with Sweetie's posse proper, which was franticly working cell phones and personal organizers to reconfigure the rest of their boss' day now that the R²Rev shoot was running long. A swing past Versace was threatening to fall out of the day altogether.

And all the while, the network was paying a New York union crew to stand around drinking coffee and smoking cigarettes. In less than 90 minutes, this stage was going to be needed to construct the set for *The Ripple Room*, the net's weekly rap/dance party, commonly known as *The Nipple Room* for the preferred dress of the kids brought in to rub up against each other for the cameras. They couldn't wait much longer.

A reluctant Hutch Posner had been called down from his office. He was going to have to do something.

"Sweetie-P!" Hutch drawled, trying to pimp it up the best he could. Bryce, the three-year-old, was yipping and squawking obnoxiously as he squeezed himself between Hutch and the throne.

"'Sup," Sweetie said with the dead-eyed indifference of an autistic child, offering his hand to receive a retro soul shake. This lazy-wristed how-do-you-do, which around the late '70s had all but vanished as a Huggy Bear-ed affectation of the worst kind, was now de rigueur for a generation and an industry steeped in hollow, caricatured gestures.

"Hutch Posner. We met at that AIDS thing in June."

Whatever... "Yeahallright."

Bryce was tugging at his father's leather-covered arm. Sweetie was starting to bristle.

"Raised a lot of money that night," Hutch said. "You really came through."

"Yeah. My first deejay, from back in the day—he died from the AIDS," Sweetie said solemnly before breaking into a leering laugh. "That nigger stuck his dick up some *skanky* holes!"

He crowed and reflexively swung downward with an open palm, expecting to lay skin on one of his crew. Someone, at all times, had to be nearby to offer affirmation to Sweetie's trenchant remarks by receiving his boneless low-five with an adulatory cry of "Nigga be sayin'!" or simply "Dat's it!" (roughly translated: "Aptly put, old bean").

But the system had broken down, and Sweetie brought his hand down into nothing but air. His posse was elsewhere, working the phones and chatting up the hos, and he was not being serviced.

He was about to explode when he noticed that young Bryce was beside him with his palm outstretched.

"Skanky holes!" the three-year-old said brightly.

His doting father burst into a smile and laid skin on the boy. The posse, suddenly aware of and horrified by its malfeasance, laughed with relief.

Hutch laughed, too. He rubbed Bryce's head affectionately, then quickly withdrew his hand. He recalled vaguely that there was something politically incorrect about rubbing a black boy's head.

He couldn't stall any longer. "So, bro—"

"*Boo!*" Bryce had leapt up between Hutch and Sweetie. Sweetie erupted. "Donna!"

"*That* one's not mine!" Donna snapped back.

Sweetie cursed bitterly at his mistake. He'd had a 50-50 shot.

The other mother—Charlayne—recognized the vicious bite in Sweetie's voice and leapt into action, pulling Bryce away quickly. Donna flew in behind her to grab the baby. Sweetie-P was done fathering for now.

He glowered at them all as they withdrew, the Santa hat drooping off his head. Charged menace hung in the air.

Hutch cleared his throat awkwardly. "Cute kids."

"Safe sex, dog," Sweetie moaned wearily. "Only way to go."

"So, Sweetie," Hutch drew in closer, burrowing on. "Bro, it's the shit, having you cut these spots for us. But you're a busy man, I want to get you on your way. Thought maybe we could reconceptualize and lay this thing down."

Sweetie dismissed him with a wave of the hand. He dug down deep and summoned up the will to endure.

"Nah, man. S'all right," he sighed. "Car's just a few blocks off. We'll be kickin' it any minute now."

Hutch coughed. "Our driver just called and said she pulled over to do some shopping. Said your son needs better clothes for the shoot."

"*Bitch!*" Sweetie seethed through clenched teeth. It was a sharp, violent curse, one that could be pictured being uttered along with a shot to the face.

He laid out his hand and instantly a phone was dropped into it. He jabbed at a button and prepared to unload.

"Hold on," Hutch said quickly, delicately. He could still pull this off. "Man, it's killing me, seeing you mess with all this drama on account of us. Tell me how I can make this work for you, right now."

"It's Christmas, bitch!" Sweetie snapped at Hutch, his voice going up an octave. "It's a Christmas-fucking-card, that's the plan. It's me and my fucking babies and Merry-fucking-Christmas! If I ain't got my babies, the fuck's the point?!?"

Hutch hung on. "I hear ya, man. I'm down with that. But, hey, look: We got *two* of your babies! Cute as hell and ready to go. Let's just go with them, get you outta here."

Sweetie-P stared at him. "The fuck's the matter with you? I got three babies. Whole fuckin' world knows I got *three* babies. Barbara Walters interviewed me, she was rollin' around on the floor with all my little pickaninnies like we's her favorite darkies on the whole plantation.

"The fuck can I show up now with just two babies? Black man in this country turn up with a baby missing, he gets social services crawling up his ass. Nigger, please."

"Well," Hutch began hopefully, when in fact he should've braked. Hard. "Supposing we could find—"

Sweetie nearly leapt off the throne. "*Find what?* Some other black baby? Stick him in the family photo and just figger nobody's gonna know, seein' as how we all look alike and all?"

"No!"

"Dat's it, we're through." The posse was already halfway to the door, forming a line of security that would stretch to the limo idling outside.

Sweetie stood and prepared to make good on his threat, but made the mistake of looking to his manager first. The manager knew that the pre-release tracking on the greatest hits package was disturbingly low and that Sweetie could not afford any bad blood with R²Rev right now.

The manager pursed his lips and shook his head with an almost complete stillness. Sweetie had seen the numbers, had heard the warnings that his move toward softer fare had caused his base to start questioning his legitimacy. Fact was, if he carried through on his plan to abandon the guns, pimps & hos entirely in favor of the mainstream, R²Rev would have no use for him at all.

He impotently flopped back down onto the throne, hissing with anger.

"Fuck y'all!" he shouted. "*No* babies. It's just me and my ass and let's do it!"

The Santa hat flopped across his face. "*And get this the fuck offa me!!*"

Without the children and the hat, the scene didn't say Christmas at all. It was just one very angry black man on a throne, staring hatefully into the camera. Anyone stumbling upon this spot might've thought the Revolution had finally come.

When little Bryce figured out he wasn't going to be on TV with his daddy, he started to bawl. The baby, fussy and hot under the lights, set to shrieking as well. The two mothers, who had gone to the trouble of getting here on time with the hope of scoring a little glory for their bastard children, fumed furiously.

Hutch felt the forceps squeezing at the base of his brain as Sweetie-P waited for the TelePrompTer to heat up, his teeth grinding.

Finally:

"Yo, you kids dreaming of a white Christmas? I know I am…"

Teach Your Children Well

And then, there she was. Waiting for him.

She had already commandeered his VCR, had already fired up that ridiculous tape she had returned with. Even more audacious, she had collared staffers from across the floor and pulled them into his office to view it.

He could hear that kid—that irredeemably common kid—from all the way down the hall.

"It's almost like we're being born just to take money off us," Joel protested on the tape. "Fuck that!"

Fresh from his run-in with Sweetie-P, this was the last thing Hutch needed. He had to pull people away from his doorway and aim them back toward their work stations just to get into his office.

"All right, thank you," he said dryly, hating the nagging, school-teacherish tone in his voice. Every month as the head of this media giant took him farther and farther away from the happening young man he once thought he was.

"Back to work. We've got a culture to bring down." He pushed more staffers out of the room.

Last to leave—in fact, as yet oblivious to Hutch's hectoring—were the interns, standing nearest to the monitor. They were young college students, much closer to high school age than the paid staffers. And, as eager-to-be-unpaid drones in the R²Rev universe, much less possessed of the cynicism and attitude that marked the staffers.

To have the best view of the TV, they must've come running when Annie first put out the call.

Or maybe she went to them first.

"Annie—" he fussed.

"Look," she said quietly. "They're paying attention. What more do you want?"

He grabbed the remote from her hand and shut Joel Kasten off. The interns turned and went pale at finding themselves busted in the boss' office.

"I'm about to hire the bunch of you just so I can fire you."

They scuttled out, averting their eyes as they squeezed past Hutch. This was the closest he'd ever come to encountering much of the intern staff.

Christ, did they all look this young?

Annie took the remote back from Hutch and started the tape again, muting it. Images of Joel, of the Happy Snack, of a persecuted Daljit Singh spilled into Hutch's office.

"What do you think?" she asked confidently.

He edged past her and reclaimed his desk. He had been dreading this encounter all week.

"Have a seat. We'll work this out."

She sat down opposite him. Her extended duty in the field had allowed Hutch to forget how attractive Annie was. Once again, he felt stirrings. No doubt she had dressed this day to produce that very effect.

He leaned back casually, adopting his most earnest guise. "Am I glad you're back. I think I've finally found a position for you that you'll soar in, and which will—by happy coincidence—drag my ass out of one very big fire."

He was dodging the issue. Annie's antennae went up as she leaned in warily.

Hutch set to rumba nimbly between the shit and the Shineola. "Executive Producer. *The Ripple Room.*"

She blinked. "You're kidding me."

"It'll keep you here in town, which I know is important to you. Ten hours a week of prime programming, all under your command. A couple specials a year, live from Spring Break. It could be a launching pad to anything you want to do in this industry."

Annie, straight-faced: "So, *I'd* be the one making sure the dancers are wearing panties before the cameras start rooting around up there?"

"Or you'd make someone else do it. The privilege of power."

"Hutch," she laughed. He also had forgotten how cutting her laugh could be. "*The Nipple Room?*"

"Annie—"

"Did you even look at this tape?" She gestured to the monitor. The silenced Joel was in mid-speech, looking fine.

Hutch went hardball.

"Annie, it's shit. It's less than shit. This is… a bunch of ugly teenagers, standing around in a parking lot, preaching about how bad cigarettes are for you. Christ, where are the kids hyping church on Sunday and chastity belts? Our viewers would shit themselves if we laid this on them."

"You—"

"How is it that you don't understand our demographic?" he said cuttingly, jabbing toward the monitor. "Bring me videotape of *our* kind of teenager kicking the shit out of *those* teenagers and I'll give you a two-hour special. I mean, Christ… Look at them!"

"This isn't an anti-smoking movement!" she said, not surprised that Hutch had missed the point entirely. "This is an anti-exploitation movement, an anti-*adult* movement. These are teenagers saying 'Go fuck yourself' to institutions that thrive on taking advantage of them. If *you* understood our demographic, you'd know that nothing would appeal to them more."

"Hey!" he cried, legitimately offended. *Never* slight a media titan's grip on his demo.

"Yeah, okay," Annie pressed on smartly. "There are no pimp clothes. There are no tattoos. There's hardly even a damned backwards baseball hat. But you know what? Most of our viewers don't look like the caricatures we sell. They look *just like that*," she said vehemently, pointing to the screen. "They look like that. And I guarantee you, they *feel* like that. Or maybe they would, if they knew kids somewhere else felt the same way."

"Annie," he said with condescension, "we are a *music* network."

"Oh, yeah right. But somehow you'll find space for multiple airings of *Anal Sex: The New Virginity*," Annie said. "Ever find anybody who would help you with your personal research on that one?"

Her shot was withering. Hutch flinched.

"That was a public service program. There was a *question mark* in that title. *Is* anal sex the new virginity? No, it is not."

"Yeah, with host Mimi SoWett , who could fit a Volkswagen up her ass she's had such a workout up there."

She bore down forcefully. "There is machinery in place right now for this network to produce and air non-music-based programming when you can find some leering angle you can exploit. All I am asking for is one half-hour to see if we can't broaden our scope just a little bit."

"A half-hour?!"

"Fine. A segment, five minutes. Drop it into *Week In Review*. Run it in place of *this* week's arraignment hearing for Phat Bastard."

Hutch had heard enough. Annie was running down R²Rev's artists and its on-air talent—she was way out of line. And her veiled hints of blackmail could only be tolerated for so long.

He looked at her grimly. "Look, you think about *The Nipple Room*. If that's not of interest to you, then maybe it's time you find a more suitable outlet for your aspirations."

Annie was struck dumb, not expecting Hutch to dig in so tenaciously. He took the remote from her hand and prepared to send Joel and his friends back to obscurity.

"Four dead in O-hi-o!"

Hutch and Annie turned. It was John Viceroy, the MediaTrust liaison. He was watching the videotape as the camera panned across the gathered Happy Snack faithful.

"What's this?"

Hutch quickly shut down the tape, portraying just the right amount of toadying for his boss. "Nothing. We were just—"

"No, no. Turn it back on," Viceroy commanded genially.

He drew closer to the monitor as Annie's tape played. He studied the teenagers closely, their placards and their youthful indignation seeming to strike a deep chord of fondness inside the powerful corporate player.

Their inflamed faces were contorted with purpose. The sound was still off, but the tenor was clear.

"Look at that," Viceroy sighed wistfully. "Christ, does that take me back..."

John Viceroy was 55-years-old—20 in 1969.

Ah, the mind grasps it: *he was from the '60s!*

He had been there, neck-deep in the revolution. He and his friends were the ones who were going to snatch the country away from the adults, the oppressors, and deliver a compromised and diseased America to the young and pure of heart to be nurtured back to wellness. Together, they would embark on their *own* adulthood, cleansed of the craven behaviors that had marked their parents' generation. When the time came, they would pass a gentle and enlightened country along to their children, who would be raised in a land in which cynicism and self-interest would know no place.

It had been a beautiful time, John Viceroy still believed, when anything seemed possible. Anything but the possibility that they were all full of shit.

"Do kids *do* this anymore?"

"Well, you know..." Hutch shrugged. "You guys had a war to protest."

"Yeah," Viceroy reflected dreamily. "You know, if you were lucky enough to take a billy club to the head in the midst of an anti-war protest? Once you came to, you'd find yourself in so much pussy and so much dope, you'd finally have to beg them to let up. Literally beg them. You were a hero!

"'Stop the War' was just the password to get into the speakeasy," he chuckled. "Might as well have been 'swordfish.'"

Annie, sensing an opportunity, ignored her turning stomach. She bit her tongue and let Viceroy ooze. His nose was practically pressed against the TV screen.

"*That's* the problem with teenagers today. Nobody's fighting anything, they don't learn the value of taking stands, taking sides." He shook his head forlornly. "Dylan, my oldest, could care less about politics."

"He's how old?" Hutch asked intently, holding up his end.

"Sixteen. Seventeen?" Viceroy whipped out his Palm and stylused his way to enlightenment. "Seventeen. Last month." He grimaced weakly and tapped in a note to his assistant to send the boy something pricey. "So what's this bunch on about?"

"Corporate disobedience," Annie said with cool but deliberate emphasis. She had all but stood herself between Hutch and Viceroy.

"These kids in Berline, Illinois, a couple hundred of them"—well, sort of—"have decided to send a message to corporate America by boycotting products that are most aggressively peddled to them. They're sticking it to The Man by withholding their money."

"The Man!!" Viceroy beamed. "Whatever became of The Man?"

"He's in Berline. And he's feeling the heat. Stores that had been making their living off teens are out tens of thousands of dollars since this started. These kids are starting to feel a real sense of empowerment."

"Yes, that's it! That's what we had: empowerment. People—*adults*—had to take notice, had to take us seriously, because we were just so fucking obnoxious!"

Viceroy saw one of Todd's *We're Not Buying This Shit!* signs. He sighed and offered his solemn blessing.

"Well, good for them."

He turned to Annie. "What're your plans for this?"

"Well…"

"We were thinking of doing a half-hour on activism among teenagers, maybe try to stoke the fires a little bit," Hutch offered without shame. Annie whirled on him.

"We have some other tape—I don't think Annie's seen it yet—of some skinheads in Portland who joined up with the ACLU to stage First Amendment rallies against their high school because the principal ordered some of their racist tattoos covered up. And somewhere in the archives, we have something about some kids boycotting a Wal-Mart somewhere because they wouldn't stock the first ScroatM album.

"You know, we could contrast today with the '60s. Run a lot of clips, from back in the day," Hutch suggested eagerly. Annie had to admire his ability to set a hook. And if this is what it took to get her piece on the air …

Viceroy grinned. "I've got a picture. I was eighteen. I had this huge bong hanging out of my pants, like it was my dick. But all the water ran out—

fucking genius, right?—so this dog that lived in this house I was crashing in, it was licking the floor in front of me. And right when they took this picture, the dog looked up at this bong hanging between my legs, and it had its tongue out, like it was going to …" He was yanked back from his reverie with the vague sense that this was not appropriate conversation for these politically correct times.

"But, hey, I love your idea! Wouldn't hurt us to bring some politics into our programming. We have a responsibility to educate as well as entertain," he concluded, recalling something he had heard at a Senate hearing or someplace.

"Sure!" Hutch sucked up effortlessly. "Most of our viewers, they're just like those kids on the tape. They're probably charged up by the same issues, but they might not even know it yet."

Annie bit down hard, praising herself for her thick-skinned pragmatism. She sat down and immediately began scribbling in her notepad, roughing out an outline for the show. By the time she delivered it for air—and she *would* be the person delivering it for air—skinheads and Wal-Mart protests would only be a sidebar. She knew she had the real story.

"Hey, look," John Viceroy said, shyly but with pride.

From his wallet, he produced a yellowed photograph of a lanky, cloudy-eyed hippie appearing to be fellated by a Labrador full of bong water. All around him, Viceroy's fucked-up teenage friends could be seen giggling and pointing with glee.

One beamed stupidly and offered a peace sign.

The future was theirs.

A Town

If anybody wanted to watch, the weekly Common Council meetings aired live every Tuesday from Berline's City Hall. A more turgid slog through municipality minutia one could not hope to find, but it was politics in motion—democracy in action—right there on public access channel 25, smack dab between professional wrestling and whatever knee to the cultural groin R²Rev was serving up.

If a bus stop was due to be relocated, if low lying neighborhoods were besieged by flooding, if the drive-thru at the new McDonald's was causing traffic to back up onto South Street—solutions were forged here. The public was invited to peer in, to see how the stultifyingly mundane decisions were made that kept a community functioning.

But no one cared. If things ran properly, no one should.

This week, though, the Council chamber was packed, and televisions were tuned in: the adults had come to shut down the Happy Snack protest.

The store's parking lot there at the corner of Cypress and Donner, always a worrisome gathering spot for Dickinson students, had grown too small to contain the hordes of young people determined that the longer they gathered in the greatest possible numbers, the better the chance of pissing somebody off. The unlikely appearance of the R²Rev crew—and the rumor that they would soon return to flesh out their story—had caused the students to dig in. They weren't going anywhere.

The neighborhood surrounding the strip mall bore the brunt of the action. Curbside parking, already sparse, was now hogged by beaters and compacts that throbbed incessantly to bass-laden hip-hop and metal roaring inside. Even with the boycott, garbage was being generated and discarded everywhere—*somebody* was doing an awful lot of buying.

Boys were seen pissing alongside Bert and Doreen Franklin's garage. Old Lady Drake found used rubbers in her front hedge. When fluids were inadvertently dribbled into the palm of Mrs. Drake's hand, her son was forced to accompany her to the family doctor for an AIDS test. She was 86-years-old.

For weeks, it was assumed that somebody responsible for the store would eventually flush the students out—if not Happy Snack or its corporate parent, then the partnership that owned the corner on which the property stood. Neighbors had had it with the traffic and the mess. Parents were disgruntled with the self-impressed air that their children were taking on as they slighted their studies, and ignored their athletic commitments and other responsibilities, in order to stand around to play at being rebels.

Now it appeared that national TV would be lending validity to their children's noisy break with conformity.

What would the world think of them?

When no one in charge of the property made a move to kick the kids out, when persistent calls to the police yielded no results, the town's adults made enough noise to prompt a public hearing in the Council chambers. For many residents—the ones who never voted, the ones who felt indefinably spiteful toward those who did—this would be their first visit to the halls of their local government.

Frank Kolak, who had arrived early for a good seat, watched as the townspeople shuffled into the modest assembly room, blurry-eyed and put upon. Some unwritten compact had been violated, the one that guaranteed them the right to never pay attention.

"Why do I pay my taxes if the cops aren't going to respond when I need them?" demanded Art Berndt, one of the unhappy Happy Snack neighbors. Just about every declaration of discontent contained an embittered reference to taxes. In even the dimmest of minds, there was the understanding that something of benefit was due in exchange for the money taken from them every year.

"This has been going on for three weeks!"

Mayor Mary Claire Vincent, the matronly wife of a retired dentist, and herself a life-long resident of Berline, sat with discomfort, in charge of a room she had never seen this full in her nearly three terms of service. The eight Council members—all white, mostly male—expressed emotions that ranged from startled unease to coiled megalomania. The more goal-oriented members sensed that, finally, here was the issue that was going to liberate them from City Hall, and propel them into elected state office.

The local media, by now checking in regularly with the boycott, were there to spotlight any politician who distinguished himself. If that obnoxious music video channel sent a crew all the way from New York, could CNN and the other news networks be far behind?

Political careers had been launched by issues less notable than this.

"The Happy Snack operates on private property," Mayor Vincent responded. "If the proprietors choose to allow large gatherings in their parking lot, there isn't a lot we can do to stop them."

"There are ordinances in this town," barked Don Salem. Salem, voted off the Council last time around, still kept his nose in everything. He was convinced the town was going to hell since his steady hand left the wheel.

"If a tenant chooses to host what has turned into a *party* involving the kinds of numbers we've been seeing," he continued, "then they are required to pull permits, provide toilets and other facilities, and make damned sure that the surrounding neighborhood is not impacted. City Code 484-A clearly states that any property owner who billa staarta dooda *violation* offa den den reetz *ordinances* eff eff sinching of the roobel *held accountable* oyah stepsss *immediate* app app app…"

Todd Noland, sitting next to Frank Kolak, sighed in bored agony, his eyelids heavy and about to close. Nothing in his young life—not church, not trips to Grandma's, not fourth year German—had ever been as abominably dull as what he was being forced to listen to here. He couldn't understand why Mr. Kolak had insisted he come, and he really couldn't understand why the Social Studies teacher was sitting on the edge of his chair in rapt attention, as if this were a monster truck rally or something.

"Sssh," the teacher hissed sharply at Todd's anguished groan. "This is getting good."

"… Article Three, Section Twelve… ordinance clearly states… Articles Six *and* Fourteen… duly noted… Section Nine, amended to reflect… *pay our taxes!…"*

Todd's skin ached. He crossed his arms bitterly and studied the two woefully scrawny video cameras that the city used to broadcast the proceedings. Jesus, he sulked. *ATMs have better cameras.*

"Obviously, Don's right," said Councilman Jerry Self, who oversaw the Sixth Ward, in which the Happy Snack operated. "I move that this issue be given top priority when the committee meets…"

"We aren't waiting until a committee meets!" said Art Berndt. "We want this dealt with right now. Tonight!"

Mayor Vincent cleared her throat. "There are procedures which we are forced to—"

"What the heck's going on here?" asked Fran Webber. Fran was on the PTA, the school board, the community Block Watch committee, the Dickinson High Booster Club, Citizens for a Better Berline, and various other civic entities that kept her sufficiently oblivious to the fact that her son—a Dickinson junior for a second consecutive year—was selling ecstasy out of her garage.

"Why are we talking about going after that store for some petty code violation, when we all know they've been selling cigarettes and liquor to our underage children for years? *That man*"—meaning Daljit Singh—"should be driven out of business!"

The crowded room blurbled with indignant approval. This is precisely how the Frankenstein monster always ended up with torch-bearing villagers on his ass.

Todd couldn't fail to be impressed by the tempers in the room. Mr. Kolak listened with anticipation.

The mayor and the Council squirmed slightly.

"Our records show that police officers have been dispatched to the store numerous times over the past few years upon reports of illegal sales to minors," Mayor Vincent responded. "We have made it very clear to the store manager that the severest possible measures would be taken if it could be proven that he was violating the law."

Jack Barber laughed bitterly. "It's happening every day! Haven't you been listening to those punks on the news? If they've got the money, that store will sell them whatever they want!"

"I've called the police over a dozen times after some of the things I've found on my son," Fran Webber sniped. "I've gone in there myself and talked to that man. He just yelled at me and told me to leave. Nothing is ever done! What kind of message are we sending our children?"

Mayor Vincent cleared her throat. "That store, in one form or another, has been a valued, tax-paying member of our business community for over twenty years. Unless we have something more substantial than anecdotal evidence—"

"Excuse me…" It was Frank Kolak. On nervous legs, he had made his way to the podium. He was still wondering if he'd regret having set his VCR to tape the broadcast before he left home.

At least he'd be easy to spot on the tape. His was the only black face in the room.

"I don't want to… I mean, I live in the Sixth Ward. I follow these meetings. I know the strip mall has been the subject of a lot of discussion over the past few years."

The mayor and the rest of the Council turned to Jerry Self. He had lived in the Sixth Ward for the past 35 years, and had watched the area deteriorate markedly for the past five.

He knew exactly what Frank was referring to. It had been discussed—in carefully couched terms—before the Council numerous times.

"The commercial viability of that property is something we've been watching closely, yes," Self said. "We've lost a certain quality in that neighborhood that we used to have."

Just east of the strip mall where the Happy Snack sat was the city line that divided Berline and Cicero. Cicero's working poor and just-plain-poor—blacks, mainly—had amassed just over the line, and every year there seemed to be more and more. As space ran out, families were crossing into Berline and taking root in the inexpensive apartment buildings that some of the town's wealthiest residents owned.

With the presence of outsiders—and their outsider ways—the tone of the neighborhood had begun to change. Long-time residents, some still living in the sturdy and austere early 20th century homes they were born in, found reason to move out, maybe down to Florida, or to the west side of town. Something smaller, now that the kids were gone.

Terms and phrases such as "encroachment," "quality of life," and "maintaining our Berline identity" were used in Council whenever the subject of the erosion of the Sixth Ward ever came up, but the unspoken truth was simply that this predominantly white section of Berline was made uncomfortable by the influx of black families. The economic viability of the Sixth Ward had dipped worrisomely as the neighborhood changed, so much so that the block of stores in which the Happy Snack operated remained one of the very few stretches of functioning commercial real estate in the area.

The Happy Snack was the strip mall's anchor, the traffic-generator that—according to theory—spilled business over to the mall's other tenants: a video store, a dry cleaner, a copy shop, a Chinese restaurant, a take-out pizza place, and a hair salon. All these operations were struggling to survive, and none was eager to find out what life would be like without the Happy Snack there to assure a constant flow of potential customers to their doors. For some of the stores—chiefly the restaurants—the parking lot protest had prompted the best business they had seen in months.

Without the Happy Snack, the city fathers feared, the rest of the mall would wither and die. With commercial space then available to be leased at desperation prices, the neighborhood's newer residents—or those seeking to exploit them—might be inclined to set up stores of their own. Rent-to-own shops, paycheck loan operations, salons, and restaurants offering services and cuisine alien to long-rooted residents would then define the neighborhood. And with welcoming signage and fare thus on display, the desirability of the area would draw newcomers in even bigger numbers.

It was like dominoes, the way neighborhoods fell, so the City Council—elected to serve their constituents and vanquish their fears—were absolutely meeting their mandate by protecting that corner. If they did run Daljit Singh out of business, or if harassment over sales to minors caused Happy Snack corporate to relocate the store to a community less pissy, the same neighbors now bitching about a glut of teenagers would be *really* thrilled to see what turned up in its place.

Happy Snack corporate, when choosing locations, had a formula for figuring this out.

Frank Kolak got it on his own.

"What's your point?" Jerry Self asked Frank.

"My point is…" Frank said warily, looking to see Todd watching him with anticipation. "My point is that I wonder if the city's priorities in this matter haven't been misplaced."

Frank heard himself speaking, heard himself sounding frail and resigned to surrender before he had even begun. He looked again to Todd, and was reminded that this kid had risked something to set his own protest in motion.

Now it was his turn.

"I think it looks like you've been willing to look the other way at some of the things that that store's been doing because you need that store to stay in business. I think you need that store to stay in business because you think it's the only thing keeping you from losing control of that neighborhood." He didn't dare pause. "I think it appears that this city's been willing to expose its children to illegal liquor and cigarette sales if it means that people you don't approve of aren't crossing over from Cicero and messing with your 'Berline identity'."

Frank swallowed hard. All around him, the public tried to decipher what he had just said. Once it sank in, they mumbled their disapproval.

The Council bristled with indignation.

"Excuse me," Mayor Vincent said in clipped terms. "May I have your name?"

"My name is Frank Kolak," Frank said. "I live here."

Leonard Fischer from the Fourth Ward clicked open his microphone and stared down Frank skeptically. "I don't think I appreciate what I hear you accusing us of."

"I'm not accusing you of anything. I'm just telling you how it looks. If there's another explanation—"

"Oh, good Christ," lamented 63-year-old Ralph Dorey, from the Third Ward. Dorey, a 28-year Council veteran, had a flattop, a beet-red face, and a generational discomfort with minority groups. He had moved his parents out of the Sixth Ward the year before.

"Are you trying to turn this into a black thing?"

Frank recoiled as if slapped, then had to suppress a laugh. The lack of discretion was stunning.

"No, all I'm saying is—"

"This is how it starts!" Dorey threw up his hands with an embittered chortle. "One minute you're just a small town council trying to keep the garbage picked up and the traffic lights working, and the next thing you know you're branded a bunch of racists, just waiting for Jesse Jackson and Al Sharpton to parachute in and run some parades up and down Main Street. Happened in Decatur a few years back. It can damned sure happen here."

"Councilman Dorey..." the mayor cautioned sternly. Nevertheless, the town fairly gasped at what Dorey was predicting.

Frank felt emboldened. "I can direct you to the minutes of any number of Council meetings in which the protection of that strip mall was given a top priority. I'd just like to know what it is you're protecting *against*."

"We're protecting against losing even more business in that neighborhood. This town can't afford to have any more boarded-up storefronts," Fran Webber explained tersely, putting on her "Citizens For a Better Berline" hat. She understood that the Happy Snack was a barricade. She would have to do better by it. "Why do you people always have to drag race into this?"

"You *teach*, don't you?" asked a skeptical Nan Caplan, councilwoman from the Eighth Ward. She seemed to be accusing Frank of something.

"Yes. At Dickinson."

"And do you think it's appropriate, then, to come down here and insert yourself into these discussions? Does Principal Keller know you're here?"

Frank was dumbstruck. "This is a town hall meeting. I live in this town. I don't have to—"

"Look, I just want those kids outta that parking lot," said Art Berndt, reclaiming the mike sheepishly, regretful for having stirred this up now that he saw the big picture. "If some of them are buying cigarettes when they're not supposed to—hey, who didn't when we were their age? But I'm not looking to that store to baby-sit my kids. That's my job, and you can be damned sure that *my* kids are not breaking the law."

"I just think the store could do a better job of checking IDs, that's all I'm saying," said Fran Webber. "I'd be happy to work with the manager to make sure he has a procedure in place."

"You know what might be a great idea?" Helen Stargell, another housewife, offered brightly. "If we made sure the store had a copy of the Yearbook every year, he'd have names and pictures of the students right there in front of him. He'd know right away who's a freshman, who's a senior…"

"Like a mug book!" Art Berndt laughed. The room broke up.

Todd was disgusted. Mr. Kolak remained at the podium. Two adults were whispering something about him behind their hands.

"I think that's something you ladies should look into," the mayor said. "I know you've got your hands full, Fran, but…"

"I'd be happy to take charge of it," she said solemnly. "We're a community. There are always answers if we work together."

"And about that parking lot," the mayor continued, sensing that the closing gavel was at hand. "Look, we were all young once. We all remember how important silly things seemed to us at the time, just as we remember how quickly we moved on when some other distraction came along."

Todd ground his teeth. He wished he was as brave as Mr. Kolak, taking the microphone against these assholes.

"As soon as they see that we're not paying attention to their little protest, they'll drift off to find some *new* way to get our goat!"

A knowing murmur and satisfied cluck rose from the gallery. They liked this mayor. They might just register and come out to vote for her next time she came up for reelection.

But probably not.

When nearly a dozen of the adults bumped into each other at the Happy Snack on the way home from the meeting, everyone suddenly inspired to shore up the store's profitability, more than one remarked at what a heady experience it had been to actually get involved.

"The system works!" marveled Connie Pike.

"Six-forty-four," said Daljit Singh, his hand outstretched.

— —

Frank Kolak drove Todd home in silence. He knew he was going to hear about this, both from the school administration and from parents.

He was going to hear about this.

"It's true, isn't it?" Todd asked suddenly, studying his teacher sullenly. "What they've been doing."

Frank said nothing as he pulled up to the curb in front of Todd's house. Todd waited, then opened his door.

"See you in class tomorrow." Mr. Kolak tried to smile. "Pop quiz. You've earned a heads-up."

"Thanks," Todd said, looking into the car from curbside. "Hey, are you—?"

"Come on. It's late."

Todd let the door close, then watched Mr. Kolak drive away.

It was only a little after nine. But it did feel very, very late.

Daypart Paydirt

Annie's story aired on a Thursday night. Titled *We're Not Buying This Sh—!* the half-hour, at John Viceroy's insistence, had received significant promotion, the saturation ads featuring the most provocative sound bites from Joel, images of him tearing his shirt off, and teasing uses of the digitally-censored word "shit." Furious metallic thrash—really mean stuff, stuff that made Rage Against the Machine sound like Abba—was used to promise ranting, teeth-bearing anarchy. It completely misrepresented the show's content, Annie knew, but it worked.

Manny Clarke, managing editor of R²Rev's alleged "news division," hosted. Sweetie-P, still looking for promotional opportunities for his greatest hits CD, agreed to a brief interview on the subject of commercialism, offering up a bloodless shout-out to the multi-tiered, savagely efficient marketing machine with which he shotgunned product (his own and that which he was hired to endorse) to his fans.

Executives at companies like Nike and Philip Morris were taped ambush-style outside their offices, refusing to address the subject of the youth market (as Annie knew they would), but looking sufficiently guilty of *something* while ducking into limos and racing away.

Annie found a youthful marketing professor at NYU who testified to the staggering buying power of the American teen, one of the most ferociously sought after components of the entire retail economy. Simple graphs, illustrating dollars spent annually by teenagers since the youth revolt of the mid-'60s, provided breathtaking proof that never before had so much money been there for the taking from a consumer group practically *begging* to be raped.

"Teenagers have the American economy by the short hairs," Manny Clarke read from Annie's script. "But what kind of power is it if all you ever do is pay them what they want?"

Cut to the Happy Snack.

Annie had worked nearly 30 hours straight with the Joel tapes, distilling his unvarnished rabble-rousing into one tightly-cut invocation. She knew she could never lose sight of the fact that the very thing that defined her target audience—the herd mentality, the miserably short attention span, the blunt, irreversible dismissal of anything that attempted to impart knowledge—could cause them to bolt in an instant if they caught even a whiff of a lecture.

She learned to watch the Happy Snack crowd on the tape as closely as she did Joel: When did their attention wander? Where were the applause lines? What made the bully boys *woof* their concurrence? What made the girls squirm? Where was the essence of what Joel was trying to say?

Alone with his image in the editing bay in the middle of the night, it was hard to not let Joel run free. There was a purity to the boy and to the fuzzy thoughts that had gone from Todd's to his own that cast a kind of spell over Annie.

On her trip back to Berline to gather more material and to confirm one last time that she wasn't completely out of her mind, she had spent some time alone with Joel. In a Burger King booth late one night, she listened with growing empathy to a boy whom she came to realize used a docile swagger and the free pass given him by virtue of his attractiveness and easy charm to mask a pretty lousy home life. She heard about his parents' hateful divorce—so common these days as to be undeserving mention, but always so lacerating for the kid living through it.

His father was an asshole, a bitter and small-dicked turd (Annie was moved to speculate) who clearly drew sustenance by taking out his own failures on his son. Apparently something of a tomcat, the old man had cheated openly on Joel's mother for years before meeting a woman for whom he wished to officially trade up. But right around the time that the first marriage was done away with, the new fiancée cut him off at the knees.

Joel was fourteen at the time, a churning bouillabaisse of hormones and tangled carnal thoughts, and this hot young thing who broke up his home had been promised to him as a new mother of sorts. When she left, she in effect walked out on both father and son, leaving the elder spiteful and obsessed with finding the razor blade hidden inside future romances, and Joel simply baffled: Dad hurt Mom, made her sad pretty much all the time now, because he wanted this other one more. But then the new one started hating Dad—Joel heard her laughing at him that last night they fought—and right away Dad was hating her *and* Mom, and now he's got different girlfriends all the time who he says really mean things about when they're not around or when they won't get out of bed in the morning and go home.

A lot of these girls, Annie didn't need to be told, were right around her age. Pretty, tin-hearted darlings with a weakness for bad boys and swarthy deadbeats. Like Hutch Posner.

Other than the increasingly strained visitation weekends, the only time Joel saw his father anymore was at sporting events. For as long as Joel could remember, sports were the one thing that drew father and son together. Even when things started to go bad with his mother, Joel's dad never missed a game, never failed to take a seat as close to the action as possible to cheer when Joel did well, and to bitch—at coaches, at refs, at the kids on the other team—when Joel was trifled with. So long as Joel competed at something—*anything*—he'd know where his father was.

But even sports had grown sour, ever since Mom and Dad started taking separate seats in the stands.

As Joel matured as an athlete and began to craft a persona, much was made of his coltish detachment during play. No matter how spectacular and game-turning his accomplishments, Joel Kasten kept his head down, his showboating in check. It was his trademark.

The thing was, he *wanted* to look to the stands for his parents' approval. Nothing had made him prouder when he was little. But now, Dad's sitting over *here*; Mom's over *there*. Dad's brought another new girlfriend, Mom's… Where's Mom? Joel knew that she often just sat out in the car and smoked during the games. Sometimes, on the drive home, he'd gently quiz her to see if she really had been watching, because he had been searching the stands for her all night and she didn't seem to be there.

So mostly he just kept his head down.

Joel told Annie all this quietly, with gangly shrugs and endearing attempts at boyish machismo. Nothing he said rang true to her life. Her folks, for all their mustiness, remained faithfully, resolutely together. Marriages imploded all around her as a kid, nearly half of her friends subjected to versions of the hurt and disruption that Joel lived with, but Annie and her siblings made it through with their originally-issued set of parents. Only recently, and even then just passingly, did she regard their fidelity as an accomplishment as opposed to a fate imposed on them by a lack of other opportunities. Surely the only reason people stayed together these days was because no one better came along.

Joel had a thing for Annie—that was obvious. She was older, good-looking, prone to doting on him, if only for the purpose of getting him to bare his soul. She would catch him looking at her and realize he had a crush.

But she was thinking of him more and more. Here was a boy—soon to be a man—who had yet to make that turn into a bastard. Thanks to his old man, he was sure to be utterly fucked up when it came to women. The victimhood of his mother, the betrayal and spitefulness of his father, the idolization that Joel had already enjoyed as a looker—these were good things to hard-wire into a kid. Once that turn came, once this handsome, charismatic boy found his balls fully dropped and his potential for conquests unlimited, he could very well end up just one more dashing toxin for a single girl to be poisoned by.

Oh, yes, let's see one more of *those* set loose amongst us.

Almost better for a young woman to take such a boy by the hand and escort him through the back end of puberty, to gently acclimate him to the harsh and cynical world of relationships beyond twelfth grade. To prove to him that, despite his father's teaching, a woman could be nurturing and kind. To show him that his charisma could be harnessed as an agent of good, instead of a tool with which to easily win him whatever he wanted.

And if in the bargain she found a man who had yet to be contaminated…

"How twisted am I?" Annie grimaced to herself, shaking off these three a.m. reveries by darting out from the editing room for a smoke. "How sad am I?"

After allowing for ads (show of hands: see the irony?), the piece ran about 22 minutes. The one concession Annie ended up making to a meddling John Viceroy was a brief interview segment with Neil Young, the grizzled rock icon who had survived with his integrity pretty much intact since the Summer of Love and who—once upon a time, like when Annie was *ten*—saw an upward spike in his iconoclastic career when he took on corporate sponsorships and advertisers' betrayal of rock and roll. Viceroy "just happened" to come by the stage when Young was interviewed, scoring an autograph and getting to hang for a moment with a demigod of his youth.

He pumped Young's hand one last time before Annie shooed him away, before he could whip that photograph out of his wallet. Then she watched as the musician wiped his hand on his pant leg, to rid himself of something gummy.

"He's a really big fan," Annie said in apology.

"Nobody cleared it with me," the artist mumbled dourly.

The interview actually wasn't a bad suggestion on Viceroy's part, and if it kept his enthusiasm up, great. To that end, Annie also wasn't above fanning what was an obvious attraction that Viceroy had for her. He was a well-known adulterer ("Use the force, Joel! Don't surrender to the dark side!"), and if she gave him reason to believe that she might fall to his scary good looks and awesome corporate power…

Well, you know: *whatever.*

She had bigger concerns. She kept waiting for Viceroy—for someone— to pull the plug on this whole thing, having recognized what was at best a Grade-A set of hypocrisies, and at worst a threat to the entire infrastructure of R²Rev. What the kids in this piece were on about, what would soon be introduced to a young audience numbering in the millions, was a disavowal of pretty much every industry and behavior that kept the network alive. As the project was fast-tracked through the pipeline, she really wanted to know: Could Viceroy really not see who they were attacking here?

She wasn't going to bring it up. Let him nurture his hippie dreams and whatever dirty thoughts he had for her. In the end, she knew that he knew that this piece was just another time-filler fed into the ravenous maw that

Like We Care

was a 24-hour cable channel. Programming—no more, no less.

This stuff just passed right through the kids on the receiving end, men like Hutch Posner and John Viceroy believed. None of it stuck. None of it mattered.

This is how they slept.

The Bump-Up

"Joel turned eighteen last week," Todd told Mr. Kolak.

The teacher was guarded, as he had been ever since the City Council meeting. Except for in class, he didn't interact with his students anymore, and stayed clear of the Happy Snack. When he opened his front door to find Todd and Joel on his front step, his first instinct was to send them away.

"Happy birthday," Frank said.

"Thanks."

"Did you see the show last night?" Todd asked.

Of course he had. In the days leading up to the R²Rev debut, the whole town had been buzzing, culminating in a huge viewing party at Jeff Regan's house. Joel, of course, was the guest of honor. Todd had pleaded with Mr. Kolak to attend, had come to see him as a crucial adviser in what they were trying to accomplish, but Frank had begged off. Principal Dave Keller had suggested that it might be a good idea for the Social Studies teacher to confine his activism to the classroom for awhile.

So he watched the show alone, and found it to be a remarkable piece of propaganda. Everything he knew to be true about the Happy Snack situation was presented accurately, and yet, through manipulative editing and production embellishments, Joel's modest campaign was pumped up into a shimmering, vibrating *happening*—literally, a true fraud. Frank still admired the stand these kids had taken, still found something almost profound about the enlightenment which his students had stumbled upon and then refused to let go of, but seeing it reduced to leering entertainment processed through the very machinery Joel was taking a stand against made the whole thing ring hollow. He suspected that whatever it was that had been noble about the campaign had just been effectively strangled.

"Yeah, it was pretty good," he lied, still not wanting to dampen their enthusiasm. "Signed your first autograph yet?"

Joel puffed up as he simultaneously blanched at the very idea. "Yeah, right!"

"You really thought it was good?" Todd asked intently. "You didn't think they kind of overdid it?"

"It was what it was," the teacher shrugged, looking past them to the street beyond to see if they were being watched. "It *was* television. What did you expect?"

"It's just that—"

"Guys, look. I'm kind of in the middle of something," he said as their eagerness sagged a little. "I'm proud of what you accomplished, I really am. I'm looking at this like the greatest extra credit project ever. You took a stand, you made a difference—no Social Studies teacher could ask for more, and you'll see that reflected in your quarter grade. But you've taken it as far as you can. I think you—everybody—has to move on."

The boys were not discouraged. When you're taking a stand, you must not be.

"Can we come in?"

Mr. Kolak sighed and thought, not about the ramifications but about why he was a teacher. There were so many things that he was not, but he *was* a teacher. A good one, he hoped.

He stepped aside, and gestured them in.

— ◆ ▬ —

The fallout from the City Council debacle had left Frank rattled long after the controversy had faded away.

Dave Keller had called him into his office the next morning, having already been pounced upon by several parents, the superintendent of schools, and the local paper. Was it really true that Frank had stood up before the city and accused the Council of racism? Had he really threatened to call in Jesse Jackson?

"I mean, *Jesus*, Frank..."

Frank felt queasy. He hadn't slept all night. "*I* didn't bring up Jesse Jackson! Do you think I'm crazy?!"

Keller stared at Frank, not knowing what to do with this situation. He and Frank were friends because they worked the same mine, but Keller barely knew him. Frank kept to himself most times, and when forced to contend with an unhappy parent or a disruptive student in Keller's presence, it always appeared that the teacher might just crumble from frailty.

Every year, rumors went around among the students that Frank was gay. Inevitably, hurtful pranks resulted.

"Look, I'm probably the only person in this whole town who watches those meetings," Frank said defensively. "I know all about what's going on in that neighborhood. I've heard the Council all but admit that if they lose that store, the *complexion* of that whole corner of town could go. They say it all the time, only they use code words. I was just trying to get them to—"

"*Frank*," Keller grimaced. "That is not your place."

"Those are our students, Dave! The city has been looking the other way while that store polluted them, and nobody was doing anything about it!"

"That's for the parents to deal with. Not us!"

"The parents!" Frank laughed. "You should have seen…"

He stopped.

He had the tape. It was still home in his VCR. All night long he had circled the machine anxiously, half of him wanting to play it to prove that it hadn't really been as awful as he believed it was, the other half wishing to erase it so as to never have to witness himself falling so short of what he had come to do.

But he had the tape. And, to his credit, Dave Keller rallied behind his teacher once he saw it. What Frank had implied at the town hall meeting was inflammatory, but Keller saw that Frank had barely put his accusation on the table before he was shut down by the Council and the townsfolk in attendance. The vehemence with which they deflected his charge—and the speed with which they declared the meeting over and fled into the night—told Keller that Frank was most likely right. And you couldn't fire a teacher for that.

Frank's union wouldn't allow it. Nor would the fact that Frank was one of the few black teachers in a school that was seeing its racial balance shift with each new semester. Things would probably be tense between Frank and certain parents in the near future, but there would be no repercussions for his botched attempt at social protest. If he knocked it off.

Therefore, calls to Frank from the local news outlets, trying to wring a racial sidebar out of the Happy Snack protests, went unanswered. Without Frank to amplify what he had only hinted at before the Council, that part of the story faded away. The city's official stance was to remain determined to see to it that the store obeyed the letter of the law, *or else*.

Sixth Ward Councilman Jerry Self, running unopposed in the upcoming elections, would see to it.

— —

So nothing would be done about the Happy Snack, but this was not what had been haunting Frank Kolak. He was right—he *knew* it—and they had not only turned it around on him and tried to paint *him* as being the problem, but they had succeeded in shutting him up and turning away any attention to what he had said. *Still*, this was not what was haunting him. He had been beaten up worse than this in his life.

What was troubling him was that he hadn't seen the lesson being taught. He had been inspired by what he had seen his students set into motion. He had marveled at the ease with which their simple truths had found potency. And he was fool enough to think he could raise a stink of his own. Having never stood out, stood up, in his whole life, he had been tricked by a bunch of teenagers into thinking that he could matter, too.

But what *really* ate at him, what made him almost angry at the two boys who now sat in his kitchen, was that Todd Noland got it right where he hadn't. Todd knew he needed Joel in order to be heard; Frank Kolak, who could not have had less armor, thought he could do it himself.

Never again...

"So..." Todd began awkwardly, the tension pressing upon them in this sad little apartment. "Joel turned eighteen."

"And... ?" the teacher asked impatiently.

"And we figure that changes everything."

Frank's spine tightened. He still found this Todd Noland kid to be as intriguing as he was shrewd, but at heart he was a tricky little bastard.

"Sure. Now you can buy your cigarettes legally. Party on, dude."

Todd and Joel winced: *Party on, dude?*

"Nah, fuck that," Joel said, then caught himself. "I mean…"

Frank sighed tiredly. "You're an adult now, Joel. You can say 'fuck' all you like. 'Fuck, fuck, fuck'—just gets better every time, doesn't it?"

Todd and Joel sat quietly. Mr. Kolak was acting weird.

"But *you* can't," the teacher pointed at Todd with a melodramatic flourish. "*You're* still a kid."

"Aw, he never says 'fuck,'" Joel offered.

"Fuck," Todd said.

Frank threw up his hands with exasperation, wondering if listening devices had been planted to bust him for continuing to play along with whatever the hell these two were up to. He still believed the school would fire him if it could.

He stood up to cut short this new mistake. "Okay, never mind. Out!" he said as he pointed them toward the door.

"Mr. Kolak, *please*," Todd said earnestly. "We need you on this."

Where did they get the balls? He spent his whole life thinking the world was trying to show him the door, and here he was, literally showing them the door, and they wouldn't go.

He crossed his arms and settled back into the corner of his kitchen table. He was not going to let them ramble.

"Quickly."

Todd coughed nervously, then commenced. "Okay, so Joel's eighteen now. A lot of seniors are. I looked at the class roster and almost eighty percent are eighteen years old, or will be by April."

This Todd, he dropped clues. Pay attention.

"April?"

"What good does it do you anymore to be eighteen?" Todd asked, pointing to Joel. "He can buy cigarettes, but he's been doing that all along. He still can't drink legally for another three years. He could get himself drafted if there was a war."

"And, dude, freshmen are jailbait now!" Joel piped in, not quite grasping the legalities but clearly vexed.

Frank rolled his eyes. The priorities of teenagers were appalling. "When you're eighteen you could, oh I don't know, *vote!*"

"Yeah," Todd smiled meaningfully. "That, he can do."

Pay attention.

"So… ?"

Joel jumped ahead. Joel was always jumping ahead. "So we think you should run for City Council. If you do, we'll get everybody behind you and you'll win. Todd says so."

It just laid there for a beat or two.

"What?"

Todd picked it up. "You nailed them on that Happy Snack business. This town *knew* that store was giving us booze and cigarettes, and all they cared about was keeping black people out. You nailed that when nobody else could see it, and then they shut you down."

Frank chuckled nervously. He felt a bad, bad itch.

"That doesn't mean that I—"

"They were selling us out!" Todd stressed. "We live in this town, too. A lot of us work and pay taxes, just like our parents. Who's looking out for us?"

"We got nobody!" Joel added.

Frank stared at them. This was a tar baby, that's what this was.

Evenly, firmly: "I don't want to be on the City Council."

"Then you're a hypocrite," Todd shot back, having loaded his verbal gun with this bullet long before he showed up. These two timid souls—Todd and Mr. Kolak—locked eyes and hoped the other would look away first.

Finally: "Thanks for stopping by."

"You're a hypocrite, Mr. Kolak." Todd softened his tone, because he was disappointed. "What were you just saying? That you were going to give us extra credit for taking a stand, for making a difference? So where do you get off taking a pass?"

That stung. But not enough to concede.

"*Why?*" Frank asked with exasperation. "What do you care who's on the

City Council? You're... You're teenagers!!"

"Yeah, and there's a bunch of us. And when we stick together, we can make things happen," Todd said.

It was not hard to miss the determined mischief in Todd's voice. Frank recognized it. Thus far the kid had called his shots pretty accurately, and Frank couldn't help wondering how far his theories could be proven.

He sat down.

"It isn't over?"

"We proved we could make a difference," Todd said. "So we cost the Happy Snack a few thousand dollars. So what? They'll just raise their prices to make up the difference and wait us out. Nobody believes we've stopped buying their crap forever."

"But we got everybody paying attention," Joel said proudly. "We can still *use* this."

Joel winked devilishly. For all their self-righteousness, Frank knew that what had gone down at the Happy Snack was first and foremost nothing more than an effort to be annoying and screw things up. Teenagers *do* this.

He was forced to admit he had been flattered by their proposal. But it sure hurt when he realized it was all just part of their game.

"So this has nothing to do with me being a credible candidate. You guys just want to cause more trouble."

Joel smiled and rocked happily. "If it works, it'll be both. That's the beauty part!"

"Does that Council want you sitting up there with them? No," Todd said, kicking into gear. "Would most of the adults in this town, those who even bother to vote, get behind someone like you? No. Which is why you need to do this!"

"Jesus, Mr. Kolak. You're the smartest adult I know," Joel pleaded. "You know all about societies and laws and how things are supposed to work, and you're a good guy, too! But it sure looks to me like if you're not white, you're not allowed to say how this town is run.

"Well, fuck that!" Joel said with indignation. "We'll ram you right up their asses!"

165

Todd sighed and cleared his throat. "That probably wouldn't be your campaign slogan."

Frank smiled. How could he not? Rather than vandalize the town with spray paint or baseball bats, these two knuckleheads were out to jigger an election. And not entirely without noble intentions.

But still…

"Look, guys. I'm flattered—I think—but I'm just not…"

"The Council meets one night a week," Todd said. "Issues come up, you study them, and you vote. If somebody in your district has a problem, you try to help. You'd still have plenty of time for all your other stuff."

If Frank didn't know Todd better, he'd think this was a shot. He had no "other stuff."

"If you win, maybe you can do something about things like the Happy Snack. If you lose, at least you tried."

"You can take what you learn and teach it in class," Joel added helpfully.

He studied them both, wanting to let them down easily.

His out was obvious. For all their sincerity, their plan wouldn't work.

"You know, I realize voter turnout is an embarrassment in this town. But getting a handful of eighteen-year-olds behind me isn't going to do it. Not even close."

"Don't worry," Joel said conspiratorially. "Todd has a plan."

Frank dropped his chin to his chest.

"If you give us the okay, we'll start talking to people tonight," Todd said. "You wouldn't have to register to run for another three weeks. If we don't see enough interest by then, we can just forget the whole thing. It'd be your call."

"*Totally*," Joel emphasized.

A clock ticked theatrically. Pretty much every night prior to this one, no one was here to hear it but Frank.

"Please?" Todd asked.

Tick tick tick…

Joel leaned in somberly. "I gotta go let fly with a dump if you need time to think about it."

Into the Void

The show had run, and that was that. For all of Annie's hard work, for the sheer force of will that had turned a vague itch to produce something into a half-hour of aired programming, the premiere of *We're Not Buying This Sh—!* seemed to be over before it had begun. She was proud of it—it bleated and throbbed and postured like R²Rev product was required to while still managing to have a credible point of view—but the event was sadly hollow.

Hutch and Viceroy had separately attempted to lure her into their own private viewing parties, no doubt certain that her gratitude at having been given such a chance would result in her making naked jump-jump with them. But she had resolved that under no circumstances would she use sex to sustain what she had started. This was no small self-promise. There remained no real role for her at R²Rev now that her show had been blasted into the void. She'd been so busy since coming in from the road and getting a green light for the show that she had yet to even secure so much as a cubicle for herself. The day after the show aired, she would have nothing. She knew that the night before.

Instead, she watched the premiere in her apartment with a small group of friends, all R²Rev staffers whom she didn't know all that well due to her lengthy exile to the boonies. There was sufficient good cheer amidst the Coronas and chips and salsa, all undercut by the requisite cattiness of player-wannabes deprived of their own professional breaks. The raw desire for promotion, for status, was lethal at the cubicle level. Annie's co-workers, who took for granted that she got the Casey gig in the first place by sleeping with Hutch, cheered her on strategically that night, knowing they'd need her benevolence if her star continued to rise, but also reserving the option to withdraw their friendship if she stumbled, as they hoped she would.

Where Annie really wished to be was back in Berline, back with Joel and Todd and the Happy Snack revolutionaries. She wanted them to like what she had done with their story, and felt confident they would. There would be no bias or gamesmanship to their excitement as they watched the show. They had simply found themselves swallowed up by the cameras that had wandered into their town, and now here was the grand regurgitation. Right there on R²Rev, like they themselves were ScroatM or Sweetie-P. For one half-hour, they were the stars.

There would be a party the night Annie's show made Berline, and she should've been there. But she had worked so hard to get back to New York, had whined for so long about wanting to leave Middle America behind, that she had convinced herself that she had to stay in town on her big night. She got Viceroy to sign off on hiring a local crew to videotape the premiere party at Jeff Regan's house, just in case there was any ancillary life to the story, but this would be the closest Annie would come to Berline that night.

Later, when she couldn't sleep, she called home to Ann Arbor, even though it was late, even though she knew her parents wouldn't be able to disguise their bafflement at what their daughter had invested so much of herself into.

"It was something," her father said of the show, being so sweet as he sat on the edge of his bed, trying to sound proud as he scratched himself sleepily. "It sure was something."

— —

The show ran again five hours after the premiere—2 a.m. East Coast time—and would get another couple airings over the weekend. After that, it would be thrown into general rotation, just another half-hour block of programming used to pad out a day. If the subject matter had an open-ended shelf life, if a musician contained within could be counted on to draw some level of viewership, if there were no contractual restrictions (i.e. single-use-only licensing of a key piece of music or performance), shows like Annie's could be expected to turn up anywhere on the schedule for the next few months. Nobody would promote it; nobody at the top would even know it was occupying airtime. It was just something to splice commercials into.

John Viceroy's enthusiasm for the project had begun to ebb before the show had even run. When Annie turned down his invitation to watch the premiere at his Park Avenue apartment, it was over. There was a congratulatory message from his office on her voice mail the next morning—left at 7:43, when she was certain not to be there—but several attempts to return the call never got her through to Viceroy himself.

"He'll return," his assistant always snipped.

"Him and Jesus," Annie thought.

Hutch had remained pissy throughout, mad at Annie for going over his head to get the show made, frustrated by her rejection of *The Nipple Room* gig (he really *did* need someone to take over that thankless job), and still not sure if she intended to make noise about the whole logo thing. What he didn't know—because there was no upside in telling him—was that she had given up on trying to force the issue. She had produced a show, for Christ's sake. It was her name alone listed as producer on an effort generally thought to be perfectly competent. If *that* didn't earn her a continued role at the net, then what was the point?

To try and use blackmail to secure a promotion was almost as bad as using sex, she decided. She was better than that.

Further Turbans Perturbed

Annie found a cubicle and a phone the Monday after the show first aired, and set to thinking about *The Nipple Room*. There was a certain tradition to television dance shows, she told herself. *American Bandstand* had some vague meaning even to someone as young as Annie. She had logged long hours watching *Club MTV* and *Yo! MTV Raps* as a teenager. To be *executive producer* of such a show, right there in Manhattan, right there at R²Rev—well, that was something, wasn't it?

She would have some control—whether a care-taker role or not, she *would* have some control—so maybe she could actually work to elevate the leering pimp 'n' ho square dance that the net fed to young white minds every afternoon. There remained something honorable about black music, *somewhere*, so maybe Annie was the person to try and restore some dignity to the form.

Little white Annie from Ann Arbor, race savior.

She sighed at her strained attempt at rationalization. Besides, for all she knew, Hutch's offer wasn't even in play anymore. At least not without giving something up to get back in his good graces.

— ⬡ —

It was just past lunch that Monday when the call found her.

"Annie? This is Ashley Harper? With the *West Central Eagle?* In Grand Island, Nebraska?"

She scrambled to think, then she got it: It was one of her stringers. One of her *ex*-stringers. Annie had never even met this one. The kid never came up with anything worthy of a Casey debasement. As far as Annie could recall, she and the crew never made it as far west as Nebraska.

"Hello," Annie said warily. One of the downsides of her interaction with high schoolers across the country was that several had had the nerve to hit her up for internships—maybe even an actual job—as graduation loomed. She figured this was one of them, although the girl only sounded about fourteen.

"Hi. Um, you know, I saw that show you did this weekend? I saw it with some friends, and we all thought it was really, really good."

Annie melted. Genuine praise for the show had been hard to come by the past few days. Too bad this kid was just buttering her up.

"And you know what? They're throwing pennies down at the 7-Eleven."

Annie stopped. And came to focus.

"What?"

Quick, in one breath: "We've got this guy? This senior? His name's Terry Beecher? And he thinks he's the bomb, and I guess maybe he is, but he like runs the school and I guess he saw your show because him and a bunch of his friends went down to the 7-Eleven Saturday night and they thought it would be a goof to do what that Joel kid is doing.

"And the guy behind the counter? At the 7-Eleven? He wears a turban, too! And now nobody will buy from him, and whenever he comes out, they throw pennies at him, and they go 'We're not buying this shit!' and everything.

"I thought you'd like to know."

A fluke, that's all.

"And they're still there?" Annie asked.

"Well, it's Monday, so we're in school. But, yeah, I was just there, and there are a few. I was gonna buy some Altoids, but then I thought, like, 'Ya-huh.'"

"Hmmm," Annie said. "Well, thank you, Ashley. That's really interesting. Hey, give me your address. I'll send you a T-shirt."

"Um," the kid mumbled shyly. She couldn't have been more than a freshman from the way she sounded. "You know that boy Joel? In your show?"

Annie heard some girlish giggles in the background.

"Have any pictures of him?"

True Sway

They split up.

Joel, at Todd's direction, went to the Dairy Queen to see Dean Stoller. Dean, who was pushing 21, was Joel from three years ago. Better than Joel, actually. A hellacious knuckleball pitcher with a tricky split-finger fastball in his holster, Dean had brought Dickinson its first state championship in eight years, earning a baseball scholarship to UCLA as a reward. He was a hottie, too. Even Joel thought so, which sometimes confused him.

Then, on a July night after graduation, Dean went to a party dizzied up on ecstasy, and put his arm through a plate glass window, severing a major tendon in his pitching arm. He had been in physical therapy three days a week ever since, but he was getting old and his arm wasn't getting any better. UCLA had left the door open if Dean should ever regain his high school form, but everyone pretty much knew it was over for him.

He was assistant manager at the Dairy Queen now. Manager loomed out there someday, if the breaks fell his way. You had to wonder why the kid didn't bust out another window and aim for an artery this time.

He was looking kind of soft, maybe even chubby, Joel thought as he worked on his Dilly Bar while waiting for Dean to take a break. That seemed to happen to everyone after graduation. Dean's friends, who lived like princes during his reign but who now seemed doomed to stay in town forever, with little chance of finding distinction ever again—all of them looked a little blurry around the edges. Sometimes, when Joel and his gang were cruising—Dickinson seniors, lords of the circuit—Joel would see Dean and a carload of his guys, driving around like they still owned the place. Like they had never left high school.

When Joel's dad kept turning down those scholarships offered by lesser colleges, Joel thought of Dean.

"I'll play for a small school. I'll play anywhere," Joel wanted to say. "Just please don't let me end up like Dean Stoller."

"'Sup?" Dean deadpanned as he sank into the booth opposite Joel. He was older and once a celebrity. Joel was suitably intimidated.

"Hey, Dean. How's the arm?"

How's the arm? How's the fucking arm? For three years, total strangers kept checking in on the status of Dean's arm, like he would be taking them with him to Southern California if things worked out. He lit a cigarette and instinctively rubbed his hand up and down the jagged scar that ran along his forearm.

"I had it halfway up your mother last night," he scowled. "How's yours?"

Joel met his glare. He couldn't believe he used to think Dean Stoller was cool.

"Good Dilly Bar."

"C'mon, kid," Dean growled. "Whaddaya want? I'm busy."

"I keep seeing you down at the Happy Snack."

"Yeah, that's right. Believe it or not, I'm not buying into this pussy-ass protest of yours." He leaned back and took a deep drag off his cigarette. "I buy my smokes, I buy my Bud, and it's damned sweet not having to stand in line with a bunch of faggot high school kids. It's really so fucking impressive what you've got going down there." His spite was eating him alive.

"Did you see me on R²Rev?"

Dean jutted forward in his seat. "*I* was on ESPN. After the perfect game? *SportsCenter*, baby."

"I remember that. That was cool," Joel recalled sincerely. "I was watching it with my dad. He said, 'You pay attention. That's gonna be *you* someday.'"

Dean eased up a little. Just a little recognition, just some acknowledgement that he was once superior—that's all he wanted anymore.

"Yeah," Dean sighed, drawn back to that night for the zillionth time. "Fucking Andy Stackhouse, if he could just come up with the ball in the ninth."

"Still, a one-hitter. Against East," Joel offered.

Dean conceded their excellence. "They went to state that year.

They were awesome."

"And you owned them that night."

"Yeah," Dean said sadly. "Whatever…"

"So," Joel pressed on to fill the void. "Do you vote?"

Dean blinked. Joel may as well have asked if his shit glowed in the dark. "*What?*"

"Since you turned eighteen, have you ever voted?"

"The fuck's the matter with you?" Dean laughed.

"'Cause you know who's thinking about running for City Council? Mr. Kolak."

The name caused Dean to ease up a bit. "Oh, yeah? How's he doin'?"

"Good."

Dean took another deep drag off his cigarette.

"The only fucking teacher who would never cut me any slack on my grades. Coach would get in his face, and he'd still make me deliver C's or he'd threaten to pull me off the team," Dean recalled with a bitter shrug. "Fuck, if I'da had a couple more teachers like that…" He trailed off, gesturing to the Dairy Queen sadly. "You know, he was the only teacher who came to see me when I messed up my arm? I wasn't even a student anymore."

"Yeah, he did the same thing when *I* was in the hospital."

Dean smiled fondly, then winced.

"God, I did some shitty things to him in tenth grade. Word was going around that he was gay."

"Yeah, you still hear that," Joel said. "But, I don't know. I think he's just lonely."

This was getting too warm-hearted. Dean drew the armor back up.

"So? So what? He's running for City Council. Tell him I said good luck. He'll need it."

"I don't know," Joel shrugged. "He's a good guy."

"Yeah, he's a good guy. He's a *black* guy. You see your parents voting for him? I know my old man wouldn't."

"But *you* could. And your guys, your crew could. And if they have younger brothers and sisters who are eighteen, or older brothers and sisters who had Mr. Kolak, who maybe aren't using their vote. Get enough of you together, you could mess things up. Might be sweet."

Dean smiled reluctantly at the thought that had gone into this. He studied Joel curiously. "This is just more of that Happy Snack shit," he said, smiling reluctantly.

"Sort of. But he'd be good at it—you know that. And if getting him elected showed the old people in this town that guys like you had to be paid attention to…"

Joel moved to set the hook as Dean began to see what was being offered him.

"*I* can't do it," Joel conceded earnestly. "We need somebody older, somebody that people listen to, who is popular enough to make things happen. Maybe do a good job if he found himself being interviewed on television."

It started to gel for Dean. The spotlight, having pivoted away, was always free to swing back.

"Shit, my parents don't even vote," Dean said.

"Mine neither. How hard could it be?"

Dean grinned. It would be nice to believe his suddenly light mood came from deciding to throw his support behind a good man.

"My old man would shit!"

Joel shrugged in summation. "There you go."

— 🖱 —

Meanwhile, Todd sought out Ira Zimbaugh.

Ira was Dickinson's leading computer dick, a spindly, pimple-faced geek whose sheer, unrelenting wretchedness would strike pity in the hardest of hearts—if it weren't so clear that one day Ira would rule the world.

Ira was poking around the internet in '92—when he was *eight*—at a time when no one but colleges and hardcore computer dweebs were out there. He was always 25 steps ahead of everyone else in town when it came to technology, and, in fact, he was among a select group of kids across the country who were quietly slipped prototype copies of new software from Silicon Valley in order to road test it. The kid was maddeningly discreet—he never let on what he was up to—but by the time the hottest new game turned up on the shelves of the nearest Best Buy, Ira had already beaten it, found all its cheats and Easter eggs, and even designed new patches that could send the game off in directions that no one else in the world had access to.

All the software companies he worked with were just waiting for the kid to get out of high school so they could hire him for twenty times what a Joel Kasten might make from a minor league contract... if he even got one. Ira figured he'd wait until he went out West before he got laid the first time. Figured the pickings would be better. Besides, he was busy.

Ira was also a genius at building websites. He put Dickinson's together, and it was a marvel—you could spend hours just playing with the cafeteria menu. Several businesses around town had hired him to establish their web presence, but he was just as likely to put one together for a student who sought him out because he needed to create an outlet for his devotion to *The Matrix*. (A year or so ago, a super-scary Goth fuck wanted Ira to put together a tribute to Harris and Klebold, the Columbine murderers; load it up with hateful high praise to their wickedness, along with bomb recipes and some homicidal whacking off of his own. Ira bred one hellacious computer virus from the hundreds that he had captured over the years, and reduced the kid's hard drive to dust. Then he called the cops.)

— 🖱 —

Ira was the guy to go to after Annie called. Todd hadn't expected to hear from her again. The show had aired, and Todd's message, processed through Joel, had reached an audience far beyond anything he could've imagined. But even though the protest soldiered on at the Happy Snack, the boost from the R²Rev exposure counteracting the practical effects of a typical Illinois winter, there didn't seem to be anywhere else to go with the idea. Todd was looking forward to having a little more fun with the spring elections, but then it was probably time to let things go—get ready for graduation and life beyond the chemo-blast that was high school.

But then Annie called a week or so after the show aired with word that the Happy Snack action had grown satellites. In some corners of the country, she said, kids had found something to latch onto in Joel's campaign, and picked up the cause. Some of it was misguided and much of it was regrettable (*towelhead* was probably not a popular teen invective prior to Berline), but here and there, kids were clogging up parking lots and asking hard questions about the ways in which adult lies were lubricating the flow of cash from their pockets. *We're Not Buying This Shit!*, which Annie knew *killed* as a title for her show, was being embraced as their rallying cry.

Todd was wary. It was awesome, even frightening, that this movement, begun as the whim of a kid who spent far too much time in solitude imagining a realignment of the universe, could continue to mutate and gain potency. That it was now in the hands of dozens (hundreds?) of Joel Kastens elsewhere was sweet. But they could have it. He was done.

But Annie wasn't letting it go. Todd had first noticed that when she called from New York the night of the premiere. When she found them all at Jeff Regan's house, Todd was thrilled that she had asked for him first over Joel, and was dizzied by the fact that, by the time the show aired, Annie was treating him not just as a partner but as a kind of visionary for having set this whole thing into motion.

That night over the phone, they laughed and preened at length, but there came a point during the conversation when Todd wanted to return to his friends to celebrate. He would've gladly handed Annie over to Joel, but Joel was busy holding court over his fans, which that night included every prime-cut honey from Dickinson—and some of their older sisters.

Several times, Todd tried to "Well, okay then..." Annie into phone surrender, but it appeared to Todd that she had nowhere else to be. Whatever was going on in Berline seemed to really matter to her.

And now, here she was again, trying to keep the campaign alive, and maybe she had a point. If Todd's plan from the outset was to test his theory on as broad a canvas as possible, why pull back just as it was taking hold? Why not give the string a little more play to see where this thing went?

R²Rev, she reported, was not unaware of the echo effect that her show was having. Viewership for the re-airings, while not significant, was holding steady, which was particularly odd, given the non-lurid content. The Promotion Department continued to get calls from kids trying to find out more about Joel and perhaps score a photo. With a half-hour to fill during a slow news week, Manny Clarke was persuaded by Annie to drop a 42-second bite into *The Week In Review*, using the field footage that Annie had ordered the night of the premiere in Berline and reporting that the Happy Snack protest, now being fed by its own hype, was entering its seventh week, and that similar protests were popping up all over the country.

But Annie couldn't be sure how long the R²Rev megaphone would be at their disposal. Unless violence broke out at one of the parking lot gatherings, or unless some kind of Spring Break wet T-shirt gimmick could be worked into the mix, there wasn't much chance of the net giving this story any more play. And even less likely was the chance that Annie would be on hand to fan any more flames. Whether she was pushed or she jumped, she knew her time with the company would soon end.

She wanted to re-conceptualize the campaign to a grassroots framework, and there sat the internet, just primed to provide the machinery. It would be easy enough for Annie to get a hold of her show and Chiron-in a web address before the next airing. Could Todd, on his end, put something together? Nothing flashy at first, just some downloadable images of Joel and the protest, maybe daily words of wisdom that Todd could spin and pass off as Joel's. Animation would be killer, if you could pull it off.

"How about a Whack-A-Mole thing with Daljit Singh's head?" Todd smirked.

Annie groaned appreciatively. "You're sick."

"Society is to blame," he drawled. *Good God*, he thought, I'm *riffing* with this girl, and she's responding. Wasn't it a few weeks ago that I was going retard just looking at her?

"Well, I think I could put something together," he said coolly. "Maybe I could link it to my candidate's page."

"What?"

"Joel and I are trying to get our Social Studies teacher to run for City Council, get young voters behind him. Just for a goof."

"*Jesus, Todd...*" Annie gasped.

He wilted. No surprise that his savoir-faire had the resolve of a pelican sucked up a jet engine. "Well, we wouldn't have to," he stammered. "It was just—never mind."

"No," she pleaded. "This is… This is your bump-up! This is how you take it to the next level. If you can—"

Her mind was racing.

"Is he going to run?"

"We think we can guilt him into it."

"And he could win?"

"Dunno. He's black, so we know we can get that vote. And Joel's out right now working on support from, like, eighteen to twenty-three-year-olds."

Annie was scribbling furiously. Right near the top of her pad, she scrawled: Call Viceroy!!!!

"No, absolutely link to your guy's site. Post a daily journal of what you're doing, but make sure *you* write it—you know what works. And then…" This was getting silly, but silly might be all she had once cast from her cubicle. "If *this* caught on, and other kids tried *this*, you could link campaigns together. You could share strategies, drive each other on. It could turn into a pissing match, everybody competing to see who can actually get a candidate into office."

Even Todd thought this was too much.

"This really is maybe just a goof."

"Bullshit, Todd. Bullshit," Annie said sternly. "You don't do anything without an endgame in mind. Don't go soft on me now!"

"Okay," he said contritely.

She plowed through the schedule log for the next couple weeks. "Okay, the show airs again a week from Saturday, noon on the coasts, eleven a.m. there in the Midwest. I can get the web address on the show by then. Can you get a site up by then?"

"I think so."

"Get back to me as soon as you can. And, remember, it doesn't have to be flash to start. We can get more repeat hits if we roll out the bells and whistles over time. Just run some photos of Joel and of the parking lot crowd, and…"

She trailed off as the idea struck. She tapped her pencil on her desk. She watched herself, tapping her pencil.

"Todd?" she asked evenly. "Did you really trademark 'We're Not Buying This Shit?'"

"Yeah. It was easy."

"Get us a site. Call me back."

— 🖱 —

"Streaming live video," Ira shrugged casually. "Right there from the Happy Snack."

Todd was skeptical. "You could do that?"

"Sure. It's not just porn sites doing this stuff anymore."

He cocked an eyebrow at Todd. Todd blushed.

"Isn't it expensive?"

"Nah. Matter of fact, I've been trying to get Centurion Used Cars to try it out on their site. They could show off their inventory and how cars are flying off the lot because of their low-low prices. But the guy who owns the place thinks that if you set up a live feed, all you're going to get is a bunch of punks showing up to give the finger and pick their noses for the camera." He shook his head sadly. "You really have to take these old farts by the hand. In fact, I'll bet I can get them to kick in the gear for a few weeks as a trial run. Might have to run a free banner ad, though. Teenagers buy used cars, teenagers are going to be your exclusive demographic—everybody wins."

Todd had met his match—somebody with a great big robot brain. "Sure. Whatever."

Ira grabbed a legal pad. "What else?"

The Happy Snack protests had not escaped Ira's attention. He appreciated their subversiveness, their elevation of a fellow nondescript kid like Todd. He had just lamented the fact that the protests were being wasted on a dying medium like cable television. So here was his chance to contribute.

"I don't know," Todd said. "Surprise me."

Ira accepted this with a wink and chuckled darkly to himself as he jotted down some ideas.

"Be good, Ira. Be good."

Hold Your Tongue and Say "Big Apple"

And then Joel was in New York.

The stunt had been Viceroy's idea, which needless to say meant that Annie had planted the seed and then waited for the bullshit to fertilize it to full flower.

She had reconnected with him after Todd had told her about the political angle they were splicing into the original campaign. This teacher, Frank Kolak, had indeed announced his candidacy, and with very little effort on his part had already jumped ahead of the incumbent Councilman. Simultaneously driven by a desire to make mischief and to help a former teacher who had earned the regard of his students from his time in the classroom, young adults in Berline—freed from much of the rote pissiness that defined them as high schoolers—took on an almost "Hey, gang! Let's put on a show in the barn!" spirit as they canvassed for their man.

One Dickinson grad, wasted as a graphic artist for a local ad agency, eagerly took on the design of the campaign literature. Inside the brochure were testimonials to Frank Kolak's successful teaching career (including a district Merit of Excellence award in '98 and a series of state victories as coach of the debate team), along with Frank's own views on local issues which, while Todd had to drag them out of him, were well thought-out and, in spots, almost visionary. The guy really had been following the Council meetings and probably knew more about the town than some of the people already on the Council.

But the key to the pamphlet was the cover. At Todd's direction, the front featured a large photo of Mr. Kolak, the picture under-exposed just a half-stop to highlight his black skin, the white of his nervous smile shining through. As the young campaigners knocked on doors in working-class neighborhoods, they could see the resistance that Frank generated from older residents, who clearly preferred their elected officials to reflect their own image. The campaigners would smile earnestly as they tried to force one of Frank's pamphlets on the inconvenienced man or woman of the house, then endure the door being slammed. Their message was coming through: This town is being passed along to us, you small-minded yokels. Here's *our* man for the future. Deal with it.

Sending a reluctant Frank out to knock on doors along with four or five of his supporters just accentuated the divide and helped fuel the campaign. Truth be told, very little outright hostility was directed at Frank. This was not the South of the early '60s, after all. And yet it was impossible to miss the reflexive dismissal of Frank's candidacy, the slap often delivered most stingingly by a smiling hausfrau who prided herself on her racial enlightenment, but whose cloying condescension was all that Frank could count on come election day.

These young people, who with hindsight had come to realize that Mr. Kolak was just about the only teacher who had given them something of himself while they were at Dickinson, squirmed uncomfortably as they watched this good man endure the awkward race dance playing out on front steps all over town. So many of the adults on the other side of those doors reminded them of their parents, who they were actively trying to distance themselves from as they forged an adult image of themselves. If their parents voted at all, they wouldn't vote for Frank—and that was good enough for them. He *had* to win.

— —

So, back in Berline, the kids had gone from undermining corporate America to pirating the electoral process, and John Viceroy fell in love all over again. His fading, acid-rattled reveries for youthful, '60s era revolt could now be fused with a wound still fresh and smarting: Election 2000, and the outrage that went down in Florida.

Viceroy, by design and mandate, was a Clinton Democrat, a genuine true believer who could, if forced, square "Lincoln freed the slaves" with "At least Bill didn't make Monica swallow." Clinton was his boy, a soul survivor who took *precisely* the right message from the Age of Aquarius ("Quick, they're stoned. Steal stuff!"). And while everyone knew the party would be over come 2001, Viceroy had worked hard for his team in the vain hope that a contact buzz from the Clinton Administration could be wafted in along with Al "He's From the *1960s?*" Gore.

But the fucking conservative Supreme Court handed the election to Bush, and overnight D.C.'s stick-up-the-ass moralizing was making life hard for John Viceroy and the media complex he helped run. It wasn't just R²Rev—MediaTrust owned two of the country's biggest publishing houses, Hollywood's most profitable movie studio, two-thirds of the nation's radio stations and, perhaps soon, one of the three major television networks. Suddenly, all its product was being assaulted by sanctimonious gasbags playing to their power bases. Some of these fucks *were still there* from the Vietnam days, but most galling to John Viceroy were the men his own age who had crustified into such joyless, unhip pussies. Bush himself was barely older than Viceroy, for Christ's sake, and according to legend, once partied hard. What the hell happened to him?

It was like the good fight was back on: heads versus straights, satyrs versus the pure—only now, both sides had lots and lots of money. Lots and lots and lots.

After the 2000 election dispute, no one was going to get caught short again. Previously uncommitted liberals and, most notably, "disenfranchised" blacks—still bitter over real and perceived slights in 2000—were due to come out in record numbers, the under-represented palpably eager to cast votes in such overwhelming quantities that not even "fuzzy math" could swing the final count in the conservatives' favor. In the aftermath of 2000, voting had nearly become *sexy*, left-leaners having learned the hard way that each and every damned vote really does count.

And now, Viceroy marveled, teenagers and young adults were feeling disenfranchised, too? True, it was just one insignificant City Council race in one nothing Illinois town, but that Joel kid had already demonstrated the wildfire quality that these campaigns could take on. Annie McCullough briefed him daily on the situation, showed him the Happy Snack and Frank Kolak websites, and the growing handful of like-minded sites springing up across the country. In Berline, the "kids" put up a black man; in a

Denver suburb, a bull dyke lesbian was being encouraged by freshmen at a community college to force herself upon the buttoned-down City Council. (In a regrettable display of missing the point entirely, a bunch of young wise-asses in Dallas tried to get a local homeless man on the ballot with the campaign slogan "A breath of fresh air—and the stale stench of urine!")

Older, more conservative residents, heretofore content to vote sporadically and trust that someone who looked and lived like them would remain in charge, were beginning to squirm.

Once again, the Good Fight: the counterculture versus the establishment, the kaleidoscopic versus the white-bread.

Kick out the jams, motherfuckers!!

With spring elections looming and the presidential elections up next, both parties were working frantically to tap into new voter streams, haunted by the recent evidence that even the smallest advantage on either side could mean everything. And now here, if cultivated carefully and with sufficient panache, was a potential goldmine—youthful, previously apathetic voters who almost certainly skewed left, particularly if they fed off R²Rev. Even the most apolitical young adult had to be bristling at the benign cultural fascism of a Bush America. Many could not yet articulate it, but there was a fire burning there to restore the country to the hillbilly bacchanalia that had been the Clinton Administration.

If there was the slightest chance that these stray voting experiments could coalesce into an actual movement, that should be encouraged, Viceroy felt. That fire should be fanned.

Once again, Annie McCullough was the key. She was able to show Viceroy some creatively crunched numbers from R²Rev's internal polling proven that awareness of Joel Kasten and his various campaigns had legs, thanks to the repeated showings of *We're Not Buying This Sh—!* and the stray mentions that Annie had been able to squeeze into *Week In Review*. As a figurehead for everything going on out there, the kid had absolutely zero negatives, and Annie was confident that, with careful tending, he could do even more. Bring him along slowly, she counseled. See how he takes to the widening spotlight.

"First," she said, "I should update the original show to introduce the political angle. That's a no-brainer. But then," she paused for effect, "suppose we bring him in for the *VideoYears*?"

Brilliant. Now gearing up for its third edition, the *VideoYear Awards* were the net's highest-rated and most hype-generating extravaganza. Movie stars and musicians, all eager to spice up their images with the outlaw juice that the net traded in, fell all over themselves to be part of the show. Artists most closely linked to R²Rev lined up to perform, each duking it out with the other to push the limits of outrageousness without throwing the live broadcast off the air and into white noise and static. This year, ScroatM was scheduled to make his first live appearance promoting his new album.

Better yet, the show had become known for its stunts, throwaway moments that milked the zeitgeist for laughs, and pop culture relevancy (last year, the voting rules—always a momentum-killing recitation of disclaimers and legalese—were livened up by having porn star Rick Rigid pretending to read them off his digitally-masked thirteen-inch penis).

Joel was hardly a celebrity, Annie admitted. You wouldn't bring him on stage to present an award or anything—most of the audience wouldn't know who the hell he was. But kids *were* calling in for his picture. His Happy Snack website continued to receive hits at an impressive clip. A Joel Kasten fan club had been proposed, for Christ's sake. There was a buzz.

We could use him for a bit, Annie said, maybe a bumper coming in or out of a commercial. He was a good-looking, charismatic kid who had been receiving some national play for his stand against corporate America (*Rolling Stone* had reportedly been sniffing around for a profile). And now here he is at the *VideoYears*, protesting something.

"He's outside Radio City," Annie riffed, "*and he's protesting the show!* We'll surround him with kids, give them signs that say 'We're Not Buying This Shit!,' and they'll make like *we're* the new thing they hate. Maybe it could be a running gag—every time we cut outside, there are more and more kids. And then we'd need a payoff, like maybe they rush the stage or something. It could be hilarious!"

Viceroy sat pensively. He tended to shut down when exposed to any form of actual creativity.

"Could it?"

"It'd be a bit, a throwaway. If nobody gets it the first time, we'd have other stuff standing by. But we got first dibs on this kid. He could break elsewhere, so we have to brand him as ours first." Annie listened to herself talk, marveling that she had learned to speak asshole by osmosis.

"Okay," Viceroy said warily. "But we are over-budget like you can't believe this year. This can't cost anything. Bring him in the day of the show and send him home the next morning. I suppose we'd have to pop for a parent to come with him."

"He's eighteen, I'm sure he can travel solo. It's one night."

"And you'll baby-sit him?"

"Absolutely."

"Great," he said decisively. "Let's do it."

He stood, flexed, and strolled behind his desk, framing himself against the Manhattan skyline as he looked to the street below.

"You know, this is when this job is really rewarding, when we can actually influence society. This story that you brought us, it really speaks to something that's been missing for so long in youth culture. Passion! Protest! An actual desire to reshape the national dialogue. And, I'm thinking. If you and I can continue to—"

He turned around. Annie was already gone.

— — —

Todd wasn't mature enough to hide the hurt. Joel was off to New York, for another taste of national TV exposure, to actually *be there* at the fucking *VideoYear Awards*, and Todd was staying behind. Yeah, he heard from Joel and from Annie herself that this trip was being done on the cheap, that Annie had to scrape and claw just to get Joel there. But Todd thought that if Joel had made an issue of it, the network would've kicked in a couple hundred bucks to include the kid who—*excuse me?*—started all this.

Hell, Todd had money. He would've paid for the plane ticket himself—he could've slept on the floor of Joel's hotel room. His parents were already giving him a long leash. He had earned their trust. They would've let him go.

But, no, it was just to be Joel.

Joel landed at LaGuardia a little before one in the afternoon, only eight hours before the nine o'clock broadcast. Annie met him at the gate and grinned, seeing him come bounding off the plane, not a trace of nerves about him. He had attempted a kind of restrained white boy hip-hop look, which she would have to chip away at throughout the day to bring him back to his Midwestern essence. But she was startled at how glad she was to see him.

"How was your flight?"

"Sweet. They had some extra kosher lunches, so I ate three of 'em. I'm burpin' like a Jew guy now."

Annie shook her head with a smile. Joel had just a carry-on for this overnighter, so they were out the door and in a cab within minutes.

"Look," she said as Joel trained a tiny video camera at the sprawl they drove toward. Ira Zimbaugh had laid the camera on him with instructions to bring back material for the website. "I know your first trip to New York, somebody's supposed to take you around to all the sights—the Empire State Building, the Statue of Liberty—but I have to work! We're just in complete meltdown on the day of these live things."

Joel didn't care. The whole experience was going to be fine no matter what happened. "That's cool."

"But I was thinking, you're going to be outside tonight, you're not going to be able to see the actual show. So how about I bring you over to the theatre this afternoon? They're doing a run-through, all the musicians will be doing their soundchecks. You can just hang out."

He struggled so hard to maintain his cool. "No way."

"Sure. But, look," she said gently, "I'm kind of in charge of keeping an eye on you, but they're going to have me running all over the place the minute we get there. I would just need you to be cool and stay out of the way. These things can get pretty intense."

"Sure. Whatever."

She gestured to his video camera. "And that has to be put away while you're there."

"No problem," he shrugged.

"We'll break for dinner at six, and get you checked into your hotel room then."

As Manhattan enveloped him, Joel grew quiet. He was just a kid, Annie had to keep reminding herself, all by himself in New York City. He was a throwaway gag, a minor bit for an enormous TV show. But Annie was the one who had to make sure he got home okay.

"You ready for this?"

He bucked up. "Rock and roll."

He looked to the cab driver and noted his turban. He pointed from behind his hand and whispered to Annie, "*Towelhead.*"

— ◉ —

It was a blur, a dream. He wished Todd had been there to share it with him.

Ambling around Radio City Music Hall with a laminated All Access pass swinging from his neck, Joel drank in everything. Over there was Nicole Fine, who had broken through R²Rev's no-diva policy by successfully cultivating the look and manner of a freshly-fucked 16-year-old in her breakthrough dance club hit "Fruit Cocktail (Not Gonna Take My...)" ("You can take my pineapple, you can take my raspberry, I might try your banana, but you're not gonna take my..."). Over there was Sweetie-P, wreathed in gold and juggling three cell phones as he barked orders at his posse.

And on stage: SuicideAll, a retro death metal band convulsing over their instruments, spasmodically and with great violence, to a song about going down on their dead mother's corpse against a backdrop of cadavers and porn stars in go-go cages.

They seethed, they snarled, they defiled all that was decent and pure—until a genteel voice on the P.A. broke in over the racket: "That's fine, thank you."

The band set their instruments down and shuffled away obediently.

Earlier, Joel had been present for a real event, the kind of thing he knew he could take back to Berline and crow about for months: ScroatM's first-ever live performance in nearly two years. A bunch of muscled men with pinkie rings had attempted to clear the theatre of all but essential personnel, but Joel—feeling bad-ass and invincible in New York City—slipped up to the balcony and watched as a lone, scrawny figure shuffled out onto the bare stage and waited dispassionately for the track to kick in.

The man himself. Scroat.

The canned backing rolled. It was the song from the upcoming album, the one that R²Rev was playing every damned hour of the day, "Dingleberry." The groove was massive, the industrialized crunch and thud of beats and scratches threatening to reduce the tacky old theatre to rubble. The sonic assault smacked Joel in the chest and reverberated throughout his body—from his groin, to his feet, to the base of his neck. Mighty, mighty phat, this was.

Joel felt the song work on him, which was a surprise: Prior to this, he thought the track was… lame. Poo-poo stuff. If it had been on the first album, released way back when Joel was 15 and the perfect age to be enthralled by such sniggering stupidity, he'd be swooning right now, awash in nostalgia at this cut from the soundtrack of his young life.

But now he was 18—an adult, for Christ's sake—and ScroatM maybe didn't matter much anymore. Joel was savvy enough to know that the first single hyped from an album was meant to represent the very tightest that the disk had to offer. If "Dingleberry" was the high-water mark of *Freakal Matter*, Joel figured that there was another thirteen bucks he was going to keep for himself.

But the dude sure was working it, Joel thought as he peered through the lens of his video camera. Down there on the stage, Scroat was screaming pure acid into the microphone, the veins on his neck straining, his lean body bent sharply at the waist as he seemed about to retch on what he was bringing up, kind of like what Joel's cat looked like when it had a hairball.

He was shirtless and newly tattooed. His boxers were riding halfway up his back. Having spent hours as a young fan studying ScroatM's image, Joel had never before considered how easy it would be to give the singer a wedgie. As the millionaire punk worked through his choreographed temper tantrum, Joel for the first time thought that maybe a wedgie might be a good thing.

The stage was empty except for ScroatM. Surely there'd be more going on during the actual show. Live hip-hop had almost nothing to do with *music:* The tracks were recorded, the rapper—if he couldn't get away with lip syncing—just stalked the stage and shouted his rhymes into a microphone. Maybe a deejay up back was working the turntables. You had to have dancers or props or special effects or *something* to keep the kids entertained. The more successful hip-hop shows had more to do with *Sesame Street On Ice* than rock and roll.

Surely the people who ran the ScroatM machine knew that—

And then he was down.

As the song built to its fist-pumping, spit-spewing finale, Scroat—who seemed not to know where his marks were on the stage—turned into a confetti cannon just as it went off. He took it right in the face.

Joel jumped as intended at the surprise, then noticed for the first time that the stage was lined with cannons that had just erupted in sync. The bits of paper snowed down over the theatre, all the way up to the balcony. This was to be ScroatM's big finale. Since he wasn't there in 1975 when Kiss did this, Joel thought it was pretty cool.

The theatre was slapped into deathly silence as the track was cut off. Somewhere, a Teamster couldn't suppress a laugh as ScroatM's handlers rushed the stage in horror to tend to their fallen meal ticket.

He was back on his feet almost immediately—it was mostly surprise that brought him down.

But his fury was red hot, raging. "Motherfucker! *Motherfucker!!*" he bellowed between spits of confetti. Joel kept the video camera running.

ScroatM dove at the first handler who reached him. It was a frenzied, arm-swinging assault, scary in its savagery. Loser kids on the playground fought like this when they snapped, Joel noted.

Several more members of Team ScroatM tried to subdue their boss as he flailed and kicked wildly.

"Get offa me, motherfuckers!! I'll fire your *fucking asses!!!* You're all— Get your fucking hands—"

His team swarmed him and started dragging him off the stage, getting in a few discreet kicks as they did. Some of these goons were knee-capping to collect bad loans when Ronald Gerber was in diapers. They didn't care who was writing the checks now. They weren't going to take shit from this kid.

Tattooed arms and legs fought wildly from inside the no-necked ScroatM entourage as his protests echoed into the wings and trailed off. There was stunned silence for a moment. Then crew men slowly emerged from the shadows with brooms. They started sweeping up the confetti.

"Okay," the stage director coughed nervously over the P.A. "Next on stage, I need to see Satan."

Roadies started wheeling the next band's gear into place.

"Hurry please, Satan. Our time is almost up."

"This is so sweet!" Joel chuckled to himself as he lowered the camera. He picked up a fistful of confetti, figuring it would make a great souvenir. He examined it: it was little balls of toilet paper, dyed shit brown.

Dingleberries! ScroatM was planning to actually shit on the crowd! *Pretend* shit, anyway. It was all pretend.

He shook it from his hand distastefully and let it flutter from the balcony to the seats below.

— ⬤— —

The dinner break didn't happen. Show prep was running way behind schedule.

Annie was right—these people were wound way too tight. Annie herself was short with Joel the couple times she checked up on him. When this trip was first proposed, Joel fantasized that this would be the opportunity to see if what appeared to be a mutual flirtation could be acted upon as a sex type deal. Joel was a man of the world, he had done it with girls several years older. But back when he was 17, Annie scared him. Now that he was an adult, he figured he might go for it.

Now, though, she was kind of… *not hot*. Watching as she barked orders at those under her, only to turn around to be yelled at by those above, Annie suddenly seemed ordinary and, worse, adult. She wore no makeup to speak of, she reeked from cigarettes, and the cameras that were set to trip live at nine sharp seemed to be driving her mad.

"Okay. So you know what you're doing, right?" she snapped.

Joel laughed. "No! You've haven't told me anything."

"Oh, Jesus," she kicked herself. "Okay, you'll be out front—"

"Where's the front?" He was a kid from Illinois standing inside Radio City Music Hall. How was he supposed to know?

She ground her teeth. "Listen, you be on this spot at eight o'clock. Okay? This is serious. Make sure I can find you *right here*, and I'll lead you out there. There'll be a bunch of kids with signs and stuff and you'll be their leader, like at the Happy Snack."

"Got it."

"And you're protesting R²Rev because…" She rubbed her forehead with exhaustion. "I don't know, you're just doing it. If we decide to cut back to you throughout the show, somebody will come out to interview you and you'll just do your thing."

"My thing?"

"The boycott thing," she said impatiently, "the 'We're Not Buying This Shit' thing. But about R²Rev. And funny." A staffer started pulling at her.

Joel squirmed. For the first time, this started to feel scary. "Todd comes up with most of that stuff."

"You'll be fine," she said, leaving to put out another fire. "Just be yourself."

"Hey, do I get dinner?"

"Craft service!" she shouted as she vanished.

Craft service. This was the damnedest thing Joel had seen so far: table upon table of snacks and junk food and soda, there for the taking—for free!—by anyone connected to the production. He learned that there were union positions, paying like forty bucks an hour, that did nothing but make sure the buffet was constantly stocked. You could take four or five donuts, which Joel did, and a half-hour later they would have magically grown back.

Every A-list performer in R²Rev's heavy rotation was downstairs doing their soundchecks, and Joel ended up hanging out at craft service, trying to catch the Teamster elf who replaced the donuts.

He was still 18 going on nine.

He bounded into the shadowy backstage nook set up for the food. The place was empty. In the final 90 minutes of live prep, the R²Rev-ers weren't going to take time to eat. Like Annie, they all seemed to exist on cigarettes and abuse, both issued and endured.

Joel circled the pristine spread strategically, trying to determine where his point of attack would come this time.

Brownies, he was thinking.

Then he heard the wet, stomach-churning sound of someone dredging a healthy wad of snot from the back of his throat. In the darkened corner of the room, Joel now saw someone slumped over in a folding chair, his elbows on his knees and his eyes to the floor.

This person slowly, meticulously let go of a long, mid-air snail trail of mucus that splattered to the floor between his feet. There was more sputum puddled there; he'd been at this for a while.

Joel gagged and moved off the brownie. Then he nearly shit.

It was ScroatM.

Joel almost ran off, remembering how pissed the singer had been earlier in the afternoon. But then he got ballsy. He cleared a spot on the table and propped up his video camera just so.

He approached warily.

"Hey. ScroatM. Right?"

Scroat looked up hazily. His cloudy eyes were elsewhere. He stunk of pot.

"'Sup?"

"Too numerous!" Joel smiled. "Fuckin' ScroatM! How you doin'? Shit, I'm a fan, dude. A *real* fan. From back in the day, absolutely. I can't—shit, I can't believe this!"

Joel stuck out his hand and the singer clasped it limply, letting his arm jiggle bonelessly as Joel attempted a clumsy soul shake.

"*Right White Nigga!* Right? The fuckin' bomb, dude. Played that CD until it fuckin' melted, seriously. That disk, man… It got me through a lot." Joel let something vulnerable get through. "It helped me."

The rapper looked up to the kid blandly. "You a fag?"

Joel flinched and laughed nervously.

"What?"

"You look like a fag. A farm fag." He laughed drunkenly and picked at a scab on his forearm.

"No," Joel smiled hopefully. "I'm, I'm on the show tonight. Me and some friends—"

ScroatM summoned up some more snot and watched it dangle to the floor. Joel looked to the camera. He couldn't believe he was taping himself being dissed this way.

"Well, hey, I better get outta your way," Joel stammered. "But, hey…"

He looked around and saw a stack of note cards. He grabbed one and a pen and offered them shyly to the rapper.

"Could you maybe… ?"

Scroat stared at the card and pen dumbly. Then an idea took shape.

He took the note card, bent down to the slime pooled between his feet, and slowly swiped the card through it, collecting a pale green glob on its edge.

He held it up to Joel.

"Lube up, Gomer. I'll fuck your ass, send you home with a real story for all your farmer friends."

His laugh rattled and sliced. He barely missed Joel as he spun the card at him.

Joel had tears in his eyes. He didn't know what to do.

ScroatM started fishing down his baggies for his dick.

"How much do you love me, kid? Show me how bad you want it."

Joel turned and ran, remembering at the last moment to grab his camera.

ScroatM crowed mockingly, then slumped forward again in the chair and fell silent.

Shattered

Joel was home just after noon the next day and went straight to Todd's. The trip had left him feeling rattled and completely un-Joel-like.

He grinned as he presented Todd with the All Access pass, which Todd accepted graciously while thinking that it was kind of like giving someone a used rubber: Hey, here's what I had on while I was having all the fun you weren't having. Enjoy!

On TV, the *VideoYears* sure looked like a blast. R²Rev's stellar roster of puppets and miscreants had paraded across the stage to accept the accolades of their peers, the rappers thanking Jesus and giving teary-eyed shout outs to their posses and illegitimate babies, and the metallers making devil horns and saying "fuck" a lot. Whoever was riding the delay at R²Rev did stellar work; not a single "fuck" got through. Even in cases where "fuck" and "Jesus" were contained within the same half-sentence, Jesus got his props while the offending word was duly censored.

All the performances were smoking, with the exception of ScroatM, who tore off a listless rendition of that stupid song from his upcoming CD. At the end, he stood triumphantly at the front of the stage, arms raised in exultation, as the audience was pelted with what Mimi SoWett later said appeared to be used toilet paper.

She sniffed at it warily.

"But it's not!" she declared brightly. "ScroatM, he so *bad!*"

The bits with Joel were brief and pretty worthless, the first showing up as the show went to commercial about 25 minutes in. There he was, in front of a bunch of fake-looking teenagers, straining to get past a mock police line that had been set up outside the theatre. Signs reading "We're Not Buying This Shit!"—the naughty word scrambled for air—were peppered throughout the crowd. Todd saw them and grew even more pissed that he wasn't there.

Manny Clarke, pretending to be a newsman, reported that these kids—led by Joel Kasten, just a regular kid from Berline, Illinois—had turned up en masse to protest R²Rev, to complain that the network had become a corrupt and cynical tool with which to exploit America's young people. There were a couple nice close-ups of Joel exhorting the crowd, but he didn't speak to the camera. There was just a lot of jostling and pretend shouting. The gag didn't last more than fifteen seconds.

"We'll cut back out here the minute the cops start firing on the crowd!" Clarke smirked.

They weren't seen again until a commercial break about 40 minutes before the scheduled conclusion of the show. There were more kids now, some of the fake cops were scuffling with some of the fake protesters, and this time Clarke elbowed his way to the center of the "insurrection" to interview the kid who had triggered the event.

Only it wasn't Joel. *Joel* stood forlornly over the shoulder of some preppy-looking kid, who mumbled something obnoxious into the microphone before losing it to giggles. Manny, seeing this was going nowhere, threw it to commercial.

And that was it. The show was running long, and the cameras never went outside again. Seeing the broadcast for the first time on the tape that Todd had recorded for him, Joel was embarrassed at how fleeting and pointless it turned out to be.

"Who was *that?*" Todd asked.

Joel fumed at the memory. "So they come out the second time," he recalled, "and they say that this time Manny Clarke is going to interview the leader of the protest. Then, all of a sudden, this preppy shit, tripping on ecstasy, is brought from inside the theatre. He's led to the middle of the crowd, and *he* gets put on camera! Annie told me later that his name was *Dylan Viceroy*," he said, mocking the pretentiousness of the name, "the kid of some R²Rev big shit. She was pissed!"

Todd could only smile bitterly. "Perfect. Just perfect."

"And that was it. They told us we were done. They wouldn't let me back into the theatre, so I couldn't find Annie. I ended up standing on the sidewalk for over an hour in the middle of fucking New York City until she finally came to get me."

Todd could tell that this had scared him.

"She took me over to the hotel, we hung out for a while, and I was in a cab to the airport by nine this morning."

"What was the hotel like?"

Joel perked up. "Dude, you won't believe it."

He produced a videotape and stuck it into the VCR. On the screen was Joel's shaky tour of his room at Le Parker Meridien, a low-end suite for the worldly traveler, but a palace to a kid who had known only Holiday Inns. The camera lingered over the marbled bathroom with its Jacuzzi tub, its gold-plated faucets, and the two-line telephone right beside the toilet. Then it ambled into the main room.

And there was Annie.

She looked exhausted. Her hair was mussed, her shoes off, and she was dragging on a cigarette. She seemed a little drunk.

"Hi, Todd!" she waved brightly, sincerely, into the lens. "I miss you! I know it stinks that you're not here, but next time… I promise!"

Todd squirmed a little.

The tape proceeded to give a dizzying display of the room's many wonders, but Todd saw only this: the bed was a tangle of sheets, the clock read 2:49, and Annie—every time Joel swung the camera back at her—seemed embarrassed, a little shy.

For just a flash, the camera caught Joel in a mirror. He was wearing only a towel, and the hotel's free shower cap. Like a wise-ass.

"New York City, bay-bee!" he bellowed on the tape.

Todd shut down and iced over. Joel went to New York *and* he got laid, by Annie. No matter how clever he was or how strong his potential might be once he left high school and merged into adulthood, Todd was reminded for the zillionth time that it was always going to be the Joel Kastens of the world who won. And this time, Todd had set everything up so that Joel could get the goodies.

What kind of dick does that? Todd asked himself.

Maybe someday he'd be old enough to withstand a jab this lacerating, but right now he just wanted to be alone to die a little.

Joel, never long on perceptiveness, rambled on. He shut down the tape and hit rewind as he turned to Todd with a devilish grin.

"Hey, what did you think of ScroatM?"

Todd shrugged listlessly. He really wanted Joel to go.

When the ScroatM part of the tape reached the playback head, Joel giggled. "Check this out."

He played the clandestine footage of ScroatM taking a faceful of dingleberries. It was brilliantly funny—the preening, cocksure superstar literally getting blown off his feet by the blast, and then shrieking like an asshole while being pummeled by his own staff and dragged offstage.

Todd couldn't suppress a grin. But it wasn't the reaction Joel expected.

"Great," Todd smiled sadly.

Joel had come to know Todd's wiring pretty well the past few months. Something was really wrong.

"Hey. What's—"

Todd was still watching the tape. The onstage fracas abruptly cut to a plate of bagels, then an image of someone slumped over in a chair in a sparsely lit room, and Joel stepping into view.

Seeing this on the TV, Joel leapt up and turned off the tape, like a kid caught by his parents with pornography.

Now Todd was intrigued. "What's that?"

Joel pulled the tape from the VCR. "Nothing. It's nothing."

"Lemme see."

"No, all right? Just no." Joel's mood turned dark.

Todd stood angrily. "Fine. Then, you know what? Just get the hell outta here. I really enjoyed your vacation video, and hearing about all the fun you had, but—" As he turned, the laminated pass that Joel had ceremoniously draped around his neck fluttered annoyingly. Todd yanked it off.

"And... what is this? Why would I *want* this??"

He threw it at Joel and glared at him, just the faintest trace of tears in his eyes. Joel had given the pass to Todd, sincerely hoping he would like it.

"Hey…" Joel spoke softly.

"Look, we're done, all right? The Happy Snack thing is gonna die off. Whatever happens with Mr. Kolak is pretty much up to Dean Stoller and his crowd. It'd be nice if *you* voted for him since you got him into this, but… do whatever the fuck you want."

Joel hadn't known much rejection in his life. As Todd stared at him hatefully and waited for him to leave, he tried to make sense of it.

"Dude," he pleaded with a timid smile. "Come on."

"I mean, we're gonna graduate before we know it. It's time to stop dicking around with this bullshit. *I've* got work to do. You, you're gonna get your scholarship. You're gonna play college ball, maybe get signed to the minors.

"The way things always seem to work out for you, you'll probably go to the Yankees. Then you and Annie—"

The reflexive hitch in his voice nearly triggered the waterworks. Todd fought them off and turned away, but even Joel was bright enough to see what was going on here. For all his newfound admiration for the kid, he had forgotten how much Todd continued to do without.

He didn't want him to hurt anymore.

"Dude. It was nothing."

That stung the worst, because it was most likely true. That you could get it so often, with such ease—that you could blow it off as "nothing"— splashed upon Todd like acid.

He kept his back to Joel, because the tears that he refused to let loose were turning his nose red and runny. He refused to sniff like a girl.

"Just go, okay? I'll see you at school."

Joel gave up sadly. He grabbed his videotape and studied it hard. He made a decision.

"It's just that, something happened. And it's not like…" He stopped, then laid the tape on the coffee table before Todd. "Just don't show it to anybody. Okay?"

Todd looked at the cassette curiously, rattled by Joel's solemnity. He wanted to cast off this funk, go back to being friends and co-conspirators—just kids for maybe a little while longer—but something complicated had come between them. He nodded silently and watched Joel leave.

He didn't want to see what was on the tape anymore, but now he figured he had to since Joel had trusted him when he didn't have to.

He fed the tape into the machine, sat down, and watched queasily as ScroatM tore Joel to pieces. It was most painful to watch because it was so clear that going into the encounter, Joel felt he could hold his own with the rapper. Scroat was a superstar, but so was Joel in his own little world. Here they both were, backstage at the *VideoYears*. They could hang.

Joel had laid himself bare, and ScroatM ground him into the floor. For the first time ever, Joel looked small in Todd's eyes. As Joel stood there dumbly and took the abuse, until he finally had to turn and run, Todd realized that Joel was experiencing what boys like Todd dealt with seemingly every day. The attack was extreme in Joel's case, but he lived a life accustomed to extremes—most of them favorable. For boys like Todd, the hurts were more benign, more insidious. And they accumulated, knife nick by knife nick.

A dispirited Joel had apparently stopped taping until he got to the hotel room hours later, because as the VCR kept playing, Todd was all of a sudden back at Le Parker Meridien, with Joel and Annie and their tangled sheets.

He lunged at the remote and drove the images back into the plastic cassette, as if they were toxic and never again to be released.

He thought of Joel and the emotional highs and pressure drops the kid must've experienced just the day before, on his own and so far from home. If he hadn't just left, they could've talked about it. There was still something that had been altered between them, something that most likely wouldn't be right anymore. But Todd would've talked to him about it.

Then he thought of ScroatM, the contempt making his stomach churn. *Lube up, Gomer.*

"Fucker," Todd muttered as he held the videotape. "The little fucker."

Mobilizations

"No, Ma. Don't come."

Frank was on the phone to his mother down South. She had been listening—first with apprehension, then with pride—as her son detailed to her the progress of his campaign. It was all still impossible for her to comprehend: her only child, always so reticent and frail, was, out of the blue, running for office up there in Illinois. And despite his protestations, she could decipher, through his efforts to downplay it all, that it was looking like he could win.

"It's not a big deal. It's a three-thousand-dollar-a-year Council seat. I'd be making sure that snow got plowed and garbage got picked up. And besides," he said, out loud this time but constantly inside his head, "you never know how these votes are gonna come out. You could come all this way for nothing."

There was one of those dramatic Mom pauses, then softly: "Your father would be so proud of you."

"*Ma...*"

But then again: *Sure, maybe.* Why wouldn't his old man have been proud of him? At 44, Frank was now older than his father had been when he died. And he was stepping outside himself for the very first time, taking that fragile self-confidence that had always lay useless and unexplored way down deep and asserting it in a way he could never have dreamed possible.

He was taking a stand in his community. His father would have respected that.

True, he had to keep reminding himself, none of this began with him. He understood early on that he was mostly a prop being used by the town's young people to challenge and mock their elders. He understood that his race was being put out there to provoke the docile, non-specific prejudice that ran through even the most genial neighbor.

But he saw this too: these kids (and they were "kids," these former students of his) respected him, and seemed genuinely grateful to have reason to be around him again. In many, he had planted the seed of political activism just now blossoming with this campaign. Who better to endorse than the man who told them, way back when they were young and stupid and so far removed from caring, that one day it would be up to them to see how the world was run?

He made the choice to actually turn his candidacy into a real thing, and to have it matter. He did know the inner workings of this town. He did know intimately the histories of past societies and the way that they grew and perished at the hands of public policy. Why *not* him?

All of a sudden, he had his very own website, with his opinions on civic matters on display for everyone to see. Even more exciting were links to similar campaigns that had popped up all over the country, each having grown out of Todd and Joel's slyly potent stab at the corporate boning their generation was constantly enduring. It was a genuine grassroots movement, facilitated by state-of-the-art media.

It was breathtaking, it really was, the way in which the technology and the message meshed to put the word out. Todd, via Joel, had articulated what teenagers kind of knew was being done to them, and the internet—where the young communed largely amongst themselves, most adults forever too dim to fully understand the web—shotgunned it cleanly:

Withhold your coin. Cast your vote. Piss somebody off. Fuck with the wiring. *Matter.*

Might be a laugh.

— —

The Happy Snack website continued to flourish, Ira Zimbaugh's technical wizardry drawing hundreds of hits a day and rewarding each repeat visitor with more diversions, more games, more of the hottest bootleg audio and video files buried deep inside the page. You had to fully explore the site, follow every banner and link, to get to the treasures Ira had hidden there. And while you're there, check out the Happy Snack parking lot *live*, where throngs remained posted—even when the snows came—to badger the little brown man who was no longer Daljit Singh. Singh had vanished one night, reportedly taking his family back to India.

It happened every afternoon around three p.m. local time, the new and instantly besieged Happy Snack proprietor emerging from the shop like a figure in a cuckoo clock to be assaulted by pennies as he emptied the trash. You could dial it up from anywhere in the world and watch the fun.

Daljit Singh did.

Dozens of mirror sites had gone up all over the country, Iras elsewhere launching pages that sought to do for their local protest what Ira had done in Berline. All of a sudden, a squadron of computer geeks, previously forced to distinguish themselves merely among their fellow brainiacs, were being hailed as key components of the insurrection. They were an intensely competitive tribe. The desire to out-flash all the other pages was nasty and strong.

The result was that the online terrain that sprang up around the Happy Snack and its offshoots was constantly fresh, constantly engaging. What should've rightfully died in an Illinois parking lot weeks ago was now being sustained by a bunch of pimple-faced cowboys in a cyber pissing match.

But only Ira's site had this: stuff you could buy.

Annie had come to Todd early on with an idea. Their slogan—"We're Not Buying This Shit!"—remained a masterstroke. It worked for the corporate fight; it worked on the political front. Throw a stick in any direction and you'll hit a teenager refusing to buy someone's shit.

Adults, too, for that matter. This was prime bumper sticker copy for the dull-witted and the put-upon.

As a catchphrase, it just worked.

"You *own* that," she reminded him. "You could do something with it."

"How hard could it be," she had wondered, "for Ira to reconfigure the site to sell merchandise? Just start with T-shirts: Find a place that could print them up in bulk, mark up the price just a little bit to make it worth your while, and open the site up for sales. You'd only make shirts as orders came in, so if no one's interested, you're not out anything. But if this thing took off…"

Sounded sweet to Todd. He'd hopefully be off to college in the fall and unlike Joel, there didn't seem to be any scholarships coming his way. If he could make a couple bucks off this thing that thus far had brought glory only to his charm-laden partner, that seemed more than fair to him.

Annie had really wanted him to do this, really wanted him to win something for himself in this whole thing. Maybe this was how she was going to make up for New York.

He came up with two designs: one that explicitly stated "We're Not Buying This Shit!" for the genuine outlaw willing to risk sanction for sporting an actual dirty word, and another that blurred the "shit" just enough to make it wearable in public while still promising to scandalize. He found a silk screen shop that would do up the shirts for as little as $5.30 per 500, so he priced out the items to fifteen bucks to cover shipping and handling and a little left over for himself, and he had Ira wire up a credit card account.

Within a week, he had nearly 625 orders. He got a neighbor kid to oversee the print run and ship the shirts out for a buck a pop. Todd was still going to clear about $5.70 per unit.

— —

Annie had an office now, and an assistant. The *VideoYear* stunt had been a wash, but Viceroy felt that Annie's instincts were to be respected. She knew something was going on out there when no one else did. Besides, the mock awards protest did manage to get Dylan, his embarrassment of a kid, on TV. That had to be worth something.

Viceroy's passion was now the potential political enlightenment of his young viewers. April was going to see hundreds of elections around the country, spring contests which would focus purely on local and state campaigns and issues—hick stuff, mostly. But if there truly was a new voter base out there to be cultivated and molded, what better time to put the machinery through a shakedown test? If even a handful of young non-voters could be prompted into action by R²Rev's coverage at a time when nothing much mattered, imagine the possibilities when no less than the White House was in play.

Some legitimate youth-driven campaigns had taken root across the land as a result of the initial Happy Snack boycott, Viceroy noted.

"Let's follow some of them through to election day. Put an R²Rev spin on the coverage, see if we can't make it hip to vote someone into—or *out* of*—office just because you can. Just because the system is there to be fucked with."

Annie listened obediently.

"I'll start hitting up our artists to get involved, to sexy it up for the Programming Department. But I want you to oversee the grassroots stuff. That's your turf."

"I'll want to go back to Berline."

"Fine," Viceroy said. "We've already tilled the soil there. We've already planted a flag."

"We've got our ducks in a row."

"Right on!" He spun around to his computer and punched up the Happy Snack site.

"Jesus," he said in admiration, "their site looks better than ours."

He scrolled down until he saw the link to the T-shirt page. He studied *the phrase* deeply and then pointed to the screen.

"We need this."

"We can't have it. It's trademarked."

"*By who?*"

"Todd Noland."

Viceroy screwed up his face. This was a name he did not know, and he knew all names worth knowing. Thus he was forced to ready himself to accept trite knowledge.

"The kid in Berline who started all this."

Viceroy dismissed that fact with a wave. "It's ours. We used it for your show."

"He had it first. We're lucky he didn't sue," Annie added.

Viceroy returned his gaze to the computer screen.

"We *need* this. We could umbrella the entire campaign under that phrase."

"Well, you can't *have* it."

This was a gnat, buzzing around John Viceroy's head. "This kid is selling shirts out of his basement for pocket change. I'm talking about an entire catalog: shirts, hats, screensavers, all that crap. Find out what he wants for it—we'll make it worth his while."

"You don't know this kid."

"Just talk to him."

With an unimpressed sigh, she stood to leave. "I'll talk to him."

— —

"Ma. I've got nowhere to put you."

"You've got a couch, don't you?"

"You are not sleeping on my couch."

"No, I am not. *You* are."

Frank sighed, surrender inevitable.

"Do you have campaign buttons? With your name on them? Frank Kolak, right on there?"

"Yes."

"I'm coming."

Monsters

For her, it was first and foremost an industry-type hug, a non-sexual, "Here we are again to further our mutual interests" embrace, with the added awkward facts that his 18-year-old penis had been inside her just a month earlier and, at the time, she had not found that to be a bad thing. Certain signals—certain spontaneous utterances—could've given the boy reason to believe she had enjoyed the encounter and might be interested in hosting his penis again.

Indeed, Joel hung onto the hug too long, went for her lips when she felt strongly that the proper message would be sent by a circumspect peck on the cheek. The kid looked a little swoony when he finally let go.

She was going to have to deal with this.

And Todd was right there to see the clumsy dance Joel and Annie performed when she first got back to town. She could tell by the chill in her relationship with Todd that he wasn't completely over what had happened in New York.

She was going to have to deal with *that*, too.

She needed to figure out what she was doing.

"So how are things looking?"

"Good, I think," Todd said. "Just asking around, it sounds like we've got commitments from a real good chunk of the eighteen to twenty-three crowd, and we're a lock with the blacks. Just about everybody we're getting has never voted before, so we're bringing in brand new numbers. Jerry Self, the current guy, won last time around with only like a thousand votes. And he's a complete tool."

"Mary Flemming, this state senator, just came out and endorsed Mr. Kolak," Joel added. "That's a big deal around here."

"Really?" Annie asked skeptically. "Where did that come from?"

"Dunno. She called me up the other day, and bought me dinner at Pizza

Hut. Said she's been following the race, and she agrees with me: Kolak's the dude."

Annie recognized the strategy. "She sees how you're flushing out votes. She's figuring out how she can use you and your friends. When *her* election comes up."

"Hey," Joel said. "Free pizza's free pizza."

"She might've broken the law by buying you dinner," said Annie.

"Excellent!" Joel beamed.

Annie stopped and studied Todd and Joel, so close to all this and so certain it was mostly just a kind of prank that they couldn't recognize they were actually effecting change. It was probably for the best.

"So are things okay between you two?" she asked, turning to Todd. "Joel told me you guys weren't talking."

Todd stared at his shoes. "No, we're okay. Yeah. It's... fine."

"Good," she said sincerely. "You guys are a team. You are *monsters* when you work together. Don't let anything screw that up."

"So where are you staying?" Joel asked, a little too eagerly.

Big Money

"What does that mean?" Todd asked, his feet sticking to the Taco Bell floor as he and Annie shared a booth.

"It means that R²Rev would pay you for the phrase. It would become theirs to do with whatever they wanted."

Todd was skeptical. "It's just a bunch of words."

"But they're the *right* bunch of words. They threw it into the last round of phone polling, and kids respond to it. Adults, too. 'We're Not Buying This Shit!' It's worth something."

"You know," Todd said guiltily. "I didn't make it up. Some kid, I don't even know who, showed up at the Happy Snack with it written on a sign. I just ran with it."

"So? You know how many people said 'Have a nice day' before someone thought to license it and stick it on T-shirts with that obnoxious smiley face?"

"Someone made money off 'Have a nice day'?"

"'*Wassup??*' Remember that one, from the beer commercial? '*Wassup??*' People retired on '*Wassup.*'"

"That's... That's not even grammatical."

"It was addictive. That's why it worked. *Was-s-s-u-u-u-u-p???*" Annie growled.

"Please stop doing that."

Annie sauced up another taco. "I'm just following orders. I was told to come here and ask your price."

"My price?" Todd laughed. "I'm a kid. I don't have a price."

She took a bite.

"I mean, are we talking thousands of dollars? *Tens* of thousands of dollars?" he asked. "I mean, Jesus, I'm doing great working it myself, and that's just the shirts. Why would I give that up, unless they're talking about..."

Big money.

"I don't think I can get in the middle of this, me running up the price against my employers," Annie said. "You should talk to a lawyer."

"Yeah, sure. Me and the wassup? guys share the same firm."

"Unless..."

"What?"

She dismissed the idea. "Nah. You'd think it was sleazy."

This woman, promising "sleazy," struck some illicit *twang* deep inside Todd. Pathetic, too, but...

"What?" he smiled hopefully.

"It's just that, I do know something about these things. If you wanted me to advise you in some way, like if we partnered up on this..."

"So you'd make money off this, too?"

"Sleazy, right?"

"I don't know," Todd said thoughtfully. He never wanted to see anyone shorted. And, if Annie made out on this, she might take him to bed. *Could* happen.

"I mean, none of this would be happening if you hadn't come along," he said. "I guess if anybody's gonna make a buck off this..."

"Look, just think about it. Regardless of how you want to handle it, this is a real opportunity for you," Annie said. "Talk to your folks. Talk to whoever you trust. Just let me know what you want to do."

I Work

To sexy up the piece, Annie needed tape of Joel the jock, some images of him suited up, sweaty and dominating, so he got most of the team to take some early batting practice even though there was still a sting in the air and traces of snow on the ground, and baseball season was still a few weeks away. It didn't take much convincing. Everyone was trying to figure out how to get themselves on R²Rev now that the crew was back in town.

Annie and Joel had already worked out their sexual issues. As soon as she got him alone, she expressed her belief that it was inappropriate for them to pursue any kind of relationship. Yes, she said sincerely, the night they spent together was special, but she was not comfortable with the age difference and with the blurring of the line between "documentarian" and subject.

Joel, while clearly still in the throes of lust, reluctantly agreed with her reasoning, adding his belief that if they fooled around again, Todd would "go mental," and he wasn't interested in causing that.

Annie smiled and said she thought that was sweet, which just made Joel go all swoony again.

"Swoony & Mental," Annie grinned to herself. "My two pals."

So, as she watched Joel dominate the practice, she tried to project a sisterly admiration. She tried to spend less time studying his physique, noting how his uniform strained a bit with the bulking up he'd apparently experienced just since last season, and watching instead how he held sway over his friends, all of whom were tripping over themselves trying to impress Annie and her camera.

"*Big dick!*" they'd shout every time somebody pulled off something exceptional.

Jeff Regan made a great diving catch in left: "*Big dick!*"

Bobby Slopes just beat out a throw to first: "*Big dick!*"

"Guys," Annie laughed. "I can't use any of this if you keep saying that!"

"Gentlemen," Wad Wendell said drolly from the pitcher's mound. "The lady wants no dick."

"Big dyke!"

Annie rolled her eyes, prepared to wait out these horny young bucks until they ran themselves to exhaustion and simply gave her the backdrop she needed.

Killing time, she looked to the bleachers behind home plate. There, a lone figure watched the practice intently. It did not take her long to figure out who it was. She wanted nothing to do with him, but she knew she'd have to.

"Excuse me," she said, having approached warily, "are you Joel's father?"

He was sizing her up before his eyes even fell upon her.

"Marty Kasten," he smiled, as if the name alone should close the deal. He shook her hand as he drank her in.

"Annie McCullough," she smiled back steadily. "I'm with R²Rev. I'm sure you know all about what we've been working on with your son."

"Sure. You're turning the kid into a star."

"Well, I don't know about that. He's—"

"Come on, Joel! Watch the ball!"

The father's tone was piercing as Joel stood at the plate, clearly unsettled at the sight of Annie and his dad together. He turned reluctantly back to Wad and proceeded to whiff pitch after pitch. He kept sneaking looks back to the bleachers.

Marty shook his head bitterly. "He knows better than that."

"You know, I'm working on a new piece, about the Kolak campaign. Do you think I could interview you? It'd help us get to know Joel better."

He looked over her shoulder to see the camera guy. He was already taping.

"Well, sure," he grinned saucily. "You can turn me into a star, too."

"I'll do what I can." She smiled, settling in beside him and allowing space for the camera to focus on Marty.

"So, have you been keeping up with Joel's involvement with this Council race?"

"Well, I know he keeps getting his name in the paper. I know he's got a lot of people intending to vote for this Kolak guy. Not sure what the point is, but if it keeps him out of trouble…"

"Do you know Frank Kolak? Maybe from a teacher's conference or…"

He scoffed at the notion. "Joel's mother handles all that. I work."

"What is it you do?"

"Sales. Computers. High-end stuff."

She acted impressed, then smiled. "So, have you snuck out for the afternoon?"

"I set my own hours." He leaned back across the bleacher behind him. He was indeed a handsome man, although age and rot were eating at the edges. "I save my sneaking out for nighttime."

"I see," she smiled. The lech. "So, I find political involvement in someone Joel's age to be really unusual. Did he get that from you?"

He clucked. "No. Maybe that's his mother."

"Do you vote?"

"Eh, I try. The presidential stuff." He swept his hand through his full head of hair. "Otherwise, you know… I work."

"The high-end stuff," she teased. Annie wasn't above spraying it around like TGI Friday's at Happy Hour if it would get this guy to hang himself.

"My specialty," he purred.

"So, tell me about Joel. Good kid?"

"You kidding? He's the best. Grades could be better, but he's only gonna need to be smart enough to know how to sign a contract."

"He's that good?"

"He can go all the way. 'Course, he's been a little distracted lately with all this nonsense you've got him tied up in," he said. "But then I got to thinking: If an athlete today is going to succeed on all levels, he's got to know how to work the media and the fans. I figure with what you've got him doing, all this TV crap, you're giving him a workout that most kids won't get until college, if they're lucky."

He winked. "I'm thinking there oughta be some way I could thank you for all you're doing for him."

"That's okay. I like the kid," she smiled. "So, you and your wife must be really proud of him."

213

"Well, sure, but..." He showed off his ringless finger, as if proof of his availability was a gift just for her. "We're not together anymore. One of those things."

"Hmm," Annie said, pretending this was not already known. "Divorce can be tough on a kid. How do you think Joel's handled it?"

He fussed with the crease of his Hilfiger slacks. "Aw, you know. I'm sure it was hard on him at first. But people have to be happy where they're at, and his mom and *me*, we just weren't happy. And that couldn't have been good for him, either.

"Now, I'm doing my thing, his mother is doing her thing, and we're both there when he needs us. If he's got a problem with the arrangement, he hasn't told *me* about it."

"Kasten, you suck!!" Bobby Slopes shouted from the outfield. This was mock haranguing—Joel pretty much never sucked—although right now he was raising quite a stench with the bat.

He really didn't want Annie talking to his father.

Marty looked to his son, who stared back nervously. He turned to Annie, then back to Joel. And he figured it out.

"Ahhhh," he sighed, a blend of awe and spite. "It was you."

The shift in attitude was queasy, unsettling. "Excuse me?"

"New York." He was checking her out again. Joel saw him do it. "He came back with a spring in his step, I figured he had hooked up with *somebody*. But..." He whistled his admiration. "Mm-mm-mmmmm."

Annie wanted out. She didn't need to tell the cameraman; he had already turned away.

Marty's grin turned icy, almost vengeful, as he returned to his boy.

"Get your head in the game, goddammit!" he barked, still smiling.

Then, under his breath, not entirely without affection:

"Little bastard."

Public Speaking

Annie's other responsibility was just to hang around with her crew during the final week of the campaign, picking up footage that could be cut into Viceroy's battle cry to young voters. In theory, this was a revolution she was covering. In actual fact, it was excruciating.

"I am very concerned about the young people who wait at the bus stop and use foul language and listen to their loud music and take up all of the benches so we can't sit down. There are no manners anymore in these children, no manners at all."

A low, arthritic rustle of approval stirred through the activity room. The Candidate's Forum, held every election season at the Holy Angel Retirement Village, had drawn 30 or so residents who had managed to come down to air their complaints, along with another couple dozen concerned citizens from throughout the district. Rest homes are goldmines for small town races. The elderly vote with astonishing reliability, and they actually study the candidates and their positions. Common sense dictates that those on the ballot should gratefully accept the invitation to come and take part in a debate in front of some of the district's most likely voters.

"Doesn't anyone teach these kids anymore to give up their seat to an older person?"

Jerry Self cleared his throat, the feedback from the microphone lost on many of the hearing-deprived in the audience. He had wowed them last time around, and their support had been a big factor in his victory.

"As I promised you I would last time I ran, I have made numerous efforts to convince the county that residents here deserve a separate bus stop of their own, or at the very least some kind of patrol presence that would, during high traffic periods, ensure that the stop here is geared to your special needs. As I am sure you understand, getting county bureaucrats to even acknowledge a problem, let alone fix it, is an arduous process that can only be accomplished through persistence and dedication. The only way I can be allowed to see this project through to its completion is for you to re-elect me on April sixteenth. Thank you."

"Kill me now," Annie's cameraman whispered painfully as the room applauded softly. She jabbed him in the side with her pen as Frank Kolak slid the microphone over and shored himself up for his first response.

"Um, you're not going to get a separate bus stop out of the county," he began, his bluntness causing a minor stir. "They've got the entire bus line timed out to the minute based on a rigid formula determined entirely by the precise spacing of stops and the average amount of time each stop requires. One new stop on just one line could knock the entire system off schedule if the stop is added to a major artery that feeds into a number of transfers, which is what you've got here.

"And while you'd never get them to admit it, you can also bet that they're aware that a stop designated specifically for Holy Angel would really slow down their schedule, seeing as how none of us are moving as quickly as we used to."

The crowd chuckled appreciatively.

"Maybe my opponent knows something I don't, but I'd just as soon not make you any promises that four years from now I'd have to come back and make all over again."

Jerry Self squirmed as Annie smiled behind her clipboard. She liked this Frank Kolak.

"Now," Frank continued, "if you all have figured out how to legislate good manners into teenagers, *please* let me know."

More laughs. Down front, Frank's mother glowed with pride.

"I'm around them every day. I know many of them are severely lacking in proper behavior. And if I were to learn that any of these kids causing you inconvenience were *my* students, then that reflects poorly on me, and I apologize."

He gestured to the room, where several of his young campaigners sat among the white heads.

"Maybe you've noticed the *youthful* quality of some of my supporters.

Many of them are my former students, and I cannot tell you how proud I am of them," he said. "They're giving up their time, they're giving up their rap music and all that other nonsense that drives us nuts, to get involved. To try and make their community a little better. They make me look good, just by being willing to lend a hand."

Frank's youth brigade blanched as the grandmas and grandpas in the room suddenly turned to smile at them and applaud dotingly.

What the hell, most shrugged. Like it's so awful to be caught caring about something.

"But I must be getting good at this politician business, because I'm avoiding the issue," Frank continued with a smile. "To be honest, I don't know what the answer is to your bus stop problem. Once I'm in office, I'd take a good long look at it and do what I could. That I *can* promise you.

"But," he added, pointing at his supporters dramatically, "win or lose, I am charging my young friends out there, if you know any kids who use that bus stop, tell them to knock it off and give these folks a break. Tell them that no matter how immortal they're feeling right now, one day it's going to be *them* looking for somewhere to take a load off. And it's going to be sooner than they think."

The room came alive with grateful applause. Frank smiled and shyly waved his acknowledgement as he handed the microphone back to Jerry Self for the next question. Self sagged visibly, his voter support draining out from under him.

Annie applauded too, then realized she was probably obligated to show some kind of impartiality. This even after Self had tried to ban Annie and the crew on the grounds that they were an entertainment entity and not a news organization. All Annie had to do was flash her permit and roll the camera—The Man caught trying to shut down R^2Rev—and Self was forced to slink away impotently.

This was precisely the type of material Annie needed for the show. Quite obviously too civil, too sincere, for the average R^2Rev viewer, but if Viceroy's quixotic, not entirely cynical desire was to change some hearts, Kolak was the kind of politician who might do it: young (compared to the stereotypical politician), plain-spoken, and an outsider by virtue of his skin. Jerry Self, with his eight-dollar haircut and his badly chosen tie, was the archetype of a musty, passionless civic administrator. Frank Kolak bested him with humor and honesty, and in the same breath had the balls to scold the town's young people—his voter base—for being such putzes when they were around old people.

Annie still didn't know how this was going to cut together. No amount of flashy editing could make this more than a bunch of old farts kvetching about a bus stop. She suspected that R²Rev would ultimately decide that Viceroy's stodgy get-out-the-vote drive had no business on the pridefully mindless network, freeing her to find a more appropriate outlet for the material. PBS, for example, did documentaries like this all the time—muted studies of some minor slice of Americana, where folks were acting up in ways unexpected.

How would *that* sound to Viceroy: A joint effort of R²Rev and PBS, television's most profane and most cerebral linking up to shed light on one oddly compelling quirk in youth culture. He could still get his message out, but now with the dignified stamp of left-leaning Public Broadcasting. He might even get an award out of it, instead of the contempt and condemnation that most of his programming brought him.

She looked across the room and listened as Frank fielded more questions, not just from the retirees but from the public at large who had bothered to show up. When he didn't know the answer, he admitted it. When the opportunity presented itself to weave some of his reticent charm into a response, he went for it. In the same way Todd had picked the ideal figurehead in Joel, the kid had found what seemed to be a compelling candidate in the intellectual but likable Social Studies teacher.

A lot of people were apparently coming out to vote for the first time; Frank was a novice at the election process, too. Maybe that was what was so appealing about him. Together they'd take a shot at this democracy business, see if it was worth the trouble.

That's That

And then it was a kid—*dammit*—who brought it all down.

Because he was sixteen, because he was mean by habit and pumped to the gills with that corrosive teenage bile that required him to piss on anything that felt sincere or hopeful—*gay*—Dickinson junior Mike Barnstall came forward to gut the campaign.

He waited until he thought he would do the most damage, then he took the tape to Channel 4, hoping he'd be paid for the scoop. He had to be content with merely destroying a man.

"With election day just three days away," anchorman Brad Knight began, "the race for councilman in Berline's Sixth Ward has been shaken by evidence of criminal behavior by Frank Kolak, a Social Studies teacher at Dickinson High School who was looking to unseat incumbent Jerry Self.

"That evidence, seen here in videotape obtained exclusively by NewsMax 4…"

Cut back to the Happy Snack. Everything, inevitably, led back to the Happy Snack.

The amateur video darted and zipped oafishly through the parking lot crowd as the anchorman set up the piece in a voiceover. The images would appear to have come from the heady, early days of the protest, as things were still ramping up.

There were the packs of kids, waving dollar bills like banners and bouncing pennies off Daljit Singh's front door. There were Bobby Slopes, Wad Wendell, and the others mugging it up for a reporter from another station.

And there were Joel and Mr. Kolak, sitting on the hood of Joel's car. It was happenstance that they were caught on tape; it would've been missed if someone hadn't called attention to it.

But there they were, chillin'. And sharing a cigarette.

The station zoomed in on the image, turning it grainy, like surveillance footage: a teacher and his underage student, passing a cigarette between themselves.

They backed it up and froze it.

As everything began to fall away…

"…a minor at the time, technically putting Kolak in violation of the law. Beyond that, it is now calling into question the judgment of a man entrusted with the education of the community's children, and running on a platform of honesty and ethics.

"Our Bonnie Swerdlow talked to Dickinson High School junior Mike Barnstall, who brought us the tape."

There he was, his zits seeming to glow red with noxiousness, a snaky smile stretched across braces caked with crud.

He was so proud of himself.

"Can you tell me how you came into possession of this tape?" the reporter asked gravely.

"Just some friends, you know, had been dinkin' around with a video camera, down at the Happy Snack," Barnstall mumbled, "and I heard about something that they had accidentally filmed and so, like, I asked to see it and, you know, it was just wrong, far as I could see. I thought people should know about it."

"Do you know Frank Kolak? Has he ever been your teacher?"

An infinitesimal twinge of guilt passed briskly across Barnstall's face. "Yeah, I mean… He's all right. He's not…" He shrugged dimly. "I don't have a problem with him."

Something, perhaps regret, was threatening to touch him deep inside, so he ratcheted up the pose so as to kill it. "Adults are just such hypocrites, y'know? I mean, they tell you to do one thing, and then you see that they're doing something else and, y'know, we're just sick of it. Knowuddumsayin'?"

And there it was, horrid to behold: In the gluey recesses of his mind, the kid was doing a Joel Kasten of his very own. Lob a bomb, get yourself on TV, be famous for a minute or two. Just for a laugh.

The movement was now folding in on itself.

The report then cut to another taped interview. Marty Kasten, pleased again to find himself on camera, feigned outrage.

"I wanna know who this guy is," he said gruffly, kind of like a TV cop. "My son is an athlete! He has a future ahead of him, and his *teacher* is handing him cigarettes!! Who knows what else this guy has been exposing him to. Some of the stuff I hear about this guy, I'm not sure why he's being left alone with our kids."

"Your son is Joel Kasten, who has been getting a lot of attention lately for his various activities around town," the reporter interjected. "Have you spoken to him about this yet?"

Marty looked into the camera. "My son has been letting himself get led around by all sorts of people who have figured out that the kid isn't bright enough to see through their act. It's time for him to cut out this crap and get his head back in the game."

The reporter delivered her wrap-up: "Berline police are studying the tape to see if there is sufficient evidence to charge Kolak with contributing to the delinquency of a minor, a misdemeanor citation that carries a fine of just over one hundred dollars. Far more worrisome for the Kolak campaign, however, are the reactions of voters in Kolak's district, as well as administrators with Dickinson High School and the Berline school district, whom we have yet to be able to reach for comment.

"But if what we appear to be seeing on this tape turns out to be true, it would seem that Frank Kolak's teaching career, let alone his political aspirations, may be in serious jeopardy."

Frank's mother was watching this, alone in his apartment. Some kind of crisis had come up earlier in the day, and a shaken Frank had left her there without an explanation.

From out of nowhere, something was now pushing in on her from all directions. A maternal alarm she had not felt since he was a boy leapt up and choked her heart.

She looked around his apartment, really noticing for the first time how sparse and unsettled it looked.

"This is nothing!" Todd said as he paced frantically. "This is *nothing!*"

Joel was there, as were Annie and her camera guy. And Frank Kolak, silent as he sat alone at a picnic table a pace or two away. They had gathered in a park on the edge of town, hiding out from the reporters who were now after the candidate for comment.

Annie's camera circled and taped. She knew she should stay back, maintain her professional distance, but she was part of this.

"Todd..."

"He took a drag off a fucking cigarette! From a kid who was less than two months away from being eighteen! This is..." He came up short for words, then laughed at the ridiculousness of it. Because he could not bear the inevitability of it. "*This is nothing!!*"

"Todd," Annie said firmly, but with care, "the appearance of it is horrible." Frank felt a needle prick. "Especially now. He could be *fired* on Monday, the day before the election! You're going to have parents and adults out there, pointing at him as some kind of threat to their kids. You've got Joel's own father implying that he's gay!" Annie continued.

Todd and Joel winced at Annie's bluntness. They turned to Mr. Kolak, who registered no reaction.

"If they couldn't muster up enough votes before to counteract what you guys have managed to pull together, they sure can now. He's hanging out with his students, during school hours, sharing cigarettes with them!"

Joel kept out of it. He was only concerned about Mr. Kolak, but he didn't know what to say to him.

"These are the same adults who didn't lift a finger to stop that store from selling us cigarettes!" Todd spit. "These are the same adults... Jesus Christ, I could show you a couple dozen parents who let their kids smoke in their house, right in front of them. Are the cops going to arrest *them?*"

She took him by the shoulders to steady him; it appeared he might stroke out. She knew him well enough to understand that he felt the full weight of what his little prank had just brought down on Mr. Kolak.

"Todd. It is the *appearance*. If they want to, the press and the other side can turn this into a huge deal for the next three days, whether it really is or not."

"But we've still got our votes!" Joel blurted out, certain that this was not the time for surrender. He was standing protectively over his teacher. "They'll all see this for what it really is, and if they see that we're gonna lose over it, they'll come out in even bigger numbers, just because it's so fucking not fair!

"This is still Mr. Kolak we're talking about," he pleaded.

They all stopped and looked to Frank, his gaze frozen on the grass between his feet. Annie's cameraman was swarming around him like a wasp. She silently told him to move back.

Todd took a step toward him. "You could make a statement. You could apologize and say that... You could say that you didn't know Joel was seventeen. He's a senior. How's a teacher supposed to know if a kid has turned eighteen or not?"

"Frank?" Annie began gently. He was never her teacher, and though she addressed men 20 years her senior with familiarity every day in her career, it felt odd using his first name. "Teachers have the toughest unions in the country. They wouldn't let you get fired just for this, right? It could get ugly, but..."

Frank drew up his spine and stood, taking in a deep breath on an exquisite spring day.

"I am not going to hide behind my union," he said casually, almost jauntily. "I am not going to hide behind a lie.

"I did it. And that's that."

He stooped to pick up some pinecones and began tossing them at a tree trunk. He never came close to hitting it.

Todd, Joel, and Annie shared a confused look. "That's that *what?*" Todd asked.

He kept throwing wide of the tree.

"I have to quit."

Todd turned away as if spun around by a blow. Joel bore down.

"What? *Why?* You don't know how people are gonna respond to this! C'mon, Mr. Kolak, we still got a chance!"

The camera captured all this. Joel's hurt was raw, his plea desperate. He was 18 years old and he had the world by the balls and nothing mattered to him more than what was unraveling before him.

Something had gotten through.

"Joel," Frank said softly. Whatever his own hurt, he saw that the kid needed help through this. "It's too hard. People are going to be coming after me, saying things about me, and I won't know how to fight back. I wish I did, but I'm not..."

Like you.

Frank stopped, embarrassed by this soul-baring. And saddened by how much it soothed him, how much it made surrender palatable.

"I just need to quit."

Todd finally turned, a steeliness behind his damp eyes.

"What else are you quitting?"

They kept their distance, Todd and Mr. Kolak. A breeze blew between them.

Frank met Todd's glare. "That school won't keep me on. I'll be sparing them a fight."

Now Joel turned away. Todd leapt up and hung from a branch just beyond his reach. He was 17. That's what the moment told him to do.

Annie could only watch. She had no business now with these three.

"You're giving up," Todd said flatly, swinging slightly as he dangled from the tree.

"I'm guilty."

"You're giving up."

Mr. Kolak shrugged idly, conceding without betraying much regret.

"I've got other things I can do."

"Name 'em."

"I can teach."

"So teach here."

Frank stooped to grab more pinecones, stepping toward the tree. He was closer now, he could hit it.

"I'm not appreciated here."

Todd's palms began to burn. He refixed his grip as his arms ached. It mattered a lot that he not let go.

"What the hell do you think this is?!" Todd shouted. He nodded toward Joel, whose back was still turned to them. He was crying.

"You're children. I'm a man," Frank said. "I want to be respected by folks like me. I'd like that for myself." He was now standing before Todd, still hanging a foot off the ground. "I'd hope you'd like that for me, too."

Todd hung on stubbornly as Mr. Kolak stood there. He'd wait this out, smiling only slightly at the boy's losing battle.

Todd finally dropped to the ground, practically the same height as his teacher but looking up to him all the same. He had to accept this.

"I'm sorry for getting you into this," he said softly. "I shoulda left you alone."

"I didn't want to be alone," the teacher said. "You chased me outside, made me see some things in myself. Don't be sorry."

Todd would try not to be.

Their bond settled, they both looked to Joel, his shoulders heaving. Todd and Mr. Kolak were both touched and, to their mutual shame, slightly amused.

"Joel... ?" Frank asked gingerly.

The kid turned, completely without words.

"Fuck, dude," he blubbered. "Just... Fuck."

He trudged over to them and they fell into an embrace, a three-man huddle. When they broke, they'd be returning to separate games.

Annie watched, tears in her eyes and a wistful smile on her face.

Her cameraman taped it all. He was just doing his job.

Another Thing

Since he withdrew so late, there hadn't been time to take Frank's name off the ballot, so the chance had still been there to cast a symbolic vote for him.

When the final tally came in, he ran a strong second. If the adults hadn't been enticed to the polls to put down this degenerate who had been teaching their children, if some of the young and the black hadn't ended up staying home, disillusioned by the brutally cynical turn their first taste of politics had taken…

One would never know.

Annie had stayed in town, hoping for just such a dispiriting, what-might-have-been finale. Todd found her at a local video house, where R²Rev had rented space for her to put together a rough edit.

"Hey," he said weakly, peering into her editing bay.

"Hey." She smiled. The wound was still fresh, the aftermath still unfolding. She had not spent enough time with Todd and Joel, so busy was she documenting the final days of the campaign.

"How are you doing?" she asked sincerely.

He shrugged cavalierly, like he was already past it. "Seen the final numbers?"

"You would've won," she stated flatly. "If they had just left him alone, your guy would've won. That's going to come through."

Todd studied the frozen images on the various monitors.

There were Frank's earnest young supporters, canvassing neighborhoods.

There was the public access video of Frank before the City Council.

There was Todd, at the park, hanging from a tree.

It didn't feel right, seeing it all there. Almost like autopsy photos. Annie sensed his unease.

"That lesbian in Denver? She won. Easily," Annie said with enthusiasm. "Four or five other local campaigns around the country that can be attributed directly to what you guys started? All winners.

"And you know what? Who cares? Winning is boring."

Todd recoiled slightly.

"*This* is the story," she insisted, pointing to the monitors. "This is what's going to get our viewers' blood boiling. You guys proved that you can make a difference. You challenged the system. You put up a perfectly qualified candidate. You had victory wrapped up, and then the adults slapped you down. Over a cigarette in a parking lot," she sneered. "Kids will get that, and they'll understand why it's bullshit."

She pointed to the image of Frank before the Council. "Frank getting forced out created an opening for this whole race angle, how he had stirred up animosity by busting the city over how they were handling the Happy Snack, how he was already on thin ice with his school. They were gunning for this guy, because of his race.

"Frank lost, and that stinks," she concluded. "But I think the *way* he lost sends your message clearer than if he had won. My bosses think so, too."

He stared at her for a long while, replaying how they got here. It felt like they had finally reached a full stop.

"You know what? I think you should just let it go."

"W-what?"

"Mr. Kolak just wants this behind him. He wouldn't be comfortable with any of this," he said calmly, recalling how traumatic Frank's stand before the City Council had been. He thought back on how garish Annie's first show had turned out, and imagined how luridly the story would be played up here. He pictured that frozen, indicting image of Joel and Mr. Kolak passing a cigarette from mouth to mouth. A black man, a trusting white boy. The *gay* thing.

Ugh...

"I'm not comfortable with it either," he said, adding simply: "This is just something that happened to us. It's not for everybody else to look at."

"Todd," she said in astonishment. "This is *all* for everybody else to look at. I mean, what have I been doing here?"

"People got hurt by this," Todd said softly. "They could still get hurt. This isn't some game anymore."

She wasn't without compassion. None of this would have happened if she hadn't understood completely the frequency this kid ran on. She respected him, she really did.

And yet this was not acceptable.

"Money has been spent on this, Todd," she said bluntly, without rancor. "People are expecting it. My boss is ready to put this on the air as soon as I deliver it to him. It's going forward, there's nothing that can be done about that now."

He nodded to his image on the monitor. He had her.

"I'm a minor. You can't use my likeness without my parents' okay, and they won't give it. Mr. Kolak sure as hell isn't going to sign anything. Joel won't. You can't use any of this if we don't want you to."

Who *was* this kid? "There are ways around all that," she said. "They'll find a way. They always do."

Todd wasn't impressed. "I really think you need to let it go."

He turned and walked out. She was beautiful and connected and, if he played along, most likely a gateway to something else, but he turned and walked out.

He'd file this away, under cool things he did once.

She processed this in disbelief for a second or two, then followed him outside. She'd been holed up in the editing room all morning. The sun was bright. She squinted painfully as she touched his shoulder.

"Wait a minute!" she begged. "You'd really do this? You'd really just walk away after all the time you've put into this?"

He shrugged his shoulders dismissively. "Sure. I don't do what's expected of me," he said with a small grin. "As seen on TV."

She studied him intently, all the more intrigued and impressed.

Or maybe she *was* out to use him. That was the thing—even she couldn't tell.

She bit her lip pensively. "Okay, look. You've still got something they want, the 'We're Not Buying This Shit' thing," she said, drawing closer. "Under the circumstances, if you were to not work against us on this other thing, I really think you could make a lot of money. I would see to it that—"

"*No!*" he laughed in disgust as he pulled away. "It's not for sale! This is our *life*, what you're trying to get your hands on. You can't have it."

"Todd," she pleaded, for him, and for her career. "You're only hurting yourself. R²Rev runs this story, or they don't. It doesn't matter to them. *You* don't matter to them. The only way you come out a winner in this thing is if you take some money away from them, instead of the other way around. That's just the way it works."

He listened, because he knew she was right.

"You don't beat companies this big. You guys tried. You saw through their shit. You put the word out, and you put a dent in a few balance sheets for a few weeks, and that was marvelous. And when I said you didn't matter to them, I was full of shit, because you can bet that a lot of people—a lot of powerful people—have been watching closely to see how far you guys could take this thing.

"But kids are still smoking," she said sadly. "Kids are still buying shitty music and one-hundred-and-fifty-dollar basketball shoes and whatever else they've tricked you into thinking you can't live without. With you guys swinging at everything, there was no way you were going to stop any of it."

She rubbed his shoulder and gave him a sympathetic smile. "There are just too many things to not buy."

Todd remained silent, as a notion struck him.

He turned inward, the way he did whenever a bold vision introduced itself. If Frank Kolak were here, he'd be rocketing for the horizon like a cartoon rabbit right about now.

Todd Noland had a new idea.

"Look, your show—it's not gonna happen," he said a little urgently, the new plot still unfurling in his mind. "You have to go home. You can't be here for this next thing."

Annie didn't like the sound of this. "What next thing?"

He was already seeing it play out. "It's gonna be…" He looked at her. He foresaw something bad befalling her.

"You have to go home."

She laughed nervously. "Todd? *What* next thing?"

"People can get hurt in these things, Annie," he said soberly. "Put some distance between us. If you do, you might be okay."

Fattening Frogs for Snakes

The machine was primed.

The *Freakal Matter* marketing assault that had been planned and incrementally rolled out over the past six months had tripped and triggered itself through a series of carefully orchestrated press availabilities and media stunts, bringing the CD-buying public to lubricated readiness for the album's April 27 release.

Scroat's undeniably flaccid performance at the *VideoYears* had been tempered somewhat by the brief scandal caused by his toilet paper prank. A hastily arranged series of live dates, in which he headlined a roster of Tok$ic's fresher hip-hop acts, shored up any concerns about the rapper's touring popularity, although more than one critic noted that the set list for these dates leaned heavily on tracks from *Right White Nigga*. After a rapid shot to the top of R²Rev's request list, "Dingleberry" had faded quickly, and there was a subdued panic among ScroatM's handlers over what to rush out as the next single. Despite fifteen available tracks on the new album, their choices were really limited to only six or seven. The harsher songs—the fag stuff, the bitch stuff, the gonna-chop-up-my-mama-and-feed-her-to-the-dog stuff—were clearly too profane to spin off as separate revenue-generating entities from the album, even with the crude censorship jobs that artists routinely allowed in order to make their work more radio-friendly. These more repellent (more satiric?) tracks would ship silently, tucked away inside the disk, and assault the 13-year-olds seduced by the sophomoric charms of "Dingleberry."

R²Rev, burned both by Scroat's performance and his pre-show meltdown at the *VideoYears,* and well aware of the subdued pre-release tracking for the new album, nevertheless honored the promotional commitments Hutch had made. Even if his musical time had passed, there was still the speculation that ScroatM could be retooled as an actor in youth-oriented thug fare, with

R²Rev⁴Films having any number of scripts in development into which he could be inserted as a marketing component. Relationships, therefore, had to be preserved.

So Scroat did his scheduled walk-ons on various R²Rev shows, and dutifully showed up to record celebrity gas for *Bowel Cloud Theatre*, although when it turned out that the artist could not deliver, the flatulence of others was credited to him.

All Tok$ic was hoping for with the new disk was a strong street date pop, one great rush of sales that might not translate into a hit down the line but would earn them a few positive headlines in the trades and the props of the industry. The gaudy influx of cash from *Right White Nigga* had allowed the label to sign and develop a wide roster of promising young acts, and the sense shared in only the most private of meetings was that their lives would be much easier (and their cut much richer) if future fortunes were tied to artists they had groomed to serve at their command, rather than the increasingly demanding and unmanageable ScroatM.

Freakal Matter, then, might best serve as a bridge of sorts to a re-dedicated Tok$ic Records. A diversified Tok$ic, their financial team had stressed, was the best hedge against the vagaries of the market and the inevitable volatility of artist-label relations.

So there was a lot riding on *Freakal Matter*.

Kill Shot

The "next thing" Todd had promised came for Annie just a few days after she got back to New York. She was still smarting over the heat she had taken for returning home without the election piece, and for the lack of professionalism she had shown by not locking up releases before they became an issue. She insisted that there were ways to finesse their way around the legalities, but she could tell that Viceroy's enthusiasm was waning yet again and that a fight was unlikely.

All for the best, Annie thought. If this thing could just fade away due to apathy, the stink of her own failures might not follow her to whatever her next job was going to be. Wherever that job was going to be.

But then she was called into Viceroy's office, where Hutch and some MediaTrust lawyers were waiting grim-faced with a couple of Guidos whom Annie quickly learned were the proprietors of Tok$ic Records. The mood in the room was black with menace-laden male fury. And they all looked to Annie as if they intended to extract something that would restore their sunshine.

A chair had been held for her in front of Viceroy's desk. She sat down, a kind of terror rising in her chest.

"Do you have any explanation for this?" Viceroy asked darkly, swiveling his computer screen towards her. She leaned in to watch some concert footage. It was ScroatM in rehearsal at the *VideoYears*. And the dingleberries. Startled when the moment came, Annie stifled a woefully ill-timed giggle as she watched the skulking rapper get blown backwards by the cannon shot. She had been elsewhere when the accident happened at Radio City, but word of the mishap had spread throughout R²Rev. It turned out to be as funny as it had sounded.

Annie composed herself and watched with professional regret as ScroatM went spastic and started getting beat up by his own men. The video was shaky, obviously amateur, but it was all there.

Viceroy shut down the image as everyone studied her.

"Where did you get that?" she asked nervously, still not knowing what this had to do with her.

"It's on the internet," Viceroy glowered.

"Oh," she said with appropriate concern. "Well, you know… It's like a blooper kind of thing. It's just an accident that happened. ScroatM has a sense of humor about himself. He could have some fun with this."

"Ain't nothing funny about any of this," one of the Tok$ic guys said through clenched teeth.

"Oh. Well, I'm not sure how I—"

"Shut up," Viceroy snapped.

He turned again to his computer, and Annie's heart sank. Because there on the screen was Joel Kasten—*her* Joel Kasten—interacting with ScroatM backstage at the awards show. And getting himself eviscerated by the cruel and seemingly unbalanced rap singer. It was gruesome to watch, a truly rare glimpse into the toxic soul of a superstar.

This was on the internet, too.

"You brought that kid here," Hutch said tersely. This was going to be good.

"Well, I… *We…*" she turned to Viceroy, who stared back with shark's eyes. He would not be taking the fall for any of this.

"You were in charge of keeping an eye on him," Hutch scolded.

Annie was in full panic. She looked from face to face, realizing that she was in desperate, desperate trouble.

"This is running on his website?"

"It's the *only* thing running on his website," Viceroy said. "He's pulled down all other content, and he's got sister sites all over the country feeding into this one.

"*It's fucking everywhere!*"

Annie gulped. "What can I—?"

Viceroy slammed his phone down in front of her and jabbed open the speaker, so that the dial tone sliced through the strain in the room.

"You give him a handjob if you have to, but you had better take care of this."

All eyes singed her as she clumsily punched in Todd's number. It rang several times before he picked up.

"Hello?"

"Todd?" she began, speaking slowly and firmly. "You have to take it down. You have to take it down right now."

He was obviously anticipating this call.

"We will. On Saturday."

Hutch lurched toward the phone, needing to beat somebody up in front of Viceroy in order to come out of this with a win.

Annie glared and thrust out a hand to silence him. She knew Todd needed to be handled.

"Saturday? Why Saturday?" she asked calmly.

"We've got something else going up Saturday. It's the best thing yet."

Annie shivered at the thought. The others in the room saw her reaction and grew even more unsettled. "You'll never get that far," she said, hoping the concern was coming through her voice. "Someone will figure out how to shut you down."

"Ira says try and find him," he said casually. "We're going to start teasing this new thing this afternoon. Keep watching."

Hutch sneered into the speaker phone.

"Look, kid, you are in some serious shit here. That video was obtained illegally. 'Dingleberry' is copyrighted material. You keep circulating that shit and I *promise* you that the entire recording industry is going to want to see your ass thrown in jail!"

"Who is this?"

"This is Hutch Posner, President of Programming at R²Rev."

"Oh," Todd said meekly. Then: "Hey, could I request a video?"

Hutch absorbed the outrage and opened his mouth to fire back, but Todd hung up. The dial tone filled the room again as Annie smiled sweatily.

"I'm really pretty," she wanted to say. "Could I cash that in here?"

The illicit, bootlegged quality of the ScroatM videos, combined with the fact that they were available freely on the net, made them perfect fare for tabloid television and hot-for-a-topic cable news shows. With ScroatM awareness already reaching its peak with the *Freakal Matter* marketing push, it made perfect sense to further sate the public's interest in all things Scroat by playing up this embarrassing, unflattering portrait of the controversial singer. Those who loved him would tune in out of curiosity, while those who despised him could enjoy the satisfaction of seeing him exposed. It was no-lose programming.

Here and there, there were actually some thoughtful discussions of what the second clip—the Joel clip—revealed about the dark truths of the relationship between fans and celebrities. For the most part, though, it was just disposable, voyeuristic nonsense, a couple days' worth of diversion until something new came along.

But not for young CD-buyers. True, many of ScroatM's earlier fans were already planning to take a pass on *Freakal Matter*, but the core, his marketers hoped, would not succumb to the vague sense that the rapper had crossed that unforgiving line into yesterday—at least not until after they bought the new CD. Everything they had originally cherished about Scroat, everything he attacked on the new album—civility, authority, those who can't fight back—teenagers hated them, too, and vastly more than when his first album came out. There was still a kind of synergy to be exploited.

But now, here he was, caught on tape attacking *them*. Joel had become a kind of stand-in for the kids following his adventures. Seeing him ripped apart by the rapper, it wasn't hard to put themselves in his place. Teenagers are an easily aggrieved bunch, and easily betrayed. They can spray their contempt in all directions without a thought to the effect it has on others. But let someone mistreat *them*, and their collective soul fairly aches at the injustice. It *is* a big, mean world, just like their years of sulking had told them.

From R²Rev, they had been inundated with countless images of ScroatM in repose, in his mansions in Miami Beach, and Manhattan, and L.A., tooling around in limos and private jets, his flesh pierced with diamonds and gold, starlets on his arm. They knew *they* had made all that possible. They had believed in this guy, even when he started covering his ass by saying that he didn't actually mean anything he rapped. It was a *character* he was playing, he said. It was just pretend.

But that was no character on the Joel tape. That was a real guy, caught raw with no handlers or producers or media to explain away the loathsomeness. ScroatM *hated* Joel. And Joel was them.

And hate has a way of coming back on you.

http://www.notbuyingthisshit.com

Lube Up, Gomer!

Here's the deal: We fucked up.

Instead of protesting one thing we protested everything, and no way we're going to win that way.

Here's how we DO win:

ScroatM's new CD goes on sale this Tuesday. DON'T BUY IT!!! If you HAVE to have it, buy it next week. Or even better, find it on the internet for free. It'll be there if you know where to look. (Hint, hint)

But DO NOT buy it on Tuesday. There are fuckers with calculators who will be standing by to see how many of us are dumb enough to buy that piece of shit. The first week is killer for them. If we stay home, they are fucked and WE WIN ha ha ha ha ha☐

ScroatM is an asshole and a fraud (LINK TO VIDEO). If you give him any more of your money, you are an idiot and a tool.

WE CAN DO THIS!!! Just don't buy ScroatM's new CD on Tuesday—how fucking hard is that? Keep your money in your pocket and the asswipes who have been fucking with us forever will know we have the power and they had better cut the shit out. OR ELSE!!

Okay? Make something of yourselves, for Christ's sake.

Signed,

Joel Kasten

Content

The new content went up early Saturday night. The hype leading up to its debut had breathlessly promised something outrageous, so some of the tens of thousands of kids seduced into checking in were bitterly disappointed by the single page of text. Ira had lobbied for some kind of aesthetic flash, but Todd knew that simplicity was the answer here. This generation had been sand-blasted with meaningless noise and imagery every conscious hour of its day. It was a gamble, but Todd felt the starkness of the new manifesto would appear sufficiently urgent. Word had to spread quickly. There was no time for distraction.

And it wasn't like he was ordering them to take to the streets or anything. For the plan to work, all Todd needed was for America's youth to do absolutely nothing—something at which they were particularly gifted. But the message sent at the cash registers, if this one specific product was left on the shelves despite millions of dollars being spent to ensure its sale, would be huge.

"It's like a chain," Todd kept saying. "We're on one end, and they're on the other. If we yank, they'll feel it."

The boycott did not need to be total, and in fact Todd planned to be first in line on Tuesday to buy the CD—so that he could hand it to Ira, who would then digitize it and send it out to the world for free.

Sales projections for the first week were easy to find. The morons from Tok$ic had been hyping grossly inflated numbers for weeks, while trade publications were offering more modest predictions. But the benchmark was there: Any number that came in dramatically lower than what was expected would be a dire warning to the industries that relied upon the lumpish compliance of its young consumers.

And if ScroatM got wrecked in the process? "That's the beauty part," as Joel would say.

Wack, Indeed

"This is wack!" ScroatM bitched, stomping his foot so hard his baggies nearly slid off his narrow hips. "I mean, what the fuck, Artie? What the fuck?"

"The fuck do I know?" shot back Artie Pistone, Scroat's manager. They were in his high-toned Manhattan office, which featured Scroat's gold and platinum albums from his first CD. "Nobody wants to buy the fuckin' record. What am I supposed to do about it?"

The first day's figures had been horrific—barely half of what had been projected. All across America, kids were staying home, or coming out to the stores specifically to make their sentiments known. Pennies were lobbed here and there. At a Target store in Tucson, some kid took bits of chewing gum and methodically cemented one single cent across Scroat's face on every unsold CD. In a FedEx package traveling somewhere between Barstow, CA, and the headquarters of Tok$ic Records, fifteen-year-old Joe Muniz had placed the busted pieces of *Right White Nigga* along with the CD packaging, with which young Mr. Muniz had apparently wiped his ass.

Dissing ScroatM had become the thing to do. It might only last a few days. But that would be enough.

"The fuck does the label say?" the artist asked anxiously.

"They're bringin' in hula girls for the big fuckin' party. The fuck do you think they're gonna say?" Pistone growled. "What they're *not* gonna say is that they're movin' on, which is exactly what they're lookin' to do. Mark my fuckin' words."

"Moving on?" ScroatM sounded small and wounded.

"Cuttin' you loose. You're over, far as they're concerned. Who needs this shit? You've got every kid in America wantin' to tear you a new asshole."

"But..." Scroat said sadly. "I was just satirizing—"

"Will you shut the fuck up? Just lemme think here. Lemme think."

Pistone struck a pose approximating deep thought as ScroatM got revved up, pacing around the office feverishly. He had spent most of the day, the day *Freakal Matter* had gone out into the world, ingesting whatever he could get his hands on to take his mind off his troubles. Now the toxins were manifesting themselves in jarring bursts of manic highs and desperate lows.

"I'm gonna kick that kid's ass, that's what I'm gonna do," he said darkly. He drew up to the plate glass window overlooking the city and drove a fist into it full force. It trembled but did not break.

"Fuckin' little hillbilly shit, fuckin' with my thing." He started bouncing on the balls of his feet, throwing punches. "*Bam!* How you like that, Gomer? *Bam!* I'll punch you dead and fuck your mama, whatja think of that, little bad-ass hillbilly motherfucker?"

Pistone wearily ignored this as he tried to think.

Finally, after much struggle, a brainstorm arrived. He mulled it over for a couple minutes, watching it play out in his mind. Then he bent his fat frame toward the intercom on his desk.

"Get me DeNunzio at Tok$ic."

"Fuck, yeah," ScroatM slurred. "Bring them on, too. I'll kick their fat fucking Mafia asses clear back to Italy."

Pistone lifted himself out of his chair and came around his desk, seemingly willing to spar with his distraught client.

"You want some, too, fat ass?" Scroat leered playfully, throwing more air punches. "Let's go. I'll take you—"

Pistone calmly placed a meaty thumb and forefinger on the pressure point at the base of ScroatM's skull. If he pinched hard, the singer would pass out. If he pinched harder, he'd die. So he had this to work with.

ScroatM immediately started flailing and whining like a little girl. "Ow. C'mon, Artie. Quit it. I mean it, man. Please? Ow!"

Pistone flung him toward the overstuffed sofa on the other side of the room. Scroat hit it and curled up in a ball to protect himself against further assault. When none came, he peeked out from behind the hands he had brought protectively to his face.

"You had a good idea," Pistone said solemnly. "About the kid."

"About kicking his ass?"

"Yeah, but not that. You're gonna go see him. And you're gonna make nice."

The singer scoffed bitterly. "Fuck dat shit."

"Tok$ic," Pistone's assistant announced. He turned and hit the speaker phone.

"Albert," Pistone began forcefully. "We got us a plan. We're gonna go to this piss-ant town, this Berline, and we're gonna mend fences. Scroat's gonna perform a free show, right there in Mayberry. We'll see how long this boycott lasts when the real deal is right there in front of them for the only live concert that fucking armpit of a town has probably ever seen."

ScroatM listened, knowing that just about anything had to be considered to ride this one out.

"Artie…" the guy from Tok$ic begged off. "We got caught with our pants down on this one. We just gotta eat shit and move on. We can't—"

"Listen, you fuck," Artie shot back. "And I know you got Jimmy and Molto standing right there with you, so you two geniuses listen, too. We gotta fix this. You get a bunch of kids thinking they can sink an album, sink a career, just 'cause they *can*, and we are fucking dead. All of us. And you cheapjack, talent-jobbing record labels are gonna be the first to go. Mark my fucking words." Pistone eased up slightly. "We gotta get those kids buyin' again. We gotta put their heads right."

Silence, then muted mumbles were heard from Tok$ic headquarters. You could feel the fear-laden surrender coming through the line.

Finally: "When?"

"I got product on the shelf *now*," Pistone said. "I need this taken care of *now*. We'll go this Saturday night."

"It's Tuesday!" the record company protested.

"What, he's gotta bring in the fucking Philharmonic? He's a fucking rap singer. His whole fucking act fits in a shoebox! You give him a microphone and a playback, and he screams 'Mary Had A Little Fucking Lamb' for forty-five minutes!"

ScroatM flinched as a long silence filled the room.

"All right," DeNunzio sighed. "Let's do it."

"*Then* you're gonna call Posner or whoever you gotta call at R²Rev, and you're gonna make sure they're there to cover it. Ain't no fucking point in doing this if the whole world don't see that these kids are puttin' out for ScroatM again. You follow? They fucked us on this in the first place," Pistone said, referring to R²Rev. "Ain't no label in town gonna do business with them if they don't put this right."

Annie had been fired—as far as she knew—that day in Viceroy's office, the day Todd had teased the ScroatM boycott and then cut all ties to the network. She slunk from the room under the hateful glares of furious, powerful men, retrieved her coat and a photo of her cat from her office, and went home. No one actually told her to not come back. No one had to. The absoluteness of her screw-up didn't require the official confirmation of an actual termination. She just had to go away.

She had a computer, though, so she holed up in her airless apartment and watched Todd pull the trigger on his kill shot. He had been right—he did set loose the troubles upon Annie, and how—but he was now also truly, breathtakingly dangerous. Amidst the hype he had generated, he had kept his head. He had sifted through the treacherousness of the marketplace, the detachment of his peers, and the mind-boggling technology available to him, and rather than let his initial brainstorm dissipate in the face of the vastness of it all, he had brought it to one fine, sharp point.

If this new campaign against ScroatM didn't work, Annie knew, the next one would. Todd had hacked his way into the guts of a system ill-equipped to deal with such a determined insurrectionist.

She was proud of him, but fearful for his safety.

And she would be seeing him soon.

"Would it work?" Viceroy asked her intently. "Would they go?"

The ringing of the phone had startled her, because absolutely no one had called her since she left work. Those above her were through with her. Those on her level could not afford to associate with her. And there was no one lower than her. Her family still didn't know what had happened, and there was no reason to have any further dealings with the boys in Berline. She was utterly alone, so she had jumped when the phone rang.

When she heard Hutch's voice on the other end, sounding gentle and concerned, she assumed he would be trying merely to weasel his way into a consolation lay. Instead, he told her that he had been given the awkward chore—with no option for failure—of bringing Annie back in to the office to help put out, once and for all, the fire that Todd and Joel had started.

"They've got no hold on you, Annie. They fired you before they even called you into Viceroy's office," said Hutch, sounding genuinely sincere—which put Annie on full alert. "You'd have every reason to tell them to go fuck themselves. But this industry has a short memory, you know? Help make this one thing go away, and you could find yourself back on the inside. You're too talented to not get a second chance. I really believe that."

"Hutch?" she asked, stretching out his name playfully. "If I don't come in, what happens to you?"

"Dunno," he said, really not knowing. "There's always *The Nipple Room*."

She laughed, so he laughed. Had they ever really laughed together before?

Sure, she'd come in. What the hell?

"You are the only one who knows those kids," Viceroy said to Annie, the moment she entered his office. "If ScroatM goes to Berline, this weekend, and does a free concert, would they show up?"

She turned to Hutch. This was their plan?

"I don't know!" she laughed derisively, now entirely free of any supplication she may have once thought was due Viceroy.

"You have to know!" he replied desperately. "If we cover this and it's a disaster, then tape of *that* will end up on the internet. It'll be the proof they need to show they're having an effect. Who will they decide to fuck with next?"

"Tok$ic won't go in unless they can be sure of a turnout," Hutch added. "They can't afford the embarrassment. They've made it very clear that they need this to work, and they're looking to us to make it work. We've got quite a mess to clean up, thanks to you."

She stared at them, astonished by their arrogance. "You can't *make* kids do something they don't want to do. I know you think you can, but it's not that simple."

"Listen to what I'm saying," Viceroy said firmly, deliberately, like he was talking to a slow child. The condescension was galling. "All we're asking of you is your best read of the situation. Given the lack of sophistication in that market, given the transient nature of their commitment, would this boycott fall apart if a genuine rap star turned up to perform, for free, just for them?"

She felt the heat pouring off these two men, these shapers of culture who were horrified at the thought of losing control. She sized up the situation and committed.

"Poll it," she said with confidence. "You've got phone crews running 'round the clock, polling kids all over the country to find out what they're interested in. Put this one in the mix, limit the sample to Berline and adjacent towns, and fold the question in with a bunch of innocuous ones so they don't get wise. Put it on fast turnaround and you could have the results by tomorrow afternoon."

Viceroy and Hutch listened intently. Why hadn't *they* thought of this? (If it worked, it'd turn out that they had.)

"Say you get a thousand Definites or Very Favorables, which I don't think would be unreasonable," Annie continued. "So you book him into a venue that only holds five hundred—you're coming in at the last minute, so you'll be limited in where he could play anyway. You'll practically be guaranteed a full house, with a pack of disappointed turnaways out front, for us to put on camera, swearing their devotion to ScroatM. Edit the piece properly and the little shit will come out looking like Elvis. Problem solved."

Both men stroked their chins pensively. It was never easy to admit that someone lesser than you had the answer.

"We could poll tonight?" Hutch asked urgently. Viceroy looked at his watch, realizing it would be close. He grabbed his phone.

"Get me Research, tell them I've got a priority project," he barked, then turned to Annie. "If it's a go, I want you there."

"I don't work here anymore."

"Don't be cute."

Viceroy waited for his call to be put through while Annie winked at Hutch with a smart smile. She rolled up onto her toes for a second, then sank back to the floor, scarcely able to contain her pride.

Then she ran to get ready. She was going to make this happen.

Definite Maybe

They found a 1,200-seat theatre in Waterville, just across the line from Berline. An AIDS hospice was holding a fundraiser Saturday night, with performances by local bands and minor celebrities, and Tok$ic simply wrote them a check for twice what they could've hoped to earn and told them to go away. The polling, which was extended to a second day just to make sure, had been remarkably strong. Almost 1,000 kids left no doubt that they'd be there, and almost that many insisted they'd try. Even with the expected drop-off, the turnout would be great. Artie Pistone listened in on some of the calls and smiled contentedly. Some of these kids sounded ready to piss their pants, they were so happy at the thought of ScroatM coming to their town.

As soon as the site was nailed down, Tok$ic's field reps hit up local hip-hop radio stations to alert them to the last-minute booking, calling in all favors to get them to announce the free concert as often and as insistently as possible. They papered the malls, clubs, skate parks, and movie theatres with fliers, and handed them out as close as they could to Dickinson and other schools without violating the law.

Anyone polled who had expressed an interest in the then-hypothetical concert would receive a call back, providing the specifics. R²Rev ran alerts hourly. Despite the franticly spontaneous origins of the gig, awareness was going to be high.

The plan was for Scroat to fly into the local airport with a drastically scaled-back entourage, partly because it was decided he needed to cool the millionaire stuff, and partly because the record company had no interest in spending any more than they had to on this potentially lost cause. Scroat would hit the town well after dinner, lay low until the eleven o'clock show—during which he would perform a truncated, hour-long set—then be back to the airport before bar time. The quality of the performance, the lack of technical aesthetics, would have to be good enough. A lot was being banked on the spectacle of ScroatM's visit wowing the locals so thoroughly that they wouldn't dare be so ungracious as to complain about any shortcomings.

R²Rev—in the form of Hutch, Annie, and a small crew—would arrive separately, making at least an effort to separate their interests from Tok$ic's.

When they were in the air, Hutch showed Annie a piece of paper as he gave her her assignment for when they hit ground. He saw the disappointment on her face as she read the transcript.

"This doesn't sound like him," she said sadly.

"It is," Hutch chortled. "They actually polled Joel Kasten! And listen to him, the little shit can't wait to see a ScroatM concert!"

Annie fought this off. "He says he *might* go. He's a sweet kid. He probably thought he'd hurt the interviewer's feelings if he said no."

"He scored a Definite Maybe. The kid who started this whole damned mess is tempted to bag all this boycott shit and come out to party. If we get him, it's over."

"He won't come," Annie shook her head confidently.

"You'd better hope he does," Hutch said ominously. "You'd better make sure he does."

The message was clear. She turned and stared out the window.

"He'll make the scene with that hot piece of ass from R²Rev," said Hutch. "He'll bring all his friends. We'll hook him up with Scroat after the show. Scroat'll apologize for dissing him the time before, load the kid up with autographs and shit. Maybe share some weed, pass the peace pipe, if that's his thing. It'll be a beautiful moment."

Hutch put his hand on Annie's knee. "Bring me that moment."

— ◉— —

Joel already knew that Wad Wendell was going to be there, and Slopes, and pretty much the whole football team. As soon as word got out about what was being offered them, the chance they'd do the right thing turned to zero. They were just teenagers, neither wise like Todd, nor smooth like Joel. They were clowns; they did dumb shit. They were gonna do what they were gonna do.

Joel's every instinct told him to stay away, to give his boys his reluctant blessing but leave them to this thing that they could not resist. He had his future to think about. If public sentiment turned against those who started this whole thing, if laws ended up broken, it could harm his career. But and—it hurt Joel to think this—for Wad and the others this could be the biggest thing that ever happens to them. *Ever.*

And yet here he was, driving to meet them. Annie had called. He knew she was back in town, down at the theatre gathering material for the network. In her sweetest voice, she told him that it was time for him to drop the act. That he should come on over, and she couldn't wait to see him.

Maybe she could put him on camera one last time.

— ◆ —

When Todd realized it was inevitable, he knew he would have to attend as well. As mastermind of all this, he felt duty bound to be there for the final blow, to pay his respects as something that had once loomed so large passed into nothingness. What was about to go down at that theatre was going to be sad, too painful to observe, but he knew he would regret it later if he weren't there.

On a whim, he called Frank Kolak to see if he'd like to join him. The disgraced teacher had had a role in this thing—and had paid the biggest price of all—so maybe he should be there, for closure. Todd worried about Frank; no one had seen him much since he resigned. Word was going around that he might drive his mother home down South, and maybe stay. There was nothing keeping him in Berline anymore.

"I don't know," Frank said, typically skittish. "It's really not appropriate that we *hang out* together."

"You're not my teacher anymore. You're just my friend. I might even start calling you Frank, Frank."

He smiled, but refused. "Look, you go on down, and let me know how it turns out. I'll want to know if it's as awful as you're making it sound."

"Please?" Todd begged. "Joel's already over there. He's got his whole thing going on with Annie." His disappointment was unmistakable. "Who knows where he's gonna be? I just don't want to do this by myself."

Frank sighed and knew that his mother would be okay alone for a couple hours. He wasn't long for this town anyway. He'd do what he felt like doing.

He told Todd to swing by and get him.

"Ha ha ha ha ha…"

If you stood to the far right corner of the window in the bridal suite of the Berline Ramada and strained an eyeball past some duct work on the roof, you could make out a few square feet of sidewalk in front of the Uptown Theatre. It wasn't an ideal view—perhaps there was more going on than he could see—but from ScroatM's vantage point, something appeared to have gone horribly wrong.

"We're fucked, Artie," he whined. "We are bare-assed fucked."

He looked to the street below, where he had expected to see legions of his fans, howling at the moon, nipping off cigarettes and beers, maybe throwing a rock through a window to announce their evening agenda as they descended on the theatre. He had watched it happen before, pretty much every night on the *Nigga* tour, and it had been glorious to behold.

But now it was under an hour to show time, and kids were only showing up in stray handfuls. For a free concert. By a guy who thought he'd have the number one album in the country right now.

"Oh, Artie," ScroatM sniffed, close to tears.

"Move!" the manager barked, shoving the singer away and wedging himself into the small corner from which he could see the theatre.

He spotted Hutch Posner. They were already linked by cell phone.

"I am not believing what I'm seeing," Pistone said darkly.

Hutch looked to the hotel across the street and understood that he was being watched. He continued to pace anxiously. The entryway of the Uptown was empty, deathly quiet. Security guards were stationed at the front door with metal detectors and menacing scowls, but they hadn't had any business for over ten minutes. Every so often, a small pack of kids would round the corner toward the theatre, one of them inevitably letting loose with the celebratory "*wooooo*" of the young male bonehead approximating debauchery. But when they were met by the library-like stillness, and by the harried glare of Hutch Posner, they lowered their eyes and skulked inside sheepishly.

Several kids, who knew a bum party when they saw one, simply turned and went off in search of something more happening. The R²Rev cameraman was ordered, at the threat of his life, not to shoot any of this.

Hutch's head ached. "I don't know. We've just got to wait."

"It's fifty minutes until the fucking show!" Pistone sneered. "How many have you let in?"

Hutch chewed the inside of his mouth. "Four hundred. Maybe."

"Four hundred! In a twelve-hundred-seat house?!" Artie wheezed. "We're gonna get fuckin' tattooed on this, you piece a shit! You and your fucking boss—"

"Look," Hutch said sternly, not willing to take this kind of abuse from a mere manager. "You saw the same numbers we did. There was a statistical certainty that we could pull this off. They *told* us they'd be here!"

Hutch turned hopefully as he heard several feet approaching. His spirits soared as he recognized Annie, Joel, Todd, and that black teacher, but they sank again when he saw no crowd trailing behind them. Something was wrong.

"Stay in the room till you hear from me!" he ordered Pistone, then he hung up and got in Joel's face.

"What? What's going on? Where is everybody?!"

Joel hunched his shoulders casually, in a fashion sure to inflame the tightly-wound New Yorker. "Dunno."

"Where are all your fucking friends?"

"They're here," Joel insisted. "Didn't you see the guys from the football team go in?"

"But…" Hutch gestured helplessly, as if waving his arms would fill the foyer of the theatre with teenagers and deliver him from this mess. Annie stifled a grin as she watched him twitch. She knew he had never been responsible for a field shoot. He had never seen how easily these things could unravel.

"You had hundreds, *thousands* doing what you said!"

"Hey, look, they're their own people. They make up their own minds. Turns out I can't influence them any easier than you can."

A fully dressed-out hip-hop caricature emerged from the shadowy sidewalk and swaggered dourly toward the theatre all alone.

"Thanks for coming out!" Joel said, waving brightly.

"Fuck you," the kid sneered as he went inside.

Joel dismissed it with a shake of his head. "Kids. They outgrow you so fast."

Hutch slapped his palm into the dossier he had been clinging to. "But they *said* they'd be here." He tore through the pages of data. "These kinds of numbers don't lie."

"Well, yeah," Todd said, rubbing his nose idly, having earned the right to bring his point home. "But teenagers do. It's one of their best things.

"Somebody polls you, you're not under oath. Make stuff up. Lie," he said. "Could cause problems."

Hutch's fingers dug into the glossy cover of the polling report. "All of them? How could they *all* have known to… ?"

Annie, Todd, and Joel girded themselves for an assault as Hutch stopped to piece it together. Frank Kolak, just now figuring it out along with Hutch Posner, shook his head with awed bemusement—yet again.

"We e-mailed alerts to everyone in the area who ever visited our site. Except you guys," Todd explained. "We knew you and the record company were giving us hits, because Ira had already hacked into your systems to compile a list of all your internal screen names. Whenever there was a match, it went into the filter. Everybody but *you* was told how to respond when the call from the polling place came. The rest was just word of mouth."

Hutch turned darkly to Annie, because he now knew her role in this. She bit her lower lip fetchingly as she eased her way behind Todd and Joel for cover.

"You knew we were going to poll?" Hutch asked Todd through gritted teeth, his eyes never leaving Annie. "You *told* everyone not to show?"

"She played you, dude," Joel drawled. "Totally."

Hutch lashed out to get at her. Todd and Joel stepped protectively in front of her, and Frank stepped in front of them. Pricked by a burst of adrenaline, he shoved the R²Rev honcho in the chest and threw him backward.

"You want trouble?" the teacher asked with a kind of strut. Joel and Todd went wide-eyed—Mr. Kolak would get his ass kicked if there was an actual fight.

Instead, Frank gestured to the curb. Patrol cars had been circling all night, on high alert because of the concert. A pair of cops were standing outside their cruiser, watching the strained exchange with bored interest.

Hutch backed down with a furious glare. He turned his back on his tormentors, thought for a second, then bitterly jabbed at his phone.

"*What?*" Pistone asked on the first ring.

"We've been fucked," Hutch said, breaking off each word brittlely as he faced the Ramada window. "Four hundred is all we're getting."

Artie was already throwing things into his valise. "All right. We're outta here."

ScroatM was standing gratefully at the door. He had hoped this would be the answer.

"Wait a minute!" Hutch shouted into the phone. Artie kept packing as he cradled the cell.

"We do not go on for four hundred fucking yokels in the middle of Buttfuck, Illinois!!"

"If he bails on this, with everything else going on, his career is fucking over, you fat son of a bitch!" Hutch shouted. Todd and Joel snorted and made mocking scared faces as they listened to such high-level music business. "This could be the last four hundred kids in the whole country who give a fuck about your boy, and now he's gonna shit on them, too?"

Artie stopped packing. He cursed the logic he was hearing.

"You put him out there for a half-hour," Hutch suggested, trying to picture the eventual media coverage. "'The turnout wasn't what he expected, but ScroatM sucked it up and put on the show of his life, because he knew he had to do right by the kids who turned out.'"

Then he adddded, "It might not work, but it might be all you get."

Hutch waited out a long pause.

"All right, we're comin' down," Pistone grumbled as ScroatM sank into despair yet again. "But the car's gonna be runnin'. We're in and we're out. They might get a half-hour if they count the part where he says, 'So long, suckers!'"

Hutch shut down the phone, composed himself, then turned to Annie with pure heat.

"You're done in this industry," he spit, jabbing a finger toward her. "You're finished!"

"Promise?"

Fan Maintenance

The houselights cut out abruptly. The sad little crowd did its best to fill the hall with hoots and cheers, their sincere anticipation echoing through the empty back of the house and the roped-off balconies.

Jungle drums, hellacious beats, exploded through the theatre's primitive P.A. system. Dust from the rafters began to rain down. Damage was being done.

The assault continued for minutes, scratches, samples, and riffs now blending in with the thundering drum machine bed. The fans pressed forward hungrily, pinning themselves to the lip of the stage.

And then there he was: ScroatM, right there before them, in the tattooed flesh. Forget about the flat *VideoYear* performance. Forget about all the sniping in the music press about the laziness heard on the new album. This was ScroatM as raw and as intense as in his early, legendary days.

Because right now, he meant it. He hated these kids, for not being more. He hated all those who stayed away. He hated the critics and his manager and the record company and his accountants and his lawyers and those fuckers from R²Rev who got him into this in the first place. He really, truly *hated* them all.

He was back in touch with something pure that had been defanged and franchised for the sake of his career. It felt good to feel it again.

"*On your feet, motherfuckers!!!!!!*"

This was how all his shows began. He'd prowl the stage from wing to wing for a minute or two, stomping around with his white boy pimp swagger, letting the kids bask in his nastiness while the recorded track pummeled them into readiness.

"*On your feet, motherfuckers!!!!!!*"

He'd give this shout three or four times, until it threatened to become boring, then he'd saunter down to the front of the stage, where the palms of the fleeced would invariably be outstretched to him worshipfully. He'd make a pass or two before them, slapping his skin against theirs, just to give them a thrill. And to see if there wasn't just one more nickel he could grab from their hands.

"*On your feet, motherfuckers!!!!!!*"

But tonight, as he made with the high-fives, they meant something. He couldn't hit these kids. He couldn't lay them out and drive the toe of his boot into their kidneys, like he did with the mother of his little girl. But he could make the high-fives sting.

He wound up and swung at the palms laid open before him, packing naked spite into each blow. His soul soared as he watched kid after kid withdraw their hand in pain. Maybe he'd just do this for a half-hour, until he drew blood.

"*On your feet, mother—*"

The meaty hand of Wad Wendell reached from the pack and grabbed the singer by the forearm. Bobby Slopes got the other. Together, they pulled.

ScroatM flew from the stage and sank into the crowd. And, as planned, the Dickinson High School football team and assorted others proceeded to beat the shit out of him.

His wireless mike remained hot. Together with the muffled thumps and knocks of the scuffle—which synced up remarkably well with the percussive throb of the track—could be heard the singer's frightened yelps.

"Hey!"

Joel was in the thick of it, not sure until it happened if he'd actually sink this low, but then surrendering enthusiastically and with surprising glee as he got in his licks. As the singer was rocked and slugged from teen to teen—some who were inflamed by the industry exploitation which ScroatM represented, some who just liked to beat people up—Joel spotted Scroat's boxers hanging out of his pants.

Wedgies were so grade school, Joel deliberated at the heart of the riot. Then again, you're only a kid once…

"Ow! Hey—*hey!*" ScroatM screamed, his voice echoing through the musty old theatre (Peggy Lee played here in 1965), accompanied—perhaps faintly, if you really listened—by the sound of ripping underpants.

Because Tok$ic Records had sent along only two bodyguards, one of whom was idling the car outside; because Artie Pistone was backstage making vague threats of mob retaliation against the theatre manager, who was protesting the damage being done to his frail sound system; because the theatre had cut loose most of its security staff when the expected crowd failed to show up; because Hutch Posner was at the back of the auditorium with the cameraman and was a pussy, there was nobody to put a stop to the thrashing.

The track kept playing, well into the portion where ScroatM should've been rapping. Some of the kids who weren't beating up the singer—maybe ten or twelve of them, all white and well-scrubbed—jumped up onto the stage and pretended to perform. Their voices couldn't be heard, but they made hateful faces and flipped gang signs and pulled at their crotches and struck the ingrained poses, and damned if it wasn't good enough.

When the mike was thrown free of the melee and tossed up on the stage, the takeover was complete. One kid after another barked lyrics and stray vulgarities to the back of the house, until a fight broke out over the microphone, and a second skirmish erupted. Kids started jumping up on stage to get in a few licks, then turned to swan dive back into the crowd. But no one bothered to catch them. The floor began to be littered with broken teenagers who, when they got out of the hospital, could add *gravity* to the list of cruel disappointments that had left them bitter and mad at the world.

Back toward the lobby, a tightly constricting circle of gangstas had found a trembling Hutch Posner and the several thousand dollars of video equipment that he was obligated to protect. He knew from countless music videos that this was not going to turn out well for him.

These were his children. This was all pretend.

They would try not to kill him.

— ◖●—

Todd, Annie, and Frank stood at the rear of the theatre, mostly queasy but slightly—regrettably—amused by the carnage unfolding before them. They had assumed that Joel and the boys would just get in a few shots—if that—before ScroatM was fished from the scrum and the show played on.

But this was turning nasty. They should have done something to prevent it. They really should have.

The cops finally moved in to break things up. The music was still blaring.

"Do you know how to arrange bail?" Todd yelled to Annie.

"What?" She was truly deafened by the noise. Todd knew it.

"So you wanna go out sometime?" he shouted, a little softer.

"*What???*"

Todd grinned at her stupidly, pleased at his own cleverness.

Frank leaned in to holler in her ear.

"He *said*—"

Todd went white with embarrassment and cut Frank off with a shot to the arm. Frank smiled at the boy playfully.

He was just having fun.

On Your Feet, Motherfucker

Todd returned to the theatre a couple hours later, still looking for Joel. When the police vans had spilled open at the police station, he was not among the arrested. In the frenzy, he had probably just slipped away and gone home. But Todd wanted to check here first to make sure he hadn't been laid out in the fight and left for dead. Todd felt responsible for all this.

He knew one of the kids on the cleanup crew, so they let him into the dark, empty theatre. The auditorium was now deathly silent compared to the roar of a few hours earlier. He stood and let the emptiness press in on him.

There wasn't much light, but he heard a groan coming from the front of the hall. Down where the dance floor met the stage—where the attack had taken place—a grate had been kicked out revealing a crawl space. Todd heard another pained whimper and saw movement. Someone was hiding down there.

"Joel?" Todd whispered, starting to get scared.

He inched forward as this figure spilled out of the hole in considerable agony. Todd recognized the costume, if not the beaten down demeanor. He had seen Artie Pistone and the body guards being hustled into the police station along with the kids that were picked up. No one had been left behind to see to him.

Todd watched as ScroatM clutched his broken ribs and wiped the blood away from a gash above his eye. With great difficulty, he pulled himself up into a sitting position and leaned back against the stage. He was breathing hard and trembling.

Todd stepped up and stood over him. The hip-hop star looked up stiffly and seemed to attempt to reactivate the pose. He'd be damned if some kid was going to catch him crawling around on the floor like this.

He sneered up at Todd and tried to stand, but his right leg wouldn't support him—if it wasn't broken, it was most certainly wrecked. He fell back down to the ground and let out a little squeak of a cry. Every part of him hurt.

He was beaten. That was all. He'd mend and come back, nastier and angrier than ever. He'd come back and personally take it out of the asses of every little fuck who did this to him. But right now, he needed help.

He looked up again to Todd, this time with almost a look of solidarity. He'd allow this kid to help him, to come away with the story of how one day he did a solid for the millionaire rap star who had made the mistake of coming to his shitty little town.

He fixed a slightly vulnerable glare on Todd and weakly offered up his hand for assistance. Even in his suffering, he clung to the act.

"Yo…"

Todd stepped closer. He kept his hands in his pockets.

"You *do* realize you're not black, don't you?"

Acknowledgments

Among other things, *Like We Care* is a book about music and kids, about how everything that was once sublime about rock and roll—the rebellion, the posing, the parental bafflement and rage—has been reduced to such a hateful, cynical, soulless *industry*. Rock and its offshoots have been distilled into nothing but simple-minded swagger and bile, infecting a generation that I fear will never know what genuine music—even at its rudest and most corrosive—can do for the soul.

I was fortunate enough to be born into the years of high cotton, so in order of my exposure to them and without apologies, thanks beyond words to the following musicians:

The Beatles, the Rolling Stones, Kiss, Rush, Cheap Trick, Warren Zevon, the Band, Elvis Costello and the Attractions, Tom Petty and the Heartbreakers, R.E.M., Muddy Waters, Sonny Boy Williamson, Howlin' Wolf, John Hiatt, Bruce Springsteen and the E Street Band, Lucinda Williams, Wilco. And NRBQ. Always NRBQ.

Thanks to Richard Chapman, who read my half-finished manuscript at precisely the point where I needed encouragement, and who championed it to completion. Thanks to my publisher, Bruce Bortz, who patiently endured a prolonged dance with a particularly skittish author, but with whom I embark on this adventure with nothing but high hopes. And thanks to Elly Zupko at Bancroft Press, who pulled my manuscript from the slush pile and started me on my way.

Thanks especially to my manager Zach Tann, who got behind this book when no one else would and worked it like a mofo.

Much love to Lori, Kathi, and Nick, whose humor and support have sustained me more than they will ever know. And to my mother, always my biggest supporter and source of strength during the lean times. Only good years from here on out, Mom.

And most of all to Kevin and Paul, whose extremities may be gnawed upon by corporate America, but whose hearts and minds have had a loyal and determined protector (me, whether they liked it or not); and, finally, to Pam, who may not always know why I write, but understands that I must. If the words come, baby, it's because you let me go out and chase them down. I'm proud to be your sweet patootie.

About the Author

Tom Matthews wrote the original screenplay *Mad City*, which hit theatres in 1997. Starring Dustin Hoffman, John Travolta, and Alan Alda, it was directed by Costa-Gavras. He has also written scripts for Universal Pictures, Warner Bros., New Line Cinema, Twentieth Century Fox, and Walt Disney Pictures, working with such producers as Steven Soderbergh (*Traffic*, *Erin Brockovich*), Steve Tisch (*Forrest Gump*), Hunt Lowry (*The Last of the Mohicans*), and Lynda Obst (*Sleepless In Seattle*).

Prior to the launching of his screenwriting and novel writing career, Matthews spent fifteen years working in the motion picture industry as a journalist, film critic, and publicist for Twentieth Century Fox. He's also done freelance work for national and regional publications that include *L.A. Weekly*, *Marquee Magazine*, *The Milwaukee Journal*, and *Creative Screenwriting*. Matthews was also a managing editor for *Boxoffice Magazine* for six years.

A Wisconsin native, he lives in Wauwatosa, WI with his wife and two sons. He is currently developing a documentary series about Las Vegas with George Knapp, the resort city's leading investigative reporter.

Like We Care is his first published novel.